"A front-row seat . . .
to the glitz and glamour
of Hollywood* . . . steamy
and scandalous** . . .
a sexy first novel from a
PLL and her BFF."***

Bliss

SHAY MITCHELL
& MICHAELA BLANEY

st. martin's griffin ⚞ new york

This is a work of fiction. All of the characters, organizations, and events portrayed in this novel are either products of the authors' imaginations or are used fictitiously.

BLISS. Copyright © 2015 by Shay Mitchell and Michaela Blaney. All rights reserved. Printed in the United States of America. For information address St. Martin's Press, 175 Fifth Avenue, New York, N.Y. 10010.

www.stmartins.com

Designed by Anna Gorovoy

The Library of Congress has cataloged the hardcover edition as follows:

Mitchell, Shay, 1987–
    Bliss : a novel / Shay Mitchell and Michaela Blaney. — First edition.
        p. cm.
    ISBN 978-1-250-07568-0 (hardcover)
    ISBN 978-1-4668-8712-1 (e-book)
    1. Young women—Fiction. 2. Female friendship—Fiction. I. Blaney, Michaela. II. Title.
    PR9199.4.M585B57 2015
    813'.6—dc23

                                                              2015032516

ISBN 978-1-250-09635-7 (trade paperback)

Our books may be purchased in bulk for promotional, educational, or business use. Please contact your local bookseller or the Macmillan Corporate and Premium Sales Department at 1-800-221-7945, extension 5442, or by e-mail at MacmillanSpecialMarkets@macmillan.com.

First St. Martin's Griffin Edition: September 2016

10 9 8 7 6 5 4 3 2 1

this book is dedicated to
everyone and anyone out there
trying to find their bliss.
dream big and never give up . . .
live the life you love.

acknowledgments

We want to thank the people closest to us in our lives; though we would love to list you all, we would need a whole chapter to do it! To our families: thank you for putting up with us and always having our backs. We love you.

For the rest of our friends and family, you know who you are. Your unwavering support never goes unnoticed and we are thankful to have you all in our lives. A special thanks to everyone who helped us shape the book into what it has become: DD, SC, Mark, Bunny, and to our co-writer Val, thank you. Taking so many ideas and stories and pouring them onto pages while making sense of it all is not for the faint of heart and we thank you all so very much, for guiding us.

This book is about finding our bliss. So it is only appropriate to send a huge thanks to everyone and anyone who has crossed our paths and made an impact big or small, positive or negative. Cutting us down taught us to build ourselves back up. Sharing a laugh in the middle of a storm taught us humility. And endless support when we needed it most taught us to trust and love. You have made us who we are and we thank each and every one of you. Impacting another person's life usually goes untold or unnoticed and this is an acknowledgment to all of you: *thank you*.

And as Shay's dad always says: "The world is your oyster."

Hey fans, I know you want to read our book (thank you), but this novel deals with some mature topics, so if you're under eighteen, talk to your parents first!

Bliss

Let's get lost.

That was their goal for the night. Demi had just gotten her license, and they decided to drive around Vancouver in her dad's Mercedes without a plan. Windows down, wind in their hair, music blasting: freedom. This was what it was all about. Getting lost in their own world in their own city. You can't really know a city until you're hopelessly lost in it.

The almost-summer night was clear and full of stars, and just warm enough to keep the windows open. They all smoked then—it was the coolest thing to do, right?—and laughed at how they must have looked, cruising down the road, a big car with three arms straight out the windows.

They headed downtown. They were too young to get into any of the cool bars and clubs, but were drawn to them anyway. The three friends gawked at the college kids and the beautiful people lined up outside. Seventeen was a frustrating age. They were so close to real life, but not quite there yet.

Demi headed south, over the Lions Gate Bridge, through Stanley Park, and made a detour into English Bay, where local hipsters and tourists sat on logs on the beach to smoke weed or cigarettes. The girls sat on the rocks, listened to the waves, and smoked without worrying about the smell. In the distance, they could make out yacht lights and the sound of the newest dance track—Bob Sinclar's "World, Hold On"—bouncing across the water.

"Party cruises," said Demi. "House music. Hot guys. Tons of booze. Three hours of fun." Demi was the most petite of the three of them— she bristled when Sophia or Leandra called her cute—with bright hazel eyes, a tiny dot of a nose, petal pink lips, and soft chestnut hair that she usually wore in a pony. She looked sweet and innocent, until she opened her mouth.

"We should go on one!" said Leandra, the self-acknowledged sexiest of the trio, with lusciously shaped long limbs; high, hard melon boobs; bouncy, aggressively blond waves (they all agreed she went too light this time); and upturned green cat eyes that made strong men weak and smart boys stupid.

"Can we bring Jesse?" asked Sophia, gorgeous and exotic, mixed race (Irish and Filipona), tall, with nearly black thick hair, a killer smile, bottomless dark eyes, olive skin, and born-that-way grace. When she walked, or sat, or just stood there, people stared at her. Jesse was her boyfriend. Even on the rare night they weren't together, he was always on her mind. Demi and Leandra, who were currently single, spent so much time together they were like a couple themselves.

"If only we could just hop on one of those yachts and get out of here," said Demi. They were all ready for high school to end, and real life to begin.

"And go where?" asked Leandra. "What place on Earth could *possibly* be more exciting than Vancouver?"

The girls all howled with laughter at that one.

"Wherever we go, we'll go together," said Demi, throwing an arm around Leandra.

"Travel is definitely on my list. And Jesse's," said Sophia. "But you guys know what my number-one priority is." The others nodded. Sophia had wanted to be an actor since forever. Her parents were on the fence about her dream. They were in business, and thought acting was a major gamble. "But being successful and traveling go together," she said. "When I'm a Bond girl, for instance, I'll have to shoot in Tokyo, Milan, and Dubai."

"Exactly," said Demi. "I'll meet you in whatever city and be your 'normal person' friend. Every celeb needs one."

"I'll retire in Tuscany. But during my Oscar and Emmy years, we'll maintain a Hollywood base so I can drive my white Range Rover to lunch at Il Pastasio in Beverly Hills." Sophia followed a lot of travel bloggers on Instagram. She knew the hot spots in LA. "You guys can come, I guess. But only if you don't give me shit about my taking a thousand pictures. It's not a choice. It's a need."

"It's your *addiction*," said Demi.

"It is," said Sophia, whipping out her phone and started snapping.

"Okay! Enough!"

"One more!"

They started laughing hysterically, and fell onto the sand. Sophia stood over Demi and Leandra, shooting away. "Stop!" Demi was laughing so hard, she didn't making a sound.

"I'm going to miss this when I move to New York," said Leandra. "Or Washington, D.C. I'm torn. Do I want a Wall Street husband and live in a penthouse on Park Avenue, or should I marry a senator, and live in a town house on Dupont Circle? Decisions, decisions."

"That's your dream? Marrying a douche bag who'll dump you for a younger model in ten years, leaving you to raise the brats by yourself?" asked Demi, grinning.

"A *rich and powerful* douche bag. And don't worry. I'll get a good settlement in the divorce."

"Goes without saying."

"What about you, Demi?" asked Sophia. "What's the five-year plan?"

"Are we doing a college interview now?"

"Quit stalling."

"I definitely want to be successful, not sure how. While I figure out what I want to do, I'll just hang out in Leandra's town house, mooching off her rich husband."

"We'll find you space, like in a closet somewhere."

"I can mooch off Sophia and Jesse, too, or be the hired caretaker of their villa in Tuscany."

Leandra smiled. "Glad we've got it all figured out."

The girls laughed on cue, but this whole conversation was making them a bit anxious. Longing for their lives to begin didn't mean they weren't scared shitless about it.

"We can have whatever we want, you realize," said Sophia. "All we have to do is stay positive and never give up."

Demi barked a laugh. "Right."

"No, it's true," said Leandra. "Don't you read all those quote boxes on Insta?"

"You mean, 'Breathe it all in,'" she said sarcastically, and then took a deep inhale of her cigarette. "'And love it all out'?" The smoke streamed out.

Sophia said, "More like, 'Follow your bliss and the universe will open doors for you where there were only walls.'"

"Who said that?" asked Demi. "The woman who wrote *The Bullshit*? I mean, *The Secret*?"

"What's the alternative? Blow off bliss, live a boring life, get old and bitter, living alone with eight cats?"

"So the choice is 'follow your bliss,' or 'die alone, with cat drool on your chin,'" said Demi.

"Yes," said Sophia. "So why not go for it?"

Why not?

They decided "Why not?" would be their mantra for life. "Let's make a pact," said Leandra. "We promise to keep each other on track, follow our bliss, and love, honor, and cherish our friendship, from this day forward."

"Is this a pact, or a vow?" asked Sophia.

"Both."

"To bliss," said Demi. "And making out with men, getting drunk, and having the time of our lives."

four
years
Later...

1   that's one way to beat meat

As soon as she got home, Demi noticed James's suitcase by the door. He wasn't supposed to get back from his bank conference in New York until later that night. She reached for her phone to check for a text and panicked to find the phone missing. Then she remembered she left it at the office. (Typical. She misplaced it every hour.) James probably caught an earlier flight to surprise her. The irony was, she came home early from work to surprise him with a special dinner to celebrate their three-year anniversary. It had been two days ago. James never remembered stuff like that, but she didn't care. Sophia always said it mattered, that the thought counted, that James took her for granted, and that Demi turned a blind eye to it. Demi's attitude was more casual. Why find faults if everything was fine?

"James?" she called out. No response. He must have dropped off his suitcase and gone right back out, probably to his office. He busted his ass at work.

Demi brought the grocery bags into the kitchen and unloaded the ingredients for a decadent osso buco with a mushroom risotto. She'd never made it before. What if she fucked up and it tasted like garbage on a warm day? "Shut up, it's going to be fine!" she told herself.

Braising the veal would take a few hours, so she hoped he would stay out for a while. She smiled at the thought of him coming through the door, saying "Something smells good!" and rushing into the kitchen to gather her up in his arms, lick the cute smudge of flour off her nose, and then kiss her like he'd been gone a year. The reunions made his trips bearable.

Demi loaded the veggies into the nearly empty fridge. She didn't cook for herself when James was away. Her joy of cooking was in watching people savor her food, especially James. When he took the first bite, he usually gave her over-the-top praise—"Oh, my god, this is the best thing I've ever eaten!" She tried to outdo herself each meal, and had become a pretty good cook in the last few years. They still went out to restaurants. Yaletown, their neighborhood, was the epicenter of Vancouver's foodie culture. But James preferred her home cooking to trendy gastronomy or fusion artisanal whatever. Plus, when they went out, he ran into a hundred people, and they would end up staying out all night.

"You could do this for a living," he said once while savoring her baked spring salmon. "I love you for your cooking and taking care of me."

"I thought you loved me for my woo-woo," she joked, pointing at her crotch.

"That, too. Why do you think I stick around?"

Demi told the story to Sophia in Toronto via Skype. "Aww, he loves you for your vag," said Sophia. "That's *so sweet.*" It wasn't a compliment. Like most of Demi's friends, Sophia wasn't on Team James. A couple of years ago when she came back to Vancouver for the holidays, the three of them went out on New Year's Eve. There was a misunderstanding. James thought he was touching Demi's leg under the table and accidentally groped Sophia's. They were all hammered and it was an honest, harmless mistake on his part. Sophia got it wrong about his intentions.

Demi shook that memory away to focus on the task at hand. She put the bundle from the butcher on the counter and unfolded the waxed brown paper to inspect the two round, red veal shanks with rings of marrow-packed thighbone at the center. Each piece cost $99. James had money, so Demi didn't worry about splurging on this kind of thing. He paid for everything else, and indulged her on weekend trips, clothes, bags. If she wanted a big-ticket item—shoes or a piece of jewelry—she'd clip a photo of it on the fridge. When he got drunk, he'd buy it for her. Some of her friends made fun of her for catering to him, like some throwback Stepford wife, but they didn't get it. James lived to please *her*. If her friends were inside the relationship instead of mocking it from the outside, they'd know. She remembered how she used to judge Leandra for wanting exactly the life she'd ended up creating for herself (one exception: James was not a douche bag). If she and Leandra were still friends, they'd laugh about it.

First step in the recipe: dredging the veal. The flour canister was in the cabinet above the counter that separated the kitchen and the living room. As she reached for it, she noticed movement in the other room.

James appeared, like a ghost. His back to her, he stood in front of the rolling bar caddy by the TV. Demi opened her mouth to say something, but then ducked out of view, her body pancaked against the fridge so he wouldn't see her. He must have come out of the bedroom and gone straight to the bar. She peeked again.

He was bare-assed naked.

She watched him pour a scotch. He drank it straight down, refilled his glass, swayed, bumped into the TV, and then stumbled down the hall toward the bedroom. No wonder he hadn't heard her come in.

He was wasted, and probably half conscious. It was three P.M. She knew his habits all too well. He self-medicated a lot. It was starting to be a problem between them. His drinking was her parents' (both sets) number two complaint about James, second only to their twelve-year age difference (he was thirty-three; Demi was twenty-one). The two times Demi brought James to dinner, her dad's killer glare would haven driven anyone to drink.

So what to do? Cook dinner while he slept it off? Or . . . Demi grinned. No, she'd lull him out of an inebriated half dream with a proper homecoming. Quietly, she undressed. It was a warm June in Vancouver, so she wasn't wearing much and stripping took seconds. Off with her clothes! Starting with her brand-new studded Valentino flats, followed by her Vince jersey tank dress and BCBG loose shawl/jacket thing. Demi liked to dress casual and cool—nothing too fussy. Her hair, blown shiny and straight, tickled her bare back. She left on the bra and panties. They were brand new, a matched silken set, green to match her eyes. The bra jacked her boobs up to her collarbone. They were among her favorite body parts, and she wasn't afraid to show them off. The undies were booty shorts with lace trim. Cute, but she could do better. She'd tape some lingerie photos to the fridge. Demi had buffed, waxed, and polished for tonight. Every inch of her skin was smooth and hairless. She'd been to see the waxing lady, a Russian who called her vag "cookie." Demi once sent a photo of a Brazilian in progress to Sophia, with the caption: "Endangered beaver." She and Sophia always sent crazy photos back and forth. It was their thing.

Heart pounding with excitement, Demi kicked aside her puddle of clothes, padded out of the kitchen and down the carpeted hallway to the bedroom. A glimpse inside confirmed that James was in bed, the sheet covering his lower half, the sheet pitched like a tent. He was perpetually hard. Demi couldn't suppress a giggle. James's muscular chest was exposed in all its glory. She could see one of the tattoos from his hockey days in university. Hockey players were her weakness.

"What're you doing?" James slurred. "Get your ass in here."

Busted. He heard her. She could still make a dramatic entrance, though. Flinging the bedroom door open, she stepped into the room and said, "Welcome home!"

James's jaw hit the floor just as she hoped it would, but his eyes went wonky. He looked kind of horrified—or just massively fucked up?

Movement drew her eye toward the bathroom door. A person was coming out of there? Who the fuck could that be? Then, to her astonishment, a girl appeared on the threshold.

"It's not what you think," said James.

"Oh, shit," said the girl.

Demi looked from James to the girl, then back again. His head rolled to one side, too wasted to work up an appropriate shame face. The girl just stood there like this happened every day, which made Demi's blood turn to ice. The girl was like a teenage version of Demi, but with longer legs and bigger tits. Her bra was black, a tacky mesh lace with rhinestone hearts around the nipples. The panties were black, too, with a rhinestone arrow over the crotch and the word "FLIRT!" in script.

"I'm not really into threesomes," said the girl.

Demi would have said the same, except she was incapable of speech.

"You're the girlfriend? James told me about you on the plane." She had a Slavic accent. "I am Svetland. Nice to meet you."

"You met on the flight?" croaked Demi.

In her head, Demi was screaming and beating the living shit out of James, but her body and mouth didn't move. What happened here? He got on a plane and grabbed some tacky model to bring back to their apartment while she was at work? This cheesy fembot was supposed to be an afternoon quickie for him that she would never know about?

How many others had there been?

Didn't he even care about getting caught?

He glanced at his phone on the night table, like it explained things. The phone? What did the phone have to do with Demi's . . . ohhhhh. Her brain cylinders fell into place. He was tracking her phone's GPS.

She'd left it at work. He thought she was twenty minutes away, and that he'd have plenty of time to get rid of FLIRT! when the GPS dot started to move. Sneaky.

Svetland had retreated into the bathroom and came back out in a knockoff Versace dress, a barfy pseudo-Chanel bag thrown over her shoulder. Fake, fake, fake. In a perverse way, Demi was disappointed in him. He could do better.

The girl's shoulder brushed Demi's as she hustled out of the room. The contact made Demi feel suddenly, painfully exposed. She reached for her robe on a nearby chair and slipped it on. "How long?" she asked him. "And, more importantly, how many?"

"Are you really that paranoid and insecure?" he asked.

"Fuck you. Don't patronize me! I caught you red-handed."

"If you give me five seconds to explain." He rubbed his forehead, and Demi hoped he had a cracking migraine. "I was nervous about the flight, so I took a couple Ambiens and had a drink or two. I guess I passed out. It's pretty fuzzy how we got back here, but Svetland told me she practically carried me off the plane and got me in a cab. She asked me if she could take a quick shower here after the long flight, and considering all she did for me, I said yes. If it weren't for her, I don't know what would have happened to me. She got me home safe. Nothing happened. As you can see, I'm in no shape to screw anyone, including you. I wish I could, though. You look stunning."

Demi was disgusted by the compliment. Did he think he could flatter his way out of this? She pulled the robe tighter. "That girl said the thing about a threesome."

"A joke, obviously. Not too funny."

Backtracking, Demi replayed the scene with the new info. Svetland's hair *was* wet. She had her carry-on in the bathroom, like she was in there to shower and change. James *was* a mess. He could barely keep his eyes open. She'd seen him dose liberally on flights before. Two drinks on top of an Ambien could drop a buffalo. Maybe she *was* being paranoid and insecure. If what he said were true, she owed them both an apology. *Now I look like a psycho*, she thought. She veered from one extreme (*it's a nightmare!*) to the other (*it's fine!*).

"You can't blame me for jumping to the wrong conclusion," she said. "Finding a strange girl in the bathroom, anyone would freak out."

"But you're not anyone," he slurred, smiling slow and sexy, the same smile that enthralled her three years ago. "You're my soul mate." Even wasted, he knew that meant the world to her.

Sophia would have vomited; Demi was so relieved to hear it, she rushed toward the bed and climbed in next to him. He opened his arms and she tucked herself inside them. James kissed the top of her head, stroked her hair, and said, "Shhhh." She hadn't realized she was crying with relief—and not from his scotch-breath fumes.

"I just missed you," she said. "We didn't have sex the night before you left."

"I know."

"All week, I've been worried you're bored with me."

"Never."

She snuggled closer to him, and put her hand on his muscular chest, right on top of his heart. Her fingers fanned to touch as much skin as possible. The sheet over his junk lifted.

Ignoring his flammable breath, Demi snuggled closer, and dipped her hand under the sheet. He saw what she was doing and shifted away from her, but not before her fingers grazed him.

It felt strange, gummy, not like normal skin. She started to pull the sheet away to get a look.

"No!" he said, holding it up.

They had a tug-of-war with the sheet. Demi was sober, and she had a better grip to start, so she had the advantage. She yanked it away, exposing James below the waist.

Demi screamed, *"Why the hell are you wearing a condom?"* His dick was dressed, like a little man in a pale blue slicker. They used them in their earliest days, but they got tested and she went on the pill. "You motherfucker," Demi blasted, and launched herself out of the bedroom.

Her clothes. She needed her clothes, and then she had to get the hell out of there. Not only was he a liar and a cheater, he tried to turn it around, and made her feel like a thick-skulled, jealous nag. She had almost apologized!

Demi's knees buckled as she ran into the living room. She tried to keep calm. Her clothes and bag were in the kitchen. She threw off the robe and scooped up her dress. As she was pulling it over her head, James stumbled through the kitchen door, his blue penis bobbing like it had a life of its own.

"Get out of my way," she said.

"We need to talk," he said.

She struggled to get on her jacket. One of the sleeves was turned inside out. Legs shaking, she could barely step into her shoes.

"Listen to me," he said. "You have every right to be upset. But it's not my fault. When I get fucked up, the drugs take over. I'm not responsible for my actions. And, believe me, Svetland is no innocent girl. She was all over me the whole flight."

Rage ripped the roof off Demi's head. The bloody veal shanks were relaxing on the counter in front of her. She grabbed one in each hand, getting a firm grip with a thumb in each bone ring. Nostrils flaring, she said, "Move!" He backpedaled into the living room, hands up, eyes on her, dick bobbing. She thought, *That would make a great GIF for Insta.*

Double fisting the veal steaks, Demi slapped him across his face with the meat. Unsteady on his feet, James went sprawling on his back in front of the TV. Demi advanced toward him on the floor and, with a blast of adrenaline-fueled fury, slapped his junk with the shanks. He rolled onto his side protectively. "Stop it, Christ!" he yelled, cycling his legs to get away.

Demi dropped the shanks and lunged back into the kitchen for her purse, quickly rinsed her hands in the sink, emptied out the catchall drawer cash stash, and banged out of the apartment. She pounded the elevator button, and said, "Come on, come on!" This didn't make it come any faster.

The twenty-minute drive to her office was dicey since she was practically blind from crying. Fortunately, her boss at the tiny marketing operation had gone home, and she was alone. The first thing she did was delete the Find My iPhone app from her phone, block James's number, and delete his contact info. Then she used her desktop to call Sophia in Toronto via Skype. When her friend's beautiful face filled the computer screen, Demi wailed.

"What's wrong? Are you okay?" asked Sophia.

Pretty fucking far from okay. "James and I broke up."

There was a gasp off-screen.

Sophia said, "Leandra's here."

"Hi, Demi," said Leandra as she came into view.

Once her friend, now an enemy. They pretended to be civil, but loathing roiled just under the surface. When Leandra got into Trinity College in Toronto, Demi was thrilled. But then Leandra sold the city hard to Sophia, and lured her away from Demi as if she'd planned it that way all along. If Sophia hadn't been so brokenhearted about Jesse, maybe she would have stayed in Vancouver. Demi was left behind without a college, a job, or a clue. She thought about moving to Toronto, too, but then she met James and you couldn't have dragged her out of Vancouver after that.

"Did he dump you?" asked Leandra, that bitch.

"N-no," Demi's diaphragm spasmed embarrassingly from sobbing. "I dumped him." Sort of.

"What happened?"

Demi took a few ragged breaths. Usually, she tried to minimize her problems—she couldn't stand the idea of Sophia and Leandra talking about what a fuckup she was—but there was no way to sugarcoat this steaming pile of horseshit. She told them everything, stopping occasionally to blow her nose.

"You hit his penis with raw veal?" Leandra's nose crinkled in disgusted confusion.

"I don't think I broke it."

"That's one way to beat his meat," said Sophia.

Demi barked a laugh . . . but then cried again. "This girl, Svetland whore face, she was a younger version of me. Really, James? I'm twenty-one!"

"You *were* eighteen when you met him," said Sophia.

"Did it ever occur to you that James might, how to put this gently, like jailbait?"

"Leandra," said Sophia. "Not helping."

"This is good news, Demi. Now you're done with him. From what Sophia tells me, he's a sleazy drunk. What? Don't deny it *now,* Sophia."

Demi started sobbing again. Sophia had tried to clue her in about James. Their New Year's Eve fight about him was brutal. It seemed insane now that Demi had thought Sophia was jealous of her glorious pure love with James when she accused him of touching her under the table. Sophia had been right all along. Her parents had been right. Demi should have listened to them. That was the worst part of this whole shit storm. She was so far gone in the lavish lifestyle, her instincts had gotten soft.

"How did I read James so wrong?" she asked.

"He was great in bed." That was Leandra.

True. "Irrelevant," said Demi, wishing Leandra would shut up and go away so she could talk to Sophia alone.

"If a man is amazing in bed, you can rationalize just about anything to keep him there," espoused Leandra.

"Where are you now?" asked Sophia.

"At the office."

"Where are you going to sleep tonight? Can you go to your mom's or dad's?"

No way. They'd be smug about the breakup. Her father would immediately push her to move back home and work for him. She'd feel like an infant.

"Go to the airport," said Sophia. "Come here for a long weekend."

Demi shook her head. "I have to work," she said. Plus, she had to pull herself together, get her stuff out of James's apartment, and find a new place to live. "I'll just go home and admit they were right all along. It'll be like giving my dad an early Christmas present."

"Are you sure?"

"Yeah, it's fine," said Demi. Sophia's concern was starting to irritate her now, too. Did she think she couldn't take care of herself? On screen, Sophia stared at Demi. A feeling passed through the cyberspace between them. Sophia knew Demi was lying about going home, but by tacit agreement, she wasn't going to push it.

"Okay," said Sophia. "I'll call you later. At your dad's."

"Call my cell," said Demi. "Or text."

Leandra waved. "Bye! Feel better!" *Bitch.*

Demi clicked "end." She spent some time cleaning up her face. What now? *Get wasted,* she thought. With whom? She'd sort of alienated herself from her friends and didn't feel like calling any of the couples they hung out with. *I'll make new friends.* In their relationship, Demi was the designated driver, the sober partner. Before him, she was the life of the party. Well, tonight, she would be again.

She would spend the night in a hotel, and belly up to the bar there. Thank god she snagged some cash on her way out. She counted it at her desk. Whoa, almost $3,000. "Hello, bar tab," she said, and it did make her feel better seeing all that money on her desk. He'd miss it, for sure, the asshole.

She drove straight to the Pacific Rim Hotel in Coal Harbour across the city; it was only ten minutes from Yaletown, but James would never look for her there. The receptionist registered her with an open checkout. He didn't ask questions when she forked over $2,000 in cash for the room and incidentals, just gave her a room key and a receipt. The room was first class and cozy. She lay on the bed, chronicling every moment over the last three years that, in hindsight, pinged her radar. The nights he stayed out until dawn with friends she didn't know. Conferences that sprang up out of the blue, requiring weekend trips. What conference was impromptu? Now she could see her willful delusion plainly. Was she really that stupid and needy?

Playing rewind on the entire relationship was too wrenching to handle, so Demi went down to the hotel lounge and ordered a drink. It was bumping. There had to be some corporate event; she counted suit after suit after suit. An older man caught her eye from across the bar and smiled. She tried to send off "don't even think about it" vibes, and tap into her single-girl persona: the rebel warrior who took no shit and didn't need anyone. It was the opposite of her relationship persona, when she turned clingy and dependent, almost overnight.

Sophia had theorized that Demi's fierce-to-fragile transformation had to do with her parents' divorce when she was ten. They fought a lot before the split, but always promised her they'd stay together, until they didn't. Hello, trust issues. When a boy broke through Demi's defenses and she let him in, on some subconscious level she was just waiting for him to betray her, so she did whatever it took to keep him happy. Cook brilliant meals. Believe his lies. Sex on demand. Would she ever find a guy she could love and trust, and not turn into a sniveling, pathetic cling-on?

Hugo Boss was still watching her. He was kind of hot, actually. Salt-and-pepper hair with a sharp jaw and good shoes. Let him come. When she didn't care about a man, she was in complete control. When she cared, she lost herself. Demi had let James control everything—her life, her surroundings, her friendships—and now she felt like she had nothing.

Only one drink down, she turned maudlin. She ordered another.

Demi believed in happily ever after. Her parents had both found love again, and she admired their second marriages. Mutually supportive, balanced relationships did exist in the world. But apparently not for her. She was probably destined to be a lone animal, roaming the world, not happy or unhappy, just surviving.

"Hello, beautiful," said Hugo Boss, now standing next to her, offering his hand to shake.

"Hi, Hugo," she said.

"It's Pete." *Rhymes with "meat,"* she thought, laughing. *Oh, shit, I must be drunk.*

"Hi, Pete. I'm Demi. You can stand there, sit down, shut up, fuck off, or buy me a glass of wine. But hurry up. You're making me nervous."

"Another round," he said to the bartender, and took the seat next to her.

When Demi woke up, it took a second to remember she was at the Pacific Rim. She rubbed her eyes and looked around. It was another few seconds before she realized that this wasn't her room. She was in someone else's room.

Her phone was on the table next to the bed. It was six-thirty A.M. Whew, she didn't have to be at work until nine.

"Come here, you beautiful thing."

She jerked at the sound of a man's voice. Who the fuck . . . Demi slowly turned around. It was Hugo . . . Pete? Celine Dion's "It's All Coming Back to Me" started playing in her head. Making out at the bar. Buying a round for everyone there. Going up to Pete's room, and assorted other sordid bits and pieces.

Oh, fuck. What have I done? she thought, and covered her face with the covers.

THE WORST PART
ABOUT BEING LIED
TO IS KNOWING THAT
YOU WEREN'T WORTH
THE TRUTH.

2

good for you, now
shut the fuck up

The Skype call with Demi came
at a bad time and now Sophia had to rush. "You think she'll be okay?"
she asked Leandra, who was sitting at her desk, applying her makeup.

Leandra said, "She's a mess. I'm sorry, but that girl is a walking
disaster."

"You don't have to sound so happy about it." Sophia *still* had no
idea what happened between Demi and Leandra. One day, they
were BFFs. The next, they could barely stand to be in the same room.
They both told her they had a fight at a party—Sophia missed it to
have a mandatory dinner with her grandparents. It was just bizarre.
She pushed them hard for info, but a few days later, Jesse broke up
with her, and that was the only thing she could deal with. That had
been four years ago. After she and Leandra moved to Toronto, the

tension between the formerly inseperable best friends wasn't an everyday issue. She gave up prying for details about Demi and Leandra's breakup, and just accepted that they now merely tolerated each other's existence for her sake.

"I'm not happy. I'm worried about *you*," said Leandra. "You did notice that Demi didn't even ask how you're doing, right? Does she even know you have an audition today?"

Sophia didn't take the bait. "I've got to go," she said. "Do I look okay?"

Leandra appraised her "not trying too hard" audition look of black JBrand jeans, black patent Jimmy Choos, and a purple off-the-shoulder top from Equipment. She'd been painstaking with her hair—bouncy, side sweep, so long it went on for days—and makeup, emphasizing her dark eyes. "You'd be gorgeous in a garbage bag," said Leandra. "I hope you break every bone in your body! And don't forget the party tonight." Then she took off, heading back to her dorm at Trinity.

Sophia quickly finished her makeup and gave herself a few minutes to stare at the vision board tacked to the wall by her bed. It was covered with photos cut from magazines. A beautiful home. The Hollywood sign. A surfboard from the Teen Choice Awards. A photo of sunset on the Sahara. Another of a beach in Bali. A white Range Rover. The collage was her inspiration, what she always relied on to remind her of her long-term goals. Recentered now, Sophia told herself, "Walk like a star," as she always did when she went into the world. Sometimes, when she was with Demi, they'd say, Strut Like a Star, and stallion it out, howling with laughter.

Sophia tried to push Demi's issues out of her mind as she rode the bus to Casting Central in Toronto, a facility used by TV, film, theater, and commercial producers to hold and record auditions. Today, she was reading for a new TV show, a *Degrassi* rip-off called *Niagara*. Her agent, Agnes Chen, had set up the audition and had been checking in repeatedly to make sure Sophia memorized the sides (aka her lines). She was a bit OCD about checking in. But better than having an agent who never did. Agnes got Sophia dozens of auditions, but callbacks were few and far between. In three years, the only acting job Sophia actually landed was as a model at a car show.

She took out the sides and read them over one more time on the bus. The part was a high school queen bee, a real manipulative bitch. As the only nonwhite in her high school, Sophia had been targeted by a few of that type, so she knew firsthand how they operated. Sophia had rehearsed the script with Leandra last night until she nailed it. It was a monologue, a neopsycho kill-or-be-killed rant about the social life at the character's school.

Casting Central looked like a lot of office spaces, except that everyone waiting in the lobby and milling around the halls was exceptionally gorgeous and muttering to him or herself. She checked in with Harriet the receptionist, a woman she knew well by now, and was directed to the right suite for the *Niagara* audition. Once there, Sophia gave her name to the assistant director holding an iPad, and took a seat among twenty other girls to wait.

"Hi, I'm Marina," said the girl to her left, a knockout blonde.

She smiled at Marina. "Hi," she said, trying to send a not-too-subtle message that she wasn't into chatting right now.

"This is my first audition."

"You'll be fine."

"It feels so *real*, not like classes at Ta-Da." Marina meant the Toronto Academy of Dramatic Arts, called (beyond ironically, with jazz hands) "Ta-Da!" by students. "I love auditions at school and cold readings. I'm addicted to performing!"

Good for you, thought Sophia. *Now shut the fuck up!*

"Am I bothering you?"

She didn't mean to be short with Marina, but Sophia was finding it hard to focus on her sides as it was. Demi's breakup had really thrown her, and she couldn't take on another person's problem at the moment. "I really need to read this," she said, holding up the page.

How much longer could she keep going on auditions that didn't pan out? She was exhausted, working at the club all night, then studying for and schlepping to auditions during the day. It was hard to stay positive when all the feedback had been neutral, negative, or nonexistent.

Marina said, "You should take some classes, too, for fun. Sometimes I go to an evening workshop at Ta-Da for drop-ins, just something to do. It's very low pressure."

The assistant director with the iPad called out, "Marina Tanner?"

"Oh, my god!" said Marina, jumping up. "Wish me luck!" She bounced into the audition room, leaving Sophia to study the sides. A few minutes later, Marina came out, beaming. She mouthed to Sophia, "Nailed it!" and then practically skipped down the hallway.

Poor delusional girl, thought Sophia. But at least she's staying positive. She thought she nailed every audition, too, especially when she first started out. Christ, did she sound like a grisly, embittered veteran at twenty-one? Wince. A few more girls went in and out of the room to read. Sophia's eyelids grew heavy, but she wasn't sleepy. More like weary. *Don't go there!* she yelled at herself in her head. *Stay positive!*

A text came from Agnes: "Are you there?"

"Here," she typed back.

"Call me the minute it's over."

After nearly an hour, Sophia's name was called. Instantly wide awake, she mentally recited her mantra—*Walk like a star! Walk like a badass!*—and entered the room of judgment.

Three people sat behind a table, two men and a woman, all middle-aged with blank expressions. *Can't you muster a little smile? Come on, people! You have jobs!* Sophia stood on the blue tape mark in the center of the room. The woman turned on the video recorder on the table. Sophia introduced herself to the writer, director, and casting agent for *Niagara.* While examining her head shot, they asked about her previous work (not much to tell). The trio sized her up to see if she matched the physical type they were looking for—slim, tall, mane, good face. Apparently, she passed the first hurdle.

"Whenever you're ready," the director said, holding out his hand in the "please proceed" gesture.

Sophia exhaled. She opened her mouth to deliver the opening

lines of the pages she'd memorized . . . and couldn't remember a single word.

"Are you okay?" asked the woman, the writer.

"I need a prompt."

The casting agent said, "'It's all about control.'"

Yes, that was the first line. Sophia cleared her throat and said, "It's all about control." And then . . . nothing. A blank. A void in her head where the words were supposed to be. "I'm so sorry, this has never happened to me before."

The CA repeated, "'It's all about control. Self-control, and controlling other people.'"

Sophia said the line, praying the rest of the material would magically pop into her head. Nope. Her mouth was dry, like she'd swallowed sand. "Can I glance at the sides? I've got this. Just a quick look and . . ."

"Thank you," said the director, this time giving her the "please leave" hand gesture. She was only halfway out the door when she heard the writer say, "Well, *that* was a complete waste of time."

Too stunned to be crushed, Sophia walked out of the room in a daze. A text came in from Agnes: "How did it go? Call me."

Sophia couldn't bring herself to reply. *What happened?* Leandra would blame Demi for upsetting her mojo. But then again, Leandra would blame Demi for climate change, the recession, aliens attacking the planet. Demi would blame Leandra for shit-stirring and suffocating her. Last night, Sophia had stared at her vision board and tried to manifest getting this part. Why wasn't *The Secret* working?

Because I'm just going through the motions, she thought.

She had to admit the truth. Her focus was off. She was staying up all night (for work and after), making out with randos, sleeping late, blowing off workouts, eating like shit. She had to get her head in the game.

Sophia rode the elevator down to the street with half a dozen other would-be stars. Some looked happy; most were dejected. She refused to put herself in that camp. She had to do something to break out of this negative mind-set and sharpen her edge.

Maybe Marina was right. Taking an acting class might be a good idea.

That evening, Sophia entered the front door of the main building at the Toronto Academy of Dramatic Arts for an evening workshop for amateurs and students. As instructed by the website, she came ready to deliver a monologue. She was going to do the *Niagara* sides, just to prove to herself that she could do it. After a fall, you have to get back on the horse. Right now, *Niagara* was her horse.

She opened the classroom door. If Marina was there, Sophia might have to turn around and leave. There was only so much perky she could stand in one day. A dozen other people were seated in plastic chairs in two rows (no Marina, thank god). It was a nice mix of older and younger, male and female, a few people of color, including herself. It wasn't a typical acting class of young beautiful people, which was a relief. Sophia took an open seat. A man went to the front of the room and introduced himself as Wesly Shamrock, a part-time professor at the school. She put him in his late thirties, handsome, thin, with a quasi-brogue like a footman on *Downton Abbey*.

"I see a new face tonight," he said. "Come on up here. Show us what you got."

Sophia jumped right up. This kind of felt like performing for her parents' guests at dinner parties when she was a kid. When she was done, maybe they'd give her candy! She clicked to the front of the room in her sensible pumps.

Wesly said, "What's your name?"

"I'm Sophia Marcus, originally from Vancouver, but I moved to Toronto for the acting opportunities."

"What are you performing for us tonight?"

"It's a monologue from a show I auditioned for today and . . ."

"Proceed," he interrupted. Okay, backstory not needed. Got it.

Sophia exhaled and imagined herself the mean girl, the reigning Regina of high school. Without the pressure of it being for real, Sophia remembered every word of the monologue, and really got into it. When she finished, the group applauded and she took a cheeky low bow. She waited for Wesly's verdict, but he just sat there, shaking his head at her.

"So?"

"Obviously, you're gorgeous and your reading was competent," said Wesly. "But I have to ask: Why on earth are you trying to slog it out in the acting world? It's dog-eat-dog, dog-puke-dog, dog-shit-dog, dog-eat-shit, and so on. This goes for all of you. Unless you can't see yourself doing anything else, get out now! Run for your lives!"

Sophia had certainly heard that before—although not in such gross detail. "Here's my advice to you, Sophia from Vancouver," he said. "Go to Los Angeles and ride shotgun in some rich man's Ferrari for the next ten years. A sexy girl like you shouldn't have to work. You won the genetic lottery! Cash it in!"

"Ka-ching!" she said, pulling an imaginary lever.

He smiled smarmily. "So who's next?"

Sophia took her seat, grinning, squinting at him, imagining she could squash his head like a bug if she wanted. He'd written her off as just a pretty face. Wesly took himself seriously, though. His comments were all borderline cruel disguised as helpful. A classic case of "those who can't do, teach drama." Throughout the rest of the class, Wesly kept up the refrain—"Quit now, before it's too late!"—no matter how good or truly awful the monologues were.

Acting school might be a good idea, but not here, and not with Wesly Shamrock. When the workshop ended, Sophia was beyond ready to bolt.

"Excuse me, Sophia?"

A guy tapped her on the shoulder as they filed out of the room. He was around her age, very handsome and as pretty as she was. "Yes?"

"I'm Scott Warren," he introduced himself. "I really enjoyed your monologue. You're really good. Don't listen to Wesly."

"You didn't do one," she said.

"I went last week, but didn't have anything new. Sometimes it's cool to just watch. If you're free sometime, we could grab a coffee. My friends are bored with my talking about acting and auditions," he said.

She laughed. "Same."

If he were hitting on her, she would have hesitated. But she didn't get that vibe. As if to confirm her suspicions, he said, "It's not a date. You're not my type."

"Really."

"Meaning female. My type has XY chromosomes."

Okay, then. "I'd love to have coffee," she said, smiling. She might not have gotten any acting tips here, but maybe she'd get a new friend.

"Fuck them all. God, I hate casting agents," said Renee, a bartender at CRUSH where Sophia was a bottle-service waitress. Like Sophia, Renee dreamed of stardom. She'd done some catalog modeling and, awhile back, starred as the Molson Canadian Girl in a commercial. They commiserated together, which Sophia appreciated. Renee was stunning. Perfect abs, toned arms, workout obsessed, beautiful face, and long brunette hair. But she was out for herself. Other people could be selfish but Renee was the ultimate "it's all about me" person.

Sophia wore her uniform of full makeup, a black minidress with a sequined bustier, and black leather thigh-high boots. The club was empty now, and freezing. In a few minutes, hundreds of people would crowd the dance floor and Sophia would run from table to table for six hours, logging a marathon in high heels. Renee didn't have it any easier behind the bar. She'd pour thousands of drinks, and do the physical labor of restocking the bar every hour and managing the guys who hit on her. She flirted huge tips out of them, which was how she paid the bills.

"I've never blanked like that before," said Sophia. "It was terrifying."

She expected Renee to give her the "It happens to everyone" speech. But instead, Renee said, "Maybe it's a blessing in disguise."

"How so?"

"I'm going to quote the Buddha now, so brace yourself. 'In the end, only three things matter: how much you loved, how gently you lived, and how gracefully you let go of things not meant for you.'"

"So I should live more gently?" asked Sophia, laughing. The two of them often talked about when to let go of the dream, if ever, and usually encouraged each other to give it more time.

"Are you still going to LA?" asked Renee.

Sophia was planning to go to Hollywood in a month for pilot casting season. Agnes had set up some auditions for her. She'd have to take time off from work, which would be a financial blow. But, as Agnes said, "Now or never." Especially after today, Sophia was wondering if a better description of her acting career was "now *and* never."

"What's going on with you?" she asked Renee. "You had an audition this week, right?"

A blast of music came through the speakers. Sophia and Renee turned to wave at DJ Squayla, tuning up her boards. On either side of the DJ booth were platforms with poles for dancers. Below the platforms were several of the club's VIP tables. More tables skirted the dance floor. The hierarchy of seating status was determined by location, location, location. The closer to the DJ, the better the table, the flashier the customers, the bigger the tips.

"Less talking, more working," boomed Vinnie Cardinale, forty-five, Toronto's poor-man's version of Tony Soprano. Fat, balding, a lover of polyester shirts, he owned CRUSH and had been her boss for three years. Renee immediately poured him two fingers of whiskey. Vinnie sipped it delicately, smacking his lips. "That's the stuff," he said. "Renee, what's this I hear about you going to Los Angeles?"

"Wait, *you're* going to LA?" asked Sophia.

"Bobby's got a big mouth." Bobby was another bartender at the club. He knew, too? "I was going to tell you tonight," said Renee, seeing Sophia's expression. "It wasn't definite until yesterday."

"What wasn't definite?"

Vinnie talked over her. "How long are you going to be gone?"

"A month. I'll be back for Canada Day in July," said Renee. "Unless."

"Unless?"

"I'm a hit and you'll never see me again."

"Bullshit!" said Vinnie. "If you make it big, I'm coming to LA and you can give *me* a job." He laughed at his own lame joke, which was his prerogative. "We open in five minutes. Sophia, you're working section one tonight. Don't say I didn't do anything for you." Section one was like a shark tank, but the tips might be enormous. She took a deep breath, found her inner superwoman. She can do this; she can do anything.

Vinnie continued on his rounds, checking the various stations and staffers before the all-night party started. Renee filled a sink with ice, and loaded more beer into the fridge behind the bar. "It's no big deal," said Renee. "It's just a commercial for Skyy vodka."

"*What?!* Congratulations! That's fucking fantastic!" It really was.

Renee must have liked Sophia's reaction. She smiled broadly, letting her happiness come out. "It's good money," she said. "Great exposure. It's going to take me places, I'm sure of it. Sorry I didn't tell you right away, but things have sucked so hard for so long for you."

"That's crazy. I'm thrilled for you."

"It's only human nature to be jealous."

"Honestly, I'm not," said Sophia. "I'm relieved! We're going to be in LA at the same time."

Renee nodded. "I'll be really busy but we'll definitely get together."

A blow off? Really? With her landing a big job, Renee's opinion of Sophia seemed to have changed. Did she see her as a thirsty wannabe now, one of the people she'd leave behind on her road to stardom?

"From Molson to Skyy vodka, from five percent alcohol to twenty percent. You went up fifteen percent in the alcohol world!" said Sophia, grinning. Renee wasn't amused, though. It was meant to be a joke, not an insult. Sophia hoped it didn't come out wrong. "You think I could meet the Skyy people?" she asked. You didn't lose anything by asking.

"Yeah, sure," said Renee. "I don't know if they'll have time. I'll ask, but no promises."

"Okay," said Sophia.

DJ Squayla cued up. The overhead house lights went off, and the LED spots came on. The club was open for business. Sophia smiled at Renee, and gladly left the bar to man her section. The conversation had been disquieting. She vowed to herself that if she ever had any kind of success, she'd be generous with it.

In the meantime, Sophia would have to accept the unfortunate truth. Renee was right. She *was* jealous, absolutely seething with it. You could be happy for someone—and she was happy for Renee—while also wishing you were the one doing the victory dance. The feeling wasn't fair, but neither was life. You could be the next Meryl Streep, but unless you got a break, no one would ever know. On the other hand, you might have all the talent of a bar of soap, but if the right person-in-a-position liked you, hello limelight.

Fuck fame, she thought. *It's not about that for me.*

Then Sophia called bullshit on herself. *I do want it all. Success and everything that comes with it*, she thought. The first step to mastering her craft was to acknowledge and explore the ugly emotions inside—including jealousy.

"Bottle of Magnum Grey Goose," shouted the silver suit with a mustache, diamond studs, and grabby hands at table one.

Sophia could barely hear him over the thudding house music. She didn't need to. When it came to brand names of premium vodka, champagne, and tequila, Sophia could read lips. The crew at table one—four creeps in Armani suits and six girls around her age—were already on their second bottle. The table charge alone was $4,000 for ten people. Each bottle was $1,500. If they didn't stiff her, her tip could be huge.

Just to confirm so there was no haggling over the immense bill later, she leaned down to speak into the guy's ear. "Magnum Grey Goose, right?"

The stachehole answered by slapping her ass, hard enough to make a solid *thwack*. The other guys in the booth laughed uproariously, because harassment was hilarious.

Sophia wagged a finger at him. "Bad touch," she said, smiling with tight lips. "I'll be right back with your bottle."

Walk like a star, she told herself, navigating through the sweaty masses. Sophia shouted the order to Renee, who sounded an air horn. It was a call to all bottle-service girls to come to the bar. Renee taped three sparklers onto the neck of the bottle and dropped it in a flashing LED-lit bucket with a stack of LED shot glasses. The other girls arrived to get their sparklers.

"Motherfucker at table ten grabbed my boob," said Brenda, a new girl. She'd only been at CRUSH for a few weeks, and was still shocked by manhandling. "I called my boyfriend. He's going to pound that asshole in the parking lot later."

Sophia said, "Good. Can he pound the guys at table one, too?"

Renee asked, "Ready?"

The girls touched their sparkler tips together. Renee flipped open her Zippo and lit them, as well as the ones on the neck of the bottle. Sophia raised the LED bucket over her head. The other servers fell in line behind her, sparklers blazing overhead. Clubgoers around them started cheering and cleared a path as the girls made their way to table one. Sophia plastered a smile across her face as she hummed the "Oompa Loompa Song" from *Willy Wonka* in her head, as always. She placed the bucket in the center of the table. She and the other girls jumped up and down, clapping like they'd just won a car on *The Price Is Right*. The bimbos at table one hopped onto the bench seats, jumping up and down and flashing their thongs.

The very second the sparklers fizzled out, the bottle-service girls stopped cavorting and returned to their own sections where they'd take orders and fetch drinks until the air horn sounded again. This ritual was repeated a dozen times a night. It lost its charm for Sophia by her fifth sparkling conga line from hell. By the five hundredth time, she despised it. Whenever she heard an air horn, her belly flopped. It was a conditioned response. She might never go to a hockey game again. What could you do but laugh . . . or audition for one of those shows about weird phobias. *Hello, I'm Sophia, and I hate air horns.*

Sophia's job at table one wasn't quite done, though. She removed the sparklers from the bottleneck, and opened the cap. She made a big show of pouring the vodka into shot glasses from high up without spilling a drop. She was on the last one when the stachehole cupped her butt, making her overshoot a glass and pour a good amount of vodka on the table. The bimbos jumped like she'd throw sulfuric acid on them.

"I'm not going to pay for that!"

"How's everyone doing?" asked a voice behind her. It was Vinnie, riding in to the rescue. His timing was eerily impeccable.

"Your waitress washed the floor with our vodka," he said.

"If you didn't grab my ass, I wouldn't have spilled it."

Vinnie put his arm around her and gently squeezed her shoulder to quiet her down. "Apologies. I'll deduct half the bottle from your check," he said.

"You should put a muzzle on that girl."

Sophia removed Vinnie's hand and stormed away from the table, knowing she'd dump the bottle over the scumbag's head if she didn't.

"A word," said Vinnie, coming after her, clearly pissed off.

"It was his fault, and I'm the one who's going to pay for it." By cutting the bottle charge, he'd also cut her tip.

"Just follow me," he said. Vinnie led her all the way around the dance floor to the club entrance. "Outside." He pointed through the front doors.

She followed him to the street, and shivered. Even in June it was cold at two o'clock in the morning, and she was practically naked. The sheen on her skin from running around instantly froze. She folded her arms over her chest, covering herself for warmth and from the eyes of gawkers on line to get in. Bruno the bouncer gestured to a group of girls off to the side. At five paces, Sophia could smell the gin.

"Do you know these ladies?" asked Vinnie.

Leandra? "What are you doing here?" asked Sophia. "I thought you had a graduation party."

"Sophia! There you are! Where have you *been*? I texted you like *five* times."

Leandra was wasted, and so were her four sorority friends. "That party sucked. We wanna *dance*! Tell this gorilla to let us in!"

"You hate house music. And you hate dancing."

"According to your friend here," said Vinnie, "you promised them a table and bottle of Belvedere. Is that true?"

Sophia gulped. It was a hard rule at CRUSH that staffers' friends were not to be given preferential treatment. They weren't allowed to cut the line, wave the cover, get free drinks, or sit at a table for free. If her friends wanted to come to the club, that was fine, as long as they paid and didn't distract Sophia from doing her job. She'd made no promises to Leandra, ever, but if she called Leandra on her lie in front of her college friends, she'd never hear the end of it.

"Tell you what," said Leandra, pressing her melon boobs into Vinnie's arm. "Come on, Vinnie. You could use some pretty young thangs at your table."

Leandra's friends howled. Vinnie's ego was too big to understand that Leandra was making fun of him. He owned a club, which made him something of a local celebrity. But Leandra had her sights set on the type of guy who owned the bank that held the mortgage on the club. For whatever reason, tonight Leandra was in the mood to slum it and flirt with men she'd rather cut off her own hand before touching with a ten-foot pole. Sophia had zero sympathy for the pseudo-VIPs who treated her like meat and dropped thousands on booze to impress girls who were into that. But she liked Vinnie. He was a sleaze and a crook, but he didn't deserve to be played by sorority girls in Prada dresses after dealing with creeps all night.

Leandra had been a rock for Sophia at some pretty low times in her life, like during the breakup, after countless audition rejections, and when she got lonely and missed her family in Vancouver (she'd learned never to talk about missing Demi; Leandra would just go off).

But sometimes, Leandra tried her patience with her sense of entitlement.

Sophia said, "It's freezing out here. I'm going in."

"Hey! What about our table? Come on, Sophia. We're college graduates!" The girls started cheering for themselves, and got some people on line to applaud them, too.

Vinnie was won over. "Okay, ladies. You can sit at my table, and Sophia will get you a round on the house."

Unheard of. Vinnie was in a generous mood, or he genuinely thought he had a shot at Leandra, an ethereal, delicate beauty who looked particularly fetching tonight. As usual, Leandra glided through life, managing to get what she wanted with a smile. If Sophia had been on the other side of it, she would have shaken her head in amazement at what she got away with. But Leandra's free ride meant just extra work for Sophia. It was the last straw. She clicked back into the club, steamed past her section, and ignored the people frantically waving at her. She went down the back stairs, and into the employee locker room in the basement. Sitting on a wooden bench, she unzipped her boots and intended to put on her Tory Burch flats. If Vinnie said anything about it, a single word, she'd quit on the spot.

She opened her locker, and noticed her phone screen lit up with a notification from Demi. "Thanks for checking in," she texted. "Means a lot. Good to know you care." Sophia's stomach dropped.

Immediately, Sophia called Demi, but it went to voice mail. She started to text, but her hands were trembling. She had no idea what to say. "I'm sorry" or "I had a rough day" sounded like excuses. Good ones! But Demi would take it the wrong way. In frustration, she threw her phone in the locker and slammed it shut.

She sat on the bench for a few minutes and willed herself to calm down. She just had to get through another couple of hours, cash out her tips, go home, cry, and sleep. This job was just an acting opportunity, a chance to test her chops. If she could get through the rest of the night as a bubbly bottle-service girl, she was Oscar worthy. She could walk like a star through a swamp, through a desert, or back up the stairs to the club. She flipped through Instagram and saw a couple of uplifting quotes, one especially stood out: "Before you see light, there must be darkness." The light was coming; she could feel it. A positive warm rush flowed through her body.

YOU'VE. GOT. THIS.

She dug deep, and forced herself to go back upstairs. She made a beeline to Vinnie's table where Leandra and her friends were sprawled and laughing hysterically at the lowlifes on the dance floor.

"What can I get you?" she asked, smiling so hard, it hurt.

At dawn, Sophia put herself to bed. As always, she stared at her vision board, wondering if her dreams were worth it. Wesly Shamrock wasn't the first person to tell her that her best shot at life was to be a bimbo. She couldn't accept that. If she let herself go down that rabbit hole there was no crawling her way out. Was she deluding herself? She could stare at her vision board until she went blind and never get any closer to her dreams. Hollywood might as well be Mars.

Demi would say, "You got this, Sophia! You were born to be a star. If anyone can make it, you can. So put on your invisible tiara, and strut, girl, strut!"

Sophia smiled, picturing her friend's face, wishing they were in the same city, hoping she was okay. She needed a Demi-shot of love and she was sure the feeling was mutual. Would it be wrong to turn to Demi for help when she might be worse off at the moment? She'd call her in the morning. Even a pity party was still a party, and it's always nice to be invited.

NOTHING
WORTH HAVING
COMES EASY.

3

you have no idea how much i love monkeys

Leandra's hangover was epic. The worst she'd ever had, although she said that every time. She and her crew stayed at CRUSH until closing—five A.M.—and she was still drunk now, twelve hours later, at the dinner her parents insisted on having to celebrate her graduation. They'd flown in from Vancouver for the ceremony and had made the reservation weeks ago at some cheesy Italian place. Even in pain, Leandra dressed well. She wore a Diane von Furstenberg wrap dress and Jeffrey Campbell sandals. When the waiter delivered her spaghetti and meatballs, she nearly barfed in her plate.

"We're so proud of you," trilled her mom. "If Stacy were here, she'd be so proud of you, too."

"Don't talk about her, Jesus," she snapped.

Dad frowned, as he always did when Mom brought up Stacy. "We have something for you," he said, thankfully changing the subject.

He presented her with an envelope. She tore it open, and pulled out a flight itinerary, a hotel reservation voucher, and $3,000 in cash. She scanned the paperwork, struggling to read with bloodshot eyes. The destination seemed to be spelled Phuket. "You're sending me to fuck it?" she asked.

"It's pronounced poo-ket," said her dad, annoyingly jovial. "Thailand's beach haven. The Phi Phi Islands are supposed to be the most beautiful spot in the world."

"The pee pee islands in fuck it? Thank you, guys, soso sososo much."

Leandra didn't mean to sound ungrateful, but her head was throbbing and, frankly, it was just the way she related to her parents. Her parents spoiled their only surviving child way past rotten. Her salesman father had always encouraged her inate desire for more. When she haggled for another cookie, he said, "That's my girl!" At twenty-one, Leandra's greediness wasn't as adorable as it used to be (if it ever was), but it was her default setting.

She'd hinted heavily about her graduation gift, dropping the phrase "exotic and expensive" many times. Her parents had done well. She would have preferred Tokyo, but whatever, Thailand was close enough. Fighting her hangover, Leandra got up—slowly—and hugged each of her parents. Her mom cried. Her dad kept a stiff upper lip, and said, "My baby is leaving the nest."

Leandra itched to fly. Going to college in Toronto wasn't far enough. She loved her parents, really. But she bore the heavy weight of their neediness and overprotectiveness. It was understandable, considering. Leandra empathized, but she had to break free of it all and start over somewhere far away.

"When do I leave?" she asked.

"Tomorrow night!" said her mom. "First, you fly to New York, then Dubai, then Phuket!"

Mom was overselling it to mask whatever real emotions she was dealing with about losing another daughter, this one to wanderlust. Leandra played along, and spent the rest of the dinner talking excitedly about her grand adventure. Her real life would begin the minute she boarded the plane.

Leandra sat in a window seat in coach for the Emirates flight from New York to Dubai. She was wedged in, trapped next to a Middle Eastern man who smelled like BO. His hefty wife didn't speak a word, but he wouldn't shut up. From takeoff until now, several hours into the thirteen-hour flight, he'd babbled about his job in tech and how he knew a guy in Mumbai who ran a Bollywood movie studio. "You're much prettier than any of those girls," he said. "If you give me your number, I can introduce you to my friend. You can live with me in Mumbai while you become a star."

Leandra iced him, but he refused to take the hint. Even if he really did know a guy in Bollywood (doubtful), she would never want to do that. She knew from watching Sophia that acting was hard work. Leandra had no intention of working at all, even a glamorous job. "Please move your face," she said when he leaned too close. "Your breath is rancid."

She took two Ambien and passed out. When she woke up, Leandra crawled over her seatmates to go to the bathroom. The man was now asleep, thank god. His wife was awake, and shot daggers at her. She was used to being despised by wives and girlfriends, and didn't take it personally.

In leggings, a blouse from Anthropologie (so ethnic!), and Silence + Noise heels, Leandra walked forward up the aisle to stretch her legs, hoping to sneak a peek at the legendary first-class cabins on the double-decker Airbus's top level. At the very front of the plane, she found a staircase leading up. It was blocked off with a red velvet rope and guarded by two stewardesses in red pillbox hats. For a woman like Leandra, velvet ropes were optional.

"What's up there?" she asked.

One of the stewardesses said, "First-class cabins and lounge."

She peered up the stairs and saw a circular bar with bottles arranged on mirrored shelves. "Can I go up there, just for one drink?"

"Only flight crew and first-class passengers."

"Just a quick look?"

A man in a suit approached. "Is there a problem?"

The stewardess said, "The young lady is returning to her seat."

"What's the big deal?" asked Leandra. "I'm just curious."

The flight attendant leaned closer to say, "If you don't leave this area now, the air marshal behind you is going to arrest you." The edge in her voice made Leandra believe it. Okay, no need to start an international incident. She used one of the economy-class bathrooms and went right back to her seat. If she got in trouble, it might delay her adventure, so best to stay out of it.

The plane landed a few hours later. At the arrival gate, Leandra noticed a large family group exit the plane. The women wore black burkas, covered head to toe. The kids, including the girls, wore Western clothes. They ran around the women standing in a tight circle. One man with a white headpiece, like a sheet, on his head seemed to be in charge. He spoke in Arabic to two other men in black suits and earpieces (bodyguards?). She took them for a sheik and his multiple wives, and their many offspring. It was so foreign, so exotic; she gawked. Couldn't help it. When the bodyguards noticed her and glared suspiciously, she scurried off to find her connecting flight to Thailand.

The family must have been in first class. She would have noticed them in coach. Leandra did the math. The Middle Eastern man told her that first-class suites—with full-size beds, hot showers, unlimited delicacies—from New York to Dubai cost $20,000 each. For a family of ten, one flight would run $200,000. Why didn't the sheik just buy his own plane? Maybe his was broken? No matter. Dude was insanely wealthy. It was hard not to be awed by that. Vast riches and mysterious men were what she'd come for. One day in the not too distant future, she would find herself in an Emirates first-class cabin, and take a hot shower at 30,000 feet. That fantasy kept her smiling for the last leg of her twenty-four-hour journey to

Phuket, including a sickening forty-five-minute taxi ride from the airport along the construction-clogged one-lane "highway" to her hotel on Karon Beach.

"This can't be it," she said when she arrived at the street-side entrance to Sawasdee House. The website photos sparkled like a jewel, but in reality, the hotel resembled a crumbling Holiday Inn tightly sandwiched between a yoga studio and a pharmacy. Leandra paid the driver in baht the exact amount on the meter. She'd read that Thai people didn't believe in tipping.

Leandra lugged her own bags into the small lobby, and had to wait a few minutes before a woman came to the desk to check her in. The whole process—filling out forms, giving her credit card—was a letdown. Where was the champagne cocktail, Thai mini-massage, the bowing-and-scraping she expected? Her room, on the first floor facing the street, was a disappointment, too, but she wasn't in Fuck It to sit in a moldy room. Leandra put on her skimpiest bikini, walked through the lobby and a shabby dining room, and out the hotel's back glass doors to the beach.

Karon Beach was glorious. Pink sand, teal blue water, sexy Asian surfers riding waves at the crest of the horseshoe shoreline. Sawasdee House might have a trashy façade, but it was right on the beach. She stationed herself on a lounge, ordered a Singha from a passing waiter, and let the Thai sunshine soak into her skin. It was divine. Heaven. Rapture.

Except.

It was kind of boring just lying there, waiting for her fabulous life to begin. She looked up and down the horizon, and caught the eye of a woman trolling the beach selling sarongs out of a plastic bag. "No!" she had to repeat five times before the woman stopped pestering her.

"They're rather persistent, aren't they?" asked a stranger on a nearby lounge in a posh English accent.

Leandra smiled at her. It was hard to guess her age with her hat and sunglasses. Asian women looked like they were twenty-five until age seventy-five, and then they looked one thousand. She was exceptional with a kitten-shaped face, a preciously pointy chin, impossibly thin with golden skin and red lips. A Chanel tote bag (that probably cost $5,000) was on the sand at her feet.

"Do I look like I want to buy a crappy sarong?" Leandra asked. The woman laughed and smiled.

"I'm Sari," she said. "Just get here?"

"Leandra. Yeah, I got in an hour ago. Isn't it obvious? I'm so pale!" But she wasn't. She'd prepped for the trip with a brown-sugar body scrub and spray tan.

"American?" asked Sari.

Why did everyone assume she was American? "I'm Canadian, actually. You sound Australian."

"I'm from Singapore," she said.

Singapore! A dot of an island off the coast of Malaysia, the epicenter of crazy rich Asians, where the streets were paved with gold and diamonds dripped from trees, or so she'd heard. "I've always wanted to go there," said Leandra. "I hear it's incredible, like the Garden of Eden."

Sari nodded. "It's just home to me."

"Oh, yeah, same for me with Ontario. People say it's one of the most stunning places in the world, but I fail to see the appeal."

"First time in Thailand?" she asked.

"First time in Asia," said Leandra. "It's incredible, obviously, and so spiritual. I counted like five hundred Buddhas just in the airport."

"Did you notice the Big Buddha?" Sari pointed down the beach to a mountain behind them. At the top sat a gigantic statue of Buddha in lotus position. It had to be a hundred feet tall.

"How did I miss that?" she asked, dumbfounded. She tried to imagine a colossal statue of Jesus, say, looming over Niagara Falls. Would never happen. Overt religiousness wasn't the Canadian way.

"Are you staying at Sawasdee?" asked Leandra.

Sari looked taken aback, as if the very question were absurd. "No, my brother and I are at the Baray on Kata Beach, about a mile that way. We were walking along Karon and stopped for a drink here."

"Your brother?"

"Here he comes," said Sari.

Leandra followed her eyeline, and saw a man emerge from the ocean. No, not a man. A god. His short hair was black and wet around an angular face, high cheekbones, a strong chin, and light blue eyes. Rippling abs dotted with seawater, a V-shaped hairless chest, leg muscles bunching and relaxing with each step as he strode along the sand. Leandra felt tased by the sight.

Sari giggled. "I know. He's a freak of nature."

"Sorry!" Had her awe been that obvious?

"No worries. He has that effect on women."

He came to the lounge between Sari and Leandra and reached for his towel. As he dried himself, Leandra quickly assumed the position. Back slightly arched, one knee up, the other leg straight, toes pointed, an arm thrown over her head, the other playing with her bikini strap. She'd learned exactly how to hold her body to draw the male gaze.

Sari said, "Nick, this is Leandra from Canada. She just arrived in Phuket and it looks like she could use another beer."

He smiled at her. "Welcome to Thailand," he said, sounding like an Aussie god and looking like Sean O'pry. If he were rich, too, Leandra was madly in love.

Nick signaled the roving waiter and ordered drinks.

"How long have you been in Phuket?" Leandra asked.

"A few days," said Nick. "We're here for a family wedding."

Sari added, "Nick refused to stay at our cousin's private island. Too much family togetherness, isn't it?"

"You're sharing a room?" asked Leandra.

They laughed pretty hard at that. "It's a villa," said Nick, his onyx eyes sparkling. "Like a little house."

She got the feeling their digs were more like a little palace. Leandra smiled, laughed along, as if she knew exactly what they meant. "Of course. Because a sister and brother in the same room would be freaking weird."

When the waiter came back with their drinks, Nick gave him a thousand-baht note, which was the equivalent of thirty dollars. He said, "Keep the change." Leandra bit her lip. Maybe she should have tipped the cabdriver? Oh, well. What was she going to do now? Hunt him down over five baht?

Nick settled on the lounge between the women and closed his eyes. Sari lay back, too, giving Leandra the chance to study this dynamic duo. She decided that the secret to her happiness was to make them her new best friends—and, if possible, get them to invite her to stay with them at their spacious villa so she could get out of this dump. Her mom and dad meant well, but they couldn't comprehend Leandra's vision of "the good life." Her mom would take one look at the peeling paint in the hotel lobby at Sawasdee and say, "Cozy!"

Leandra drank her beer and tried closing her eyes, too. But she was just too jacked up from sleeping on the plane and being in this splendid place with Sari and Nick. She decided to take a dip. She waded into the clear, warm ocean, and walked pretty far before the water reached her prominent hip bones. She thought, *This is the first hour of my real life. I've arrived.*

Something big swum in the water near her, a dark shadow. Then Nick surfaced a few feet away. She splashed at him. "I thought you were a shark!"

He laughed. "I just wanted to tell you that we're going back to our villa now."

Leandra glanced toward the beach. Sari waved, and went about packing her book and hat into her Chanel tote. Leandra pouted. She barely had a chance to get to know them and now they were leaving? Before she could subtly hint that she had no plans for later, Nick said, "We'd like to invite you to dinner . . . if you're not too jet-lagged."

"I love dinner!" she blurted, way too eager.

Nick laughed. "I love dinner, too." He gave her the details about how to find their hotel, and instructions to meet in the lobby at seven. Then Nick swam back to the beach, his crawl seamless and speedy as a dolphin. Sari waited for him on shore. When he reached her, she gave him a towel and waved again at Leandra. The most glamorous siblings she'd ever seen strolled down the beach, looking like a travel poster for paradise. Leandra watched them until they were too small to see, then she raced back to the beach and up to her room. Her plan: a shower, nap, and then blow away the Singaporeans with her wholesome white-girl sexiness. Honestly, she didn't care which one of them she ended up with—or both. A sibling threesome? How Asian *Game of Thrones* could she get?

Walking into the Baray Hotel lobby was like going back in time to the Siam of *The King and I* with its draped, sumptuous, shining gold silk, blue and green ceramic tiles, the dazzling mosaic floor, and the intricately carved tables and chairs covered in red cushions. The lobby building was round, with a high domed ceiling, also painted gold, with murals of Buddha riding a tortoise across the sea, jumping orange fish, and a white monkey riding a white elephant through a dense bamboo and banana forest. Built into the floor in the center of the lobby, directly under the high point of the dome, was a reflecting pool lined with smooth gray rocks and dotted with pink water lilies. Fragrant orchids and lilies filled waist-high ceramic urns.

Leandra beheld the wonders. She decided that she would never leave the beautiful lobby. The private villas must be fit for an emperor. She couldn't wait to see one. A Thai woman in a red dress approached her. Leandra was about to say she was waiting for someone when Nick came into the domed lobby from another door.

"Right on time," he said. "Sari wasn't feeling well. Too much sun, I think. She asked me to apologize." Nick looked hot in jeans, a white shirt, and black Pumas.

"Too bad. I was looking forward to having both of you. I mean, having dinner with both of you."

Nick's eyebrows went up. "You look lovely," he said. "I'm glad Sari decided to stay in. I get you all to myself."

"We'll see about that," she said.

He grinned wolfishly. "We could eat here," he said. Yes, please! Leandra asked the Sawasdee concierge about the Baray just to know what to wear. The concierge rhapsodized in broken English about the Baray's thousand-dollar fourteen-course tasting menu. "Or," Nick continued, "since it's your first night in Thailand, we could walk around outside. You have *got* to experience the street food."

Leandra masked her disappointment with a bright smile. Men didn't like whiners. Tonight, she'd be fun and easy and eat cheap. Tomorrow night, she'd push for fancy. "I love street food!" she said. "Lead the way."

"Can you walk in those?" He pointed at her wedge espadrilles.

"I could climb a mountain in these."

He led her out of the lobby, toward Kata Beach. At night, it was lit up with orange and red lanterns, string lights, and small bonfires along the shoreline. Several open-air restaurants were bustling with loud happy diners, the tables laden with platters of shrimp, noodles, fish, and tropical drinks. She thought he'd steer her into one, but he guided her (his hand on the small of her back) toward some food carts lined up on a side road. "Try the dumplings," he said. He went to a particular cart and spoke to the vendor in Thai, who put some dumplings in a clear plastic bag, then scooped in spices and sauces, and plunked in a wooden stick. Nick handed her a bag, and showed her how to use the stick to pierce the dumpling, swish it around in the sauce, and pop it into her mouth.

She nearly died. It was that delicious. No way the $1,000 food could taste better than this. "Oh, my god," she said, stabbing another dumpling with her stick and shoveling it in.

"Slow down," said Nick. "We've got a lot of carts to cover."

They spent an hour sampling shrimp on sticks, sticky rice balls, noodle soup (also served in a plastic bag), and pork skewers. Nick paid for everything, although it was all ridiculously cheap. Each bite was more incredible than the last. She had to laugh about the Toronto food-truck scene, how snobby and pretentious it was. Every single one of these Thai vendors with a two-wheel cart, pot of boiling water, and makeshift grill produced tastier goodies than the gourmet trucks in North America.

"Ready to sit?" Nick asked, wiping his delectable lips with a paper napkin.

Honestly, with a full belly, Leandra was ready to lie down. She hadn't been able to nap earlier, too excited about her plans for later. The traveling and sun were finally catching up with her. "I could use some coffee," she said.

"In Thailand, we drink tea," he said. He brought her to a small beach bar and ordered a pot of green tea. They drank and watched some kids and a few dogs run around on the sand.

"I'm so glad I'm here," said Leandra, feeling genuinely grateful. Her parents worked hard to give her everything, and she hadn't always been as grateful as she should be. She felt far from home all of the sudden, and uncharacteristically emotional.

"You okay?"

She shook off that shock of sentimentality, and aimed her sexiest smile at Nick. "It's just so beautiful."

He nodded, staring right at her. "Exactly what I was thinking."

She willed him to lean toward her and make a move. *Do it! Kiss me NOW.*

Nick sipped his tea. "I really admire you," he said. "It takes a lot of courage to come halfway around the world by yourself, not knowing a soul in the whole country."

"Oh, well, I do know someone here," she said. Her mom insisted she take the phone number for her friend's nephew, an American who worked for a bank in Bangkok. Apparently, she met him once in New York, but he was so forgettable, she had no memory of him. "A family friend. I'm supposed to call him, but he's kind of a loser."

Nick smiled. "So what do you have planned for tomorrow?"

"Nothing yet. Any ideas?"

"Sari and I are renting a long-tail boat for a ride out to the Phi Phi Islands," he said. "One of the islands is overrun with macaque monkeys. Whenever a boat pulls up, the monkeys swarm the beach, looking to be fed longan berries."

She had no idea what a longan berry was, but whatever. "That's awesome!" she said. "Friendly monkeys?"

"Completely tame. They eat fruit right out of your hand. Why don't you come along? We can fit one more in the boat. Sari arranged a picnic lunch. We'll make a day of it. Monkeys, snorkeling, Singha."

"You have no idea how much I love monkeys," she said, beaming. "It's always been a fantasy of mine to feed a primate. Seriously! The closest I've come is throwing a pretzel to a squirrel."

Nick stared at her mouth for a count of three, and then, finally, he came in for a kiss. His lips were warm from the tea, and he smelled like lemon and ginger. In a word: yummy. She'd never kissed an Asian man before. His cheeks were silken, and his hair, which she ran her fingers through, was thick as mink and just as soft. She sighed against his mouth, opening up, letting him in. His tongue was smooth and slippery as a mango. In one deft move, Nick pulled her onto his lap and held her tightly around her tiny waist. The only thing that stopped their kiss from going on forever was the cluck of the old woman behind the bar. Nick pulled back and rested his cheek against hers. "She doesn't approve," he whispered in Leandra's ear.

She climbed off his lap, but couldn't let the moment pass unrecorded. "A quick selfie?" she asked, taking her phone out. He nodded and they posed, the beach behind them. Leandra immediately texted it to Sophia with the message, "In love with Phuket." She wasn't trying to make her friend jealous or flaunt her new life while Sophia was flailing so horribly. But Leandra shouldn't have to tamp down her own happiness. That wasn't how friendship worked.

Smiling at the idea, Leandra said to Nick, "Let's go back to your place." She had to see that villa! It probably had a king-size bed and a private pool right out the back door with jasmine and orange blossoms winding around a hidden terrace.

Nick frowned. "Sari's there."

"She won't hear us."

"She might," he said. "I can't really relax with her nearby. It'd be too bizarre. You understand, right?" Oh, god, his accent when he said "bizarre." It sounded like bizzz-ahhhhh. To die for.

"We could go back to my room," she said hesitantly. "But don't judge me for what a dump it is. The pictures on the website are totally fake."

He grinned. "I'll only be looking at you."

"Let's go," she said.

Leandra took off her shoes and they walked back along the beach, stopping every few minutes to make out. When they got to the hotel, they laughed as they ran past a worker fixing a crack in the lobby wall. As soon as they were safely alone in her room, they fell on the bed before they could turn on the lights. Neon street signs filtered in, giving the room a pink glow.

Nick said, "I want to give you a massage."

"Okay," she said, confused. "Should I be naked?"

"Not usually for a Thai massage, but why not?"

He peeled off her dress. He'd already seen most of her, the bikini leaving little to the imagination, but he gasped when he saw her breasts, like every man did. "Is there any part of you that's not perfect?"

She wished her feet were smaller, but she wasn't going to argue with him.

"Lie on your belly," he instructed. He found some lotion in the bathroom, and started rubbing her shoulders and back. She hadn't realized how tense and stiff she was, probably from the flights. Nick's hands were masterful. Leandra sank into his touch as his fingers and knuckles loosened her muscles and inhibitions. Her breathing slowed, and she fought to stay awake. Nick said, "Just relax," and that was it. Oblivion.

Leandra woke up to street sounds, some men yammering in Thai and a car horn. She jerked upright and checked the time. It was two P.M. She'd slept for twelve hours. "Nick?" she called out. No answer.

Damn. She must have fallen asleep last night while he gave her the massage. He probably realized she was out for the count, and left her to sleep off her jet lag. He'd even pulled the sheets up, thoughtfully. She was surprised he didn't stay. And why hadn't he called her room to wake her up for the long-tail boat ride? It was way past lunchtime. They probably went without her. Leandra decided to clean herself up, get something to eat, and go back to the Baray to track down her friends. She jumped in the shower, and stayed there for about forty-five minutes until the water ran cold, which annoyed her. What kind of hotel ran out of hot water? Three stars? In New York, it'd be lucky to get half a cockroach.

While she showered, Leandra planned her outfit. She'd wear her rainbow-striped bikini under a gray sleeveless shirtdress. It'd be a great reveal. Conservative dress and then, *BAM!*, a teeny bikini in bright colors. Her espadrilles got a workout last night with all that walking, and didn't look so great in daylight. She'd wear her silver sandals and bangles.

All dried off, Leandra went to the closet. She'd painstakingly hung up all her clothes yesterday so they didn't get wrinkled. But when she opened the closet door, it was empty.

She turned around, looking for her hard-shell silver suitcase at the foot of the bed. Maybe a maid put her stuff back into the suitcase? Why the hell would she do that? And when? She'd been in the room all day. Leandra couldn't find the suitcase either. It wasn't under the bed, or anywhere in the room.

In fact, nothing was in the room besides the furniture and other stuff that was bolted down. It seemed embarrassingly sparse, but then again, Leandra had thought that much when she got a first look at it before she unpacked.

Her bag with her wallet and phone and the key to the room safe . . . where the fuck was that? She tore the room apart, hunted every inch, but it wasn't there. Shaking with pure adrenaline, Leandra lurched back to the closet and checked the safe. The little key was in the lock, and the door was slightly ajar. She swung it open and found a black, empty space.

Her money—the $3,000 her parents gave her, plus another $1,000 of her own savings—*gone*.

Her passport—*gone*.

The diamond and gold jewelry she'd packed to catch the eye of wealthy men—*gone*.

Her open-return plane ticket—*gone*.

Leandra had been cleaned out. Everything she'd brought with her was stolen while she slept. Wearing just a towel, she ran out to the front desk and started screaming. A housekeeper and the concierge, a different woman from yesterday, followed her back to her room. Neither of them spoke English, but Leandra was able to get her message across. They looked around, as if they'd be able to find the stuff that was clearly gone.

"Yours?" asked the maid, holding Leandra's iPhone.

It was hidden in the bedsheets. She must have fallen asleep right on top of it. Leandra grabbed it and hugged it to her chest. It wasn't much, but it was something.

Leandra said, "What the fuck kind of security do you have here? Can anyone walk in and rob your guests blind? It's an outrage! I should sue!" Her rant about lax security went on for a while. The housekeeper and concierge nodded and grew smaller with every angry word they didn't understand. Someone came in with a beach sarong for Leandra to wear. Someone else brought fruit and a glass of green guava juice.

A man arrived who spoke English. "I'm Mr. Mookba, the manager," he said, bowing. "Can you say what happened, please?"

She went over it again, waking up to find she'd been robbed. "I feel violated! This is the worst hotel in Phuket!"

"Forgive me, Ms. Hunting. A maintenance worker said you brought a young man to your room last night."

"Oh, that's rich. The janitor was probably the thief! My friend could buy and sell this entire hotel ten times before breakfast."

"This man has worked here for twenty years. He is not a thief."

"Someone is! It's got to be one of the staff or a guest, unless you're saying someone could walk in off the street and right into my freakin' room."

"Are you sure it wasn't the man you were with?"

That launched another high-volume rant from Leandra that ended with the challenge, "Call the Baray! Call them!"

The manager nodded. He went to her room phone and dialed. He spoke in Thai to the person who answered over there. To Leandra, he said, "What is your friend's name, please?"

"Nick. Nick and Sari."

"Family name?"

"I don't know! Christ. Nick and Sari. Brother and sister from Singapore in one of the villas. How hard can it be to find them?"

The manager spoke to his counterpart at the Baray. "He says no one is staying there by that description."

"Bullshit! I met Nick there last night," she said.

One more round of Thai talk, and then the manager hung up. "I'm sorry, Ms. Hunting. They don't know these people."

Leandra shook her head in disbelief. It was like *The Thailight Zone.* "This is bullshit," she said. "We're going over there right now."

"We?"

"Yes, you and me. I can't afford a taxi because your crappy hotel doesn't have digital safe locks!"

The manager agreed to take her to the Baray by taxi. Upon arrival, she stormed into the lobby in her sarong, spinning around until she found the woman in the red sash dress from the evening before. "You saw me and Nick last night! You were here."

Mr. Mookba bowed to the red dress woman, and explained in Thai what was going on. The woman nodded along, looking shocked and saddened by the story. Leandra scrolled through her iPhone photos and found the selfie with Nick. "This guy! You must remember him," she said. "He was here with his sister."

When Leandra said the word "sister," the woman blushed and shook her head. "Not brother sister," she said. "Husband wife."

"WHAT?" Leandra roared.

Then the story came out, as translated by the Sawasdee manager. The man and woman came to the Baray last evening. They said they were from Hong Kong, newlyweds on their honeymoon, staying at another hotel. They asked for a quick tour of the Baray, to see if they liked it enough to book it for an anniversary trip a year from now. Right before the tour began, the woman got a call. They kissed passionately good-bye and she left. The man took a tour. When it was over, he excused himself to the restroom. A minute later, Leandra walked in. The man came back into the lobby, and left with her.

It was all suddenly, disastrously clear. She'd been scammed. Nick and Sari were con artists. They saw her on the beach, a solo woman traveler, a first-timer to Asia, someone easily impressed and eager for companions. They painted a big red target on her back, hit hard and hit fast. It took less than seven hours for them to steal everything she owned. They'd never had such an easy mark.

How could a person ever recover from such a profound humiliation? It wasn't only that she was a sucker—the biggest sucker Nick and Sari, or whatever their names were, had ever taken. She'd orchestrated her own undoing by inviting him back to her room and being a besotted idiot. No wonder he bought her cheap street food! No wonder he wouldn't bring her back to his room. It was too much truth to swallow in one gulp. Shame engulfed her. She had fucked up monumentally with no one to help her. The sudden reality of how alone she was hit her like a tsunami.

Leandra felt dizzy. Her hand went to her temples, and then next thing she knew, she was on the mosaic floor, Mr. Mookba's face hovering over her, asking, "Can you hear me?"

A crowd gathered around her. She heard someone say, "Call the American embassy."

"I'm CANADIAN!" she sobbed.

The manager got her into a taxi, and brought her back to the Sawasdee. He volunteered to make some calls on her behalf. She nodded mutely, in a state of shock. "The worst part is," she said as the concierge held her hand, "I really wanted to feed those monkeys."

The road to happiness is always under construction.

only serial killers
don't like pumpkin

A week after the breakup, driv-ing home in the middle of the night from Opus, her favorite bar, Demi made a few lefts, a few rights, and then ripped into a parking spot like a race car driver. She tripped out of the car when her foot didn't land on the curb. And why would it? She parked two feet away from it. Should she get back in the car, pull out, and try to park again, or just leave it for four hours until she had to drive to work? She might get a ticket.

"Screw it," she said.

She walked to the front door of the building. But the key didn't go in. She jammed it a few times to no avail. "What's wrong with this thing?" she said, glancing at the door and looking around.

Then it hit her. Nothing wrong with the key, but she was trying to use it on the wrong door. She'd driven herself to James's building on automatic pilot. She had sworn she'd never come back here, and yet here she was, standing at her ex's doorway. If he appeared right now, he'd think she'd come crawling back to him, drunk in the middle of the night.

Instead of sprinting back to her car to peel out of there, Demi paused. *What would happen if I buzzed?* Buzzing when buzzed, like bootie texting or drunk dialing. Not advisable. But she was here, and James was probably asleep in bed next to some rank slut. When he got up to see who was buzzing, he might trip and break his neck in the dark, so there was an upside. She slurred out a laugh, followed by a hiccup.

What would Sophia say? "Get back in your car and leave!" Followed by, "Don't drive drunk! Get out of the car and walk!"

Yes, that would be the wise thing to do. Instead, Demi leaned her full weight on James's buzzer for ten solid seconds.

Cackling, she weaved back to her Audi, jumped in, and made her getaway, almost clipping a parked car in her rush. As she drove through empty streets toward her new building five miles away, Demi's smile turned thin and mean.

This is not me, she thought. *He's turned me into a drunken jaded bitch.* So he'd cheated on her with countless hoes for the entire three years they were together. Was that inexcusable? James apparently thought so. It'd been a whole week since Demi left, and he hadn't called to ask for forgiveness. Not a peep from him. No missed calls or "let's talk" texts. She'd expected him to beg for mercy once or twice a day, across several different platforms and devices. She had blocked his number, but he could have found a way. Depending on her mood and the medium, Demi would have heard him out. She might even have considered taking him back, albeit on a short leash with a choke collar. But that selfish prick didn't give her the courtesy of groveling. Of all the ways he'd hurt her, his radio silence post-breakup might be the worst. It made her want another drink.

When in doubt, wine not. It's Wine O'Clock. She laughed to herself. The ironic part: Demi hadn't been much of a drinker with James. Two wasted people in one couple was a recipe for disaster. Single Demi was making up for lost time. Her long-neglected friends were all too happy to celebrate the breakup with her, especially if she were buying the drinks. James had transferred some money into her bank account, like a parting gift. She was burning through it, in a blur. At some point soon, Demi would stop drowning her sorrows, get on dry land, and deal. Her parents—both sets—didn't know about the breakup yet. She wasn't ready for "we knew he wasn't The One," followed by mature and responsible suggestions about how to live her life. She'd only just figured out *where* to live.

Her new apartment complex was called the Grace. She had toured a dozen apartments, and this one-bedroom was the only decent place in her price range that was available immediately. She'd moved in a couple of days ago with the suitcases she'd packed when James was at work. No furniture yet, so she slept on a mattress on the floor. Her schedule—going to work by nine A.M., coming home in the middle of the night, wasted—wasn't conducive to bonding with the neighbors. She hadn't met any of them yet.

She parked tighter this time, her rear tire rising onto the curb, lifting the back right corner of the car off the pavement. Bone tired and queasy, Demi eased out of the car carefully this time. She made it halfway up the walk toward the front door when the world tilted to one side. Her legs buckled. The ground rushed up to meet her face.

It was a semi-soft landing. Demi crashed through some bushes on the way down. The sound of snapping branches and an oomph when she hit the dirt seemed to come from a distance, as if someone *else* had taken a header into the shrubs. Demi thought of herself as a down-to-earth person, but . . . *Fuck me, I just ate it big-time.* She wheezed out a laugh that sounded a bit like a dying seal.

She tried to push herself upright, but her hair was tangled in the twigs. The trickle on her cheek could be blood, or tears, or saliva. Struggling to move, she managed to roll over and see the brightening sky. The stars were gone. It was getting light out. Her best bet, her only feasible option, was to just lie here, close her eyes for a minute, and wait for her head to stop spinning. Like Demi, time collapsed. The next thing she knew, it was morning.

"Is she dead?" asked a female voice over her.

"Dead drunk."

Demi opened her eyes a slit, and made out a pair of wrinkly faces hovering above, haloed with nimbuses of white hair. "Call the cops," said the woman in an orange windbreaker.

"I know this girl," said the other in Lululemon yoga pants and jacket. "She moved into Miriam's apartment last week. May she rest in peace." They both made the sign across their chests.

Rest in peace sounded perfect. Demi would love to close her eyes and snuggle into her pillow of mulch. But the two oldies each took an arm, and pulled her upright. She hoped she didn't pull them down with her, and forced herself to focus.

"That's a very pretty windbreaker," said Demi. "I don't want to heave on it." The ladies instantly dropped her arms, and she fell backward, landing on the ground.

"Here's Wally," said Yoga Pants, waving at someone Demi couldn't see. An ancient dude, the one who winked at her every day when she left for work as he set out on his snail-paced morning walk.

"She's cute," he said, studying Demi through thick bifocals. "Except she smells like a distillery."

"We can't just leave her here," said Yoga Pants with a soft English accent. "The dog walker comes by every morning with those five poodles. This is their favorite pee stop."

Demi sniffed and could pick up traces of dog piss. That did it. Her stomach convulsed.

"Incoming!" yelled the man.

Demi was impressed by how quickly the seniors jumped out of the way. Except for Orange Windbreaker. She was kind of doddering.

"My new arch supporters!"

"Sorry!"

"Let's get her inside," said Yoga Pants. "She needs a shower and coffee."

Wally said with a chuckle, "If I were her age, I'd volunteer to undress her."

Demi liked the pervy old man. He kept it light. The three of them were on her again, pulling her upright to standing. Her stomach spasmed again, but she swallowed hard to keep it down. "Who's Miriam?" she asked.

They ignored the question. Instead, Yoga Pants asked, "What happened to you, dear?"

"Do you mean last night, or my whole life?"

"Oh, honey," she said, double dose of sympathy, like she genuinely cared.

Demi looked into her warm blue eyes, and found an ocean of compassion in them. The affect was sobering, and Demi was suddenly, mortally embarrassed. "I'm fine," she said, standing taller, steadier. "Just another Wednesday night."

"Thursday morning," said Wally.

"I'm going to pay for your shoes, and wash the sidewalk. I promise. I just need, like, a hose. Is there a hose somewhere?"

"Over there." Wally pointed toward the side of the building. "I'll get it."

"Let him clean up," said Yoga Pants. "He loves a project."

Hosing puke was a project? Like scrapbooking? "I need a hobby," said Demi. "Hobbies are good."

"Hobbies are essential to happiness," said Yoga Pants. "Come on, I'll help you get inside."

"What about our walk?" That was Orange Windbreaker.

"Go on your walk, really. I'm okay," said Demi, bending down to pick up her bag and backing toward the Grace's front door. A handsome senior couple in matching workout gear, sunglasses, and hand weights stormed past them. *Great,* she thought. *The one day I meet all the neighbors.*

Hands shaking, Demi managed to turn the key and crawl up the two flights to her apartment. Alone finally, Demi stripped, and stood under a scalding hot shower until her skin turned bright pink. After two Tylenol and a coconut water, she set her phone alarm for two hours from then, and lay down on the mattress on the floor to sleep.

Demi rolled into the office at midday in her standard work clothes: Citizens of Humanity jeans, a close-fitting American Apparel long-sleeved navy T-shirt, and suede Vans. Maya Lundy, her boss and friend, was on the phone and waved hello. Lundy Events was a micro company, just the two desks in one room. You'd think Demi and Maya would get on each other's nerves from all that togetherness, and you'd be right. Their personalities chafed, but only occasionally. For the most part, their collaboration worked pretty well. Demi really looked up to Maya. She was forty-two, but they would go out for drinks and chat for hours. Sometimes, she babysat Maya's daughters. Not lately, though. When work slowed down—rarely—Maya told Demi about her days at Pepperdine, her years living in Venice. Demi would love to live in California!

Maya developed several businesses, Lundy Events being the last and most successful. It was the go-to outfit for promoting and launching new restaurant ventures in downtown Vancouver. Their current project was Maya's baby, from inception to installation, called First @ Second, a weekend food festival on Second Beach. If all went well, next year's festival would be called Second @ Second, and so on until eternity, if Maya got her wish. They'd been working on it for months, and had only another few weeks to go. Maya had to do most of the heavy lifting last week, with Demi's apartment search and move, her post-breakup malaise, and her constant hangover. Thank god for Maya, but Demi knew the ice was getting thin. It was only a matter of time before Maya cracked and Demi sank.

"You look better than you must feel," said Maya correctly after she hung up the phone. She was out with Demi and her friends last night, but left after one drink, hours before things got weird.

"Don't expect much from me today. I think I have to cut out early again. Just some stuff to take care of." Demi didn't really have anything urgent, other than the need to nap, and to bake some apology muffins for her neighbors. They hosed her vomit. It was the least she could do.

Maya wasn't having it. "I need a full day, Demi. Crunch time. You can either do the phones or deal with the alcohol permit. If we don't get it sorted out ASAP, we're screwed."

A food festival without beer was like Christmas without presents. Given the choice between schmoozing forty people on the phone, each with a complaint, or going to City Hall to stand in a long line, Demi would have to take . . . god, both sounded awful. She liked Maya, and she was pretty good at organization, but she didn't feel anything close to passion for this job. It was something to do until the blurry big picture came into focus. Maya's enthusiasm was usually contagious, but it wasn't spreading today.

"Did I tell you, I figured out that the whole time James said he was in Chicago last May he was really in Miami? I checked the credit card records." In her nonwork, nonblotto hours, Demi had become obsessed with logging into their Visa account and comparing past statements with her calendars. It was all there. Each statement was proof of his lies. If only she'd looked at their financials sooner. In her years with James, she'd never once checked. James handled all the bills.

"Yeah, James is a prick, was always a prick, and will continue to be one for as long as he slimes his way across North America. You should have known. You were an idiot, yes, we agree."

Demi said, "I sense . . . annoyance."

Maya laughed. "I'm not *annoyed*. I'm freaking out! As soon as First @ Second is over, I want to hear every despicable James story you've got. But until then, we have shit to do."

"I just sat down. Let me have one cup of coffee first, okay? Then I'm off to City Hall. Just half a cup."

"A Demi?" asked Maya. Two phones rang at once, and she was off to the races. Her day would continue like this for another twelve hours.

Demi filled a mug, and scrolled through her work emails. Seventy-eight messages, most of them marked Urgent, re: First @ Second. One address popped out at her. The email was from Mrs. Rydell, the building manager who showed her the apartment at the Grace. The message had an attachment—her signed and executed lease.

She called Mrs. Rydell, who picked up on the first ring. "Hello, Demi. Did you get the lease?"

"Yeah, thanks."

"Do you *love* the place?"

"I like it. But I couldn't help noticing, everyone there is really old."

Mrs. Rydell was such a fast talker when she was walking her through the place. Now, she took a pause. "I told you the residents were mature."

"By *mature*, I thought you meant *employed*."

"More like *retired*."

"Did someone die in my apartment?"

"People die everywhere."

"The lease is signed. I can't get out of it now. Just tell me the truth."

Another pause. "The apartment's quirky history is why it's so affordable."

"How quirky?"

"All I know is that the deaths were from natural causes, like heart attacks and strokes. It's just a coincidence that they happened in the same apartment."

Demi choked on her coffee. "Deaths, plural? How many?"

"Four?"

"You rented me a death trap!"

"The place is completely safe. It's been checked and rechecked. The water is clean. No mold, bugs, toxins, or rodents. The elderly are very good neighbors. No loud music, they go to bed early, and keep the place spotless. If you have some kind of prejudice against old people, then you can always break the lease. But you'll forfeit the security deposit and your first month's rent."

Demi was too hungover to be angry. It *was* a large apartment in an immaculate building and a great location. She didn't hate old people. It was just a bit disconcerting to be the youngest person in the building by fifty years. She put her head down on her desk, and tried to picture Miriam and the gang of ghosts who might be lurking in her bathroom. Friendly ghosts, she was sure, and not necessarily a bad thing. Demi could stand to meet some new people.

She might've dozed a bit, because the next thing she knew, Maya was shaking her shoulder. "I'm up!" she said, and busily tidied her

desk like a kid caught snoozing through history class. "I was just resting my eyes."

Maya was not amused. "Permit?" she said.

"Going." Demi grabbed her bag, left the office, and got in the Audi.
It made some suspicious grinding noises, but she ignored them.
Should she even be driving this hungover? She drove last night. How
could she have done that? *Never again, you idiot!* She went down to
City Hall, parked, and found the right room in the labyrinth of offices,
only to find out that the clerk was out to lunch until two P.M., an
hour from now. She texted Maya and said, "Office closed until after
lunch. Will go back then. Running errands."

Demi made the snap decision do a quick food shop and then head
back to the Grace. It was so close, and she could still smell pinot
grigio coming out of her pores. She'd bake muffins, take another
shower, then get the permit and be back at work with at least five
minutes to spare before Maya's nervous breakdown.

The oven was as old as the average resident at the Grace, so Demi
wasn't optimistic about baking there. Plus, she wasn't much of a baker
at all. She followed the recipe and measured and mixed the ingredients carefully. The pumpkin spice muffin recipe was a James favorite. She'd perfected it over the years and was quite proud of it. She
hoped her neighbors liked it. Who *didn't* like pumpkin? You'd have
to be insane not to, a deranged, twisted psychopath. Bonus: It was
packed with vitamins A and C, good news for the olds. Demi could
use a double dose of antioxidants, too. She'd been treating her body
like a garbage dump since the breakup.

Since the breakup. Her life was now divided between "before the
breakup" and "since the breakup." James's betrayal defined her life,
and probably would for a long time. She could sum up her existence
to a new person, "Hi, my name is Demi Michaels. I'm twenty-one
and have no clue what to do with my life. My boyfriend cheated on
me for years. When I found out, I had to break up with him. I'm des-
perately lonely. I wish I could bury my head in the sand, and pretend

I never caught him. But I did, and now I'm stuck with the anger, zero trust, a jaded perspective on love, an open invitation to AA, pity money, party friends, and no confidence." Man, she was a real treat these days.

Demi poured the batter into the muffin pans, and put them in the oven. While they baked, she showered again, changed her clothes, and cleaned up her space. The light was fantastic at this time of day. It gave her a freshly scrubbed, clean feeling.

Speaking of which, she had a mountain of laundry to do. While the muffins cooled on a rack, she took a duffel bag down to the basement to the washer-dryer room, no quarters required. She stuffed two of the washers, one with whites, one with coloreds, set the dials, and started them off.

As she was leaving the room, Yoga Pants came in, lugging a basket of her own dirty drawers. When she noticed both machines were running, she said, "Both yours?" and pointed at the two churning washing machines. "House rules: You're not supposed to take two at a time."

I can't do anything right, she thought. "I'll take my stuff out if you want."

"No, forget it."

"Just leave your stuff. I'll put it in when mine's done. I'll even fold. It's the least I can do after this morning."

"Are you feeling better?" The woman placed her basket on top of one of the washers.

"Much, except for the abject humiliation."

Yoga Pants smiled. "You certainly gave us something to talk about."

"I'm Demi, by the way."

"Catherine." They shook hands.

"I'm never tangling with shrubs again. I'm never drinking again. It was a one-time thing. I've learned my lesson."

Catherine said, "Bullshit!" Whoa, Demi's grandmother never cursed like that.

"You're right. I am going to drink again."

"You can come upstairs and have a sip right now, if you'd like. I put some Bailey's in my coffee at this time of day."

Be neighborly! "Um, sure. Sounds great."

They took the stairs together. Catherine zoomed up the stairs, shockingly. "I do yoga five days a week."

"You're in better shape than I am."

"Considering the shape you were in this morning . . ."

What a sassy old bird! They got to the second floor. "Here you are," said Catherine. "I'm right across the hall."

It was after two P.M. Demi really should go back to City Hall, but she couldn't very well abandon the laundry and turn down her neighbor's hospitality after accepting it. That would be rude and make a bad second impression. She'd have one coffee, transfer the wash into the dryer, then run back to City Hall and get the permit. She'd deliver it to Maya, and then race home and fold.

They got to their floor, and Catherine said, "I'll get the bottle. We can christen your place."

As she opened her door, Demi warned, "I don't have anywhere to sit, but you do yoga, right?" They both smiled. Demi felt better already.

When they were settled on boxes in Demi's apartment, she had to ask, "Were you and Miriam friends? I know about the portal of doom, by the way."

Catherine laughed. "We call your apartment 'God's Waiting Room.'"

"God's going to have to wait a long time for me."

"Don't curse yourself."

"Okay, okay. I'm going to die tomorrow. Is that better?"

Catherine liked her little joke, and gave Demi the brightest smile she'd seen in weeks. It was like sunshine and lemonade, and warmed Demi inside out.

"Something smells really good," said Catherine.

"My muffins. I baked them for you, for all of you, to say 'thanks' and 'sorry' for this morning." Demi dashed around the kitchen to put a hot cake on a plate.

Catherine took a bite, made yummy sounds, and asked, "Who doesn't love pumpkin? You'd have to be insane not to. Only serial killers don't love pumpkin."

"I couldn't agree more," said Demi as they clinked their coffees and took another bite.

demi's pumpkin spice raisin and walnut muffins

ingredients

3 cups gluten-free baking flour
2 tsps baking powder
2 tsps baking soda
1 tsp salt
1 tbsp ground cinnamon
1 tbsp ground ginger
¼ tsp allspice
¼ tsp ground nutmeg
4 eggs
⅔ cup applesauce
⅓ cup maple syrup
⅔ cup almond milk
2 tbsps vanilla extract
one can pumpkin puree
½ cup chopped walnuts
1 cup golden raisins

instructions

1. Preheat the oven to 350 degrees. Line a standard 12-cup muffin tin with paper liners.

2. In a medium bowl, whisk together the flour, baking powder, baking soda, salt, cinnamon, ginger, allspice, and nutmeg.

3. Add the 4 eggs, applesauce, maple syrup, almond milk, and vanilla directly to the dry ingredients. Stir until the batter is smooth and thick. Using a plastic spatula, fold in the pumpkin, walnuts, and raisins until all are evenly distributed throughout the batter.

4. Pour the batter into each prepared cup ¾ full. Bake the muffins on the center rack for 25 minutes, rotating the tin 180 degrees halfway through. The finished muffins will be soft to the touch, and a toothpick inserted in the center will come out clean.

5. Let the muffins stand in the tin for 15 minutes, then transfer them to a wire rack and cool completely. Store the muffins in an airtight container at room temperature for up to three days.

5

rock that invisible tiara!

A month post-breakup, Sophia studied Demi carefully on her laptop screen, checking her face for blotches and bloat, and her psyche for cracks. The breakup had taken a toll, although today she seemed okay. Better. "Any bootie texts from James yet?" asked Sophia.

"If only! He'd be shocked if I showed up at his place . . . with a chain saw."

"What's the feelings update?" Sophia asked, hoping Demi would keep it brief. Not to offend her or be rude, but she loathed James and was so glad that was over. But she understood the pain her friend was in. When Jesse broke up with her—totally out of the blue, just announced one day that he wanted out—she was shellshocked. But after a month of daily emotional check-ins with Demi, Sophia was suffering from chronic sympathy fatigue, and was ready to be done with it.

"I'm fine."

"Really?"

Demi waved off the concern. "I don't recognize that wall. Where are you?"

"I'm in a Days Inn in Los Angeles for pilot casting week," said Sophia, reflexively glancing over her shoulder at the cheesy print of fruit and cats on the wall. Usually, for their Skype chats, Sophia was on her bed with her vision board behind her.

"We're in the same time zone!"

"I can almost smell Vancouver from here. Fresh air, good food, and boringness." They laughed together.

"What's pilot season?"

"It's when every actor in North America flocks to Hollywood, trying to get a TV job. Agnes has arranged auditions for sitcoms, family dramas. I spent the day with a hundred girls in a soundstage, re-applying lip gloss every five minutes."

"I've been such an absentee friend! Sorry to be so selfish lately. I'm done with that, promise So, Days Inn, huh," said Demi.

"It's fine. Check out the room service," said Sophia, holding up the bag of Lays she got from the vending machine down the hall.

"Are you lonely?"

An odd question, but Demi could always sense Sophia's moods. "Not lonely exactly. More like invisible. I'm walking like a star, believe me, but so is every other girl. The casting people and producers don't look you in the eye. They talk to my head shot, not my actual head."

"No eye-to-eye contact," said Demi.

"Eye-to-ass, eye-to-boob."

"Eye-to-crotch. So humanizing!" As Demi spoke, she stood up to give Sophia a close-up view of her underwear. Then turned around and pushed her ass to the camera. Sophia got up and started dancing in her robe.

They laughed, instantly cheering each other up. In all this serious career stuff, Sophia needed the strong hit of goofy that only Demi could provide. If only Demi were here! It had been a long day for Sophia, with another one tomorrow. "You know that actor I met at Ta-Da I told you about? Scott? He's in the room next to me. He's been coming to LA for pilot season for ten years already. He's either a masochist or my hero."

Demi started putting on makeup, using the Skype window like a mirror. "I can't talk long. I'm meeting Sarah and Jo for dinner in an hour and I have to get ready."

"How's the new place?" Sophia didn't want to let her go yet.

"It's okay. I made friends with my across-the-hall neighbor. We hang out after work drinking Bailey's. You have to meet her when you come home."

"Another drinking buddy?" asked Sophia.

Demi snorted. "She's eighty. We bake casseroles and watch *Real Housewives*. She's just someone to talk to."

"And I'm chopped liver."

"No! You are in Hollywood, becoming a movie star." She used this stupid accent. Sometimes it veered Irish, sometimes Indian, and always hilarious.

"Yes," she replied in the same accent. Sophia missed Demi more than ever. The irony of it was that at first, Sophia was relieved when Leandra left for Thailand, to get a break from her intensity and have some mental space to think about herself. But after a week she couldn't ignore the widening sinkhole of her social life.

"Isn't Renee in LA now?" asked Demi. "Can you call her to hang out?"

Sophia marveled at how Demi could read her mind over hundreds of miles. "I left a voice mail and a text. She didn't call back."

"Bitch."

"Scott is taking me to a party in the Hills tonight, so that's something."

"Maybe you'll meet the man of your dreams."

"You mean a producer who casts me as the star of a cool new show? Ideally, he's gay, or has no hands."

"Yes, exactly!"

"You realize you haven't said a thing about James this entire time," said Sophia. "Not that I'm complaining."

"I'm giving you a heartbreak breather. Catherine lets me talk her ear off about him. To be honest, I'm kind of tired of beating a dead horse. C'est la vie!"

"You should have some French wine to go with the attitude," said Sophia.

"Way ahead of you," said Demi, lifting a glass into the frame.

"Whoa, that's a healthy dose. You're not driving are you?" A knock on the door. "That's Scott. Okay, wish me luck at my first Hollywood party."

"Wear your invisible tiara," sang Demi. "And have fun in 'the Hills,' whatever that means."

She hung up feeling calm. They were so different, but they wanted the same things: for both of them to find their bliss, ideally, at the same time so they could love their lives together.

Driving to the party via Uber was like a sightseeing tour of famous movie titles: Laurel Canyon, Mulholland Drive, the Hollywood Hills. As the car climbed higher and higher into the mountain, the houses were farther and farther back from the road. The hidden ones were the real gems, and she wished she could get out, sneak through the hedge, and take photos of them all. They drove still higher, then made a turn to see the valley stretched out below.

"Sensational view," said Scott.

"Unbelievable," she agreed.

"Just wait until you see the house."

Sophia felt the heat of the city in her body. She adjusted her invisible tiara in her mind and smiled.

According to conventional wisdom, everyone who lived in these mansions worked in the entertainment biz or had parents who did. If Sophia lived here, her imagination would spark up like a forest fire. She would have loved to stop and take photos for her vision board, but Scott would mock her for gawking like a tourist. Instead, she snapped discreetly out of the car window. She loved a good drive-by Snapchat. There was something artistic about it. They scaled the side of the hill until they reached the home on Hilldale of Adam Schlock, the writer/director of the horror series *Butcher*. (Cue stabbing music.)

"I met Adam on *Butcher 1* about ten years ago when I was young and hot," said Scott, who was only thirty years old. The car pulled to a stop at the end of the driveway. "It was a hit, and he went on to make three more of them, with another currently in the works. You would think he'd run out of ideas after *Butcher 2, 3,* and *4,* but there's always another sick, perverted way to hack up a co-ed."

"Were you disemboweled on-screen? Because that would be the centerpiece of my highlight reel," said Sophia.

"I wish! I was an extra on the beach, just another idiot screaming over a gore-covered body. Fake gore and a dummy, but still thoroughly revolting. I screamed for real the first few takes. But after the seventeenth, I could have curled up next to it and taken a nap. When the day was over, Adam told me I had the best little girl scream of any grown man he'd ever met. We bonded. I haven't managed to get many jobs out here, but I have made some friends. Then again, in LA, everyone is your friend as long as you give them something they want." They wound down the driveway toward the house, where a few party stragglers smoked or yelled on their phones outside.

"What does Adam want from you?" she asked.

Scott raised his eyebrows. "Are you from Vancouver . . . or Kansas?"

O-kay, she thought. Sophia felt herself blush.

Cracking up, Scott said, "Oh, my god, you should see your face! I'm kidding! Once upon a time, Adam and I enjoyed some friendly benefits. But it's been awhile. I call him when I'm in town, and, if possible, we catch up. He always invites me to his all-day parties. And now I'm inviting you."

"Maybe Adam will want to disembowel me for *Butcher 5.*"

"Please never say that again, you little bitch!"

Sophia made a sexual little face and strutted along down the driveway. The house that *Butcher* built, from the outside, was a seventies retro boring bungalow. Sophia couldn't help feeling disappointed. But then they walked in, and it was like waking up in Oz. The entire back wall of the house was a window. The decorating was midcentury modern, deceptively minimalist, understated elegance. The fixtures and furniture were probably authentic stuff from the thirties and forties. It wasn't her taste, but it was stunning. Demi would die. She snapped a few pictures to send her later. Sophia would have loved to photograph each stick of furniture—she had a fetish for beautiful chairs—but the room was packed with nearly naked models, guys sweating from open and obvious coke consumption, and every piece of riffraff from the Hollywood freak show. It felt like an episode of *Californication*, and Sophia was wowed by it.

It was late afternoon, still plenty of sunlight. Everywhere she looked, Sophia saw bikinis and waxed, tanned flesh—and that was just the dudes. The women wore triangular scraps of fabric that barely covered their nipples and miniscule vag slings. A lot of them were draped in elaborate chain systems that wound around their necks, between the implants, and around their tiny waists. Sophia had worried she was underdressed in a sheer, blowy frock. Compared to these nude goddesses, she might as well have been wearing a bathrobe. It wasn't just the skin on display that astonished her. They were all gorgeous. Each specimen was more perfect than the next, and nothing was left to the imagination.

Scott put a finger under her chin and lifted her jaw back into place. "Welcome to LA. This is why I can't live here," he said, sweeping his hand to take it all in, the house, the models, the view. "I'd throw myself off those cliffs if I had to see perfection day in, day out." Sophia must have looked confused. "Let me ask you: Are you appreciating the view, or feeling envious of it? Are you amazed by the beauty, or comparing yourself to them?"

She loved it, and what it represented. She wasn't bothered by the models. They weren't competition, just simply beautiful things to look at while she sipped a cocktail. Before she could tell Scott, a middle-aged man in a white shirt, faded jeans, and loafers came over. "Scott! You made it." This must be Adam. He looked exactly like she thought a horror producer would, with a neat graying beard, slicked back hair, and bushy eyebrows. He was slim with a colorful tinge to his skin, like he'd been on a carrot juice cleanse for a week. He hugged Scott and then showed her his too-white veneers. "Who's this?"

"My friend Sophia Marcus, a very talented actor I found under a rock in Toronto," said Scott.

"Is that so? Be sure to introduce yourself around, Sophia," said Adam. "Now, Scott, you must remember Carlos. He's just back from Belize and looks fabulous. Come say hello."

Scott shot her an apologetic glance before being led away by the host. So much for Sophia's three-second fantasy that Adam would offer her an audition on the spot. She wondered how many people at this party had the same dream of being discovered, of having their lives change in an instant. She surveyed the room, trying to get a lay of the land. Who seemed approachable? Sophia ventured into the vast living room that opened onto a pool deck. A 360-degree view of nubile bodies, like a Slim Aarons photograph on crack. She took a quick picture on her phone without anyone seeing, and snapped an even more permanent picture in her mind.

"You look lost," said a guy in a white tank top that showed off his elaborate sleeve tattoos, and board shorts that hung low, exposing abs that were like an arrow pointing to his package. His trucker hat read "Boy." *Thanks for the tip,* she thought. Now she was embarrassed she forgot a hat that said "Girl." He had olive skin and green eyes. She'd guess he was mixed race, like she was. "I'm Gavin."

"Sophia."

"What brings a girl like you to a party like this?"

"I'm here with my friend Scott who said he was taking me to a little house party, and now I'm *here*!" She bent to the side, palms up like she was presenting the room to him.

"Ah, you're not from here. Canadian, eh?!" *Original.*

"How'd you know?" she asked, a touch of coy.

"The way you said HOW-sss," he said. So annoying.

"Nice to meet you, Gavin, You have a good night." One douche bag down, a million to go.

Sophia circulated. It'd be extremely helpful if she knew who all these people were. If only there was an app for that. Point the camera at a face, and get a complete IMDB profile. One of the models stuck a key up her nose and snorted like she had a sinus infection. *Classy,* she thought.

The pool was breathtaking. It jutted out over the side of the hill in a stunning feat of architectural engineering. It seemed to be suspended in midair. She couldn't resist taking another photo—the cliff, the glowing lights, the Hollywood sign in the distance. Leandra would appreciate the opulence. She'd text the picture to her later with the caption "Jealous much?"

She made a lap around the pool. Although everyone was in swimsuits, no one was in the water. That would probably change as the night wore on and drinking and drugs got serious. Sophia hoped the water was heavily chlorinated, for all of their sakes. Then again, in this perfect house, it was probably salt water. She stood at the railing overlooking the LA lights below and took a few more photos while eavesdropping on some people nearby. One of the women—Afro, leopard-print bikini—mentioned the name of a show Sophia had auditioned for that morning. She had to get into this conversation.

"Hi, I love your bikini," Sophia said.

The woman scrutinized her closely. It was almost like visiting the gynecologist. "Thanks," she said finally.

"I think I auditioned for the show you were just talking about."

"Which part?"

"The blind daughter."

"I read for 'urban neighbor.'"

A pretty blond boy at her side in a purple banana hammock said, "I read for the closeted gay son. Like anyone would believe I could pass for straight!"

The sexy redhead next to him said, "I read for the alcoholic mother."

"The *mother*?" asked Sophia. The redhead was in her late twenties. "Aren't you kind of young for that?"

"Once you hit twenty-eight, you read for the mother, even if you're supposed to have an eighteen-year-old kid."

"That's crazy!"

The three of them shrugged, like *No duh, but whatcha gonna do?*

The "mother" said, "Big news. I made an appointment with Dr. Loveglove."

"Lucky!"

"Who?" asked Sophia.

Urban said, "Celeb diet doc. He's got magic pills that, supposedly, can make you lose, like, ten pounds in two weeks."

"My friend Blair went to him, and it totally worked."

"I need his number, like yesterday, bitch!" said the guy.

That launched a debate among them about the merits of bone-broth soup cleanses vs. an old-school coke binge for weight loss. Sophia stood to the side, pretending to be fascinated. She'd always been slim, and worked out (when she could) but never did anything fucking crazy like go to a doctor to prescribe pills, air, and water to fulfill your nutritional needs. The three actors didn't seem aware that she was zoning out. In fact, they were barely aware she was still standing there.

It got awkward, nodding along, as the three of them carried on their chat. She had to melt away, and find another group to pretend to listen to. Better still, she'd strike up a pleasant conversation and make a genuine human connection, which seemed about as likely at this party as finding gold in a bucket of mud. But you had to keep digging. Who knows what can happen?

Sophia got a text from Scott, saving her. "Find me by the pool. I might have a job for you!"

A job! He could have said, "It's true love!" and she wouldn't have felt a thing. But a job! That gave her a jolt. No need to excuse herself, she just walked away, squeezing through the thickening crowd, and spotted Scott by the sushi buffet in a small circle of two other men and one girl.

She joined them and was shocked to find a familiar face among them. "Hey, Renee!" she said, leaning in to give her a hug. "I hoped I'd run into you."

"Sophia, good to see you," said Renee, not nearly as excited to see Sophia.

"I left you a message."

"Oh," said Renee, not bothering to pretend she didn't receive it. What was wrong with her?

"You two know each other?" asked Scott.

"We work at the same club in Toronto," said Sophia, smiling.

"Worked. I quit," said Renee. To the other two men, she said, "That was before I starred in a Skyy vodka ad. We just finished the shoot. The ad should start running internationally in a few months. TV. Bus shelters. Internet. I'll be all over the place."

Scott paused after Renee's self-promo moment. Then he said, "Sophia, I'd like you to meet Tom and Chuck. They run Rx Studios."

Chuck was around forty, with a cracked-leather tan, slicked-back hair, and a single diamond stud in his left ear. He was the West Coast equivalent of the jerks in the VIP section at CRUSH.

"What's Rx Studios?" she asked.

"A production company," said Tom, the shorter version of Chuck. "We produce TV ads. Some are for products. You've heard of Shampow? We did that. Some are for health care products. So if you have pills or drops for dry eyes, or a dry mouth, or a dry vagina, you come to us."

When Tom said "vagina," they smirked at each other.

Attn: Demi. Please appear out of thin air! They'd have a field day with this. *Once a frat boy, always a frat boy.* Sophia said to Renee, "This is so weird, bumping into each other. Who do you know at the party?"

Renee glared at her. "I'm here with a friend." Then she beamed at Chuck and Tom. "Tell me about the ad campaign you're working on."

Scott said, "Yes, that's why I called you over, Sophia. I couldn't help overhearing Tom and Chuck talking to . . . Reba? Renee, yes. They were discussing some of the ads they're currently casting."

Chuck said, "The big one right now is for a chat line called Hot Links."

"Chat lines? They still exist?" asked Scott.

Sophia said, "And they advertise on TV?"

The ad guys said, "It's low-budge, late-night stuff. But it's still a big market. We need a girl to hold a phone like it's her boyfriend's dick, and say, 'Call Hot Links for a Hot Night!'"

Renee nodded, like this was the job opportunity of a lifetime. "Sounds so fun!" Seriously?

Tom (or Chuck?) said to Sophia, "Turn profile, sweetheart. Good. Now the other. Do a spin. You are a gorgeous girl. You don't have a bad side. Including the back side."

Scott skillfully blocked the ad man from taking a swat at Sophia's butt.

"Can I have my agent send you my reel?" asked Renee.

"We're looking for actors," said Tom. "The girl will have to read a few lines. Models are better seen, not heard."

"I have more acting credits than she does," said Renee petulantly. "Sophia's never been called back for anything." Turning toward her, Renee added, "But don't get discouraged. You hang in there. Something will come up."

Sophia's blood boiled, and her smile got bigger. When pissed, she smiled and nodded. It was a defense mechanism.

Renee had been in LA for a few weeks, and the transformation was complete. Not a trace of her Canadian party girl persona remained. She was a shark now, ready to fight to the death over a chat line ad. Sophia wasn't going to take the bait. She was better than that, and preferred the high road. Renee was welcome to Tom and Chuck. She apparently needed them, badly.

Renee smiled at her, eyes telegraphing, *Try me, little girl.*

Scott said, "Now, now. Plenty of hot links to go around."

Tom pointed at Sophia's strappy sandals. "I couldn't help noticing your feet, Sophia. We're also doing an ad for a toe fungus medication. You'd be a shoe in for it!"

He and Chuck laughed and high-fived each other.

Scott rolled his eyes, and mouthed, *Sorry*.

"I'm auditioning for some TV pilots, so I can't commit to anything else right now," she said. A graceful rejection. "But Renee seems to be available for any body part you need." She smiled and tried to steer Scott away from the others.

Before they got five steps, Renee spun her around to face her. "I get it," she said. "I really do. If I were you, I'd be jealous of me, too. I'm getting work, and you're striking out. When the princess doesn't get what she wants, she has to shit on everyone else."

"I can't believe I ever thought you were my friend," said Sophia.

"You always thought you were better than me," said Renee. "Now we know the truth."

Damn right! The truth was, Renee hadn't been cheering on and supporting Sophia, like she thought they were for each other. Renee had been rooting for Sophia to fail. The difference between them was suddenly blazingly clear. She wondered what in her manner came off as superior or smug. She had no idea. Sophia didn't look down on Renee, she just believed in herself. They'd talked a few times about Renee's hardscrabble childhood, and she remembered Renee saying, "You can always fall back on your parents, Sophia. I don't have that luxury." It seemed, at the time, like an observation, not a condemnation. Renee's resentment toward her was scalding. All along Renee had secretly hated her.

"It was great to see you, Renee," said Sophia diplomatically. "Maybe we'll run into each other again."

"Now you're going to tell everyone back home that I've turned into an asshole."

"If the fungus fits," muttered Scott, which made Sophia laugh, and Renee furious.

"You'll never be a star, Sophia. You don't deserve it. You don't have the talent. In five years, you won't have your looks either."

Sophia had reached her limit. On pure, angry impulse, she pushed Renee into the pool. When the bartender came sputtering to the surface, she shrieked, "You bitch! I borrowed this dress from the set!"

Scott and Sophia watched her splash around the shallow end. He said, "You just threw her in the pool. On purpose."

"By accident," she lied. A girl can only be pushed so far before she has to push back. She wasn't proud of it, but . . . well, maybe a little.

"Remind me not to get on your bad side," he said.

"I don't have a bad side, remember?" she said.

Every
SETBACK
is a
SETUP
for a
COMEBACK.

6

sometimes, destination kicks journey's ass

Leandra received a text from Sophia with a picture of some pool in Hollywood.

She lowered her sunglasses to get a better look at it. "How quaint," she said to herself. She lifted her delicately pointed chin to take in her own view of an open-air infinity pool on the top floor of the highest building in Bangkok. A waiter in a crisp white jacket had just brought breakfast—croissants, sticky rice, dragon fruit, purple mangosteens, and a steaming porcelain pot of Thai tea—to her private cabana, where she lounged on a cushioned sofa. After she ate, she'd sun herself and then do a few laps. Swimming to the edge of the pool was like gliding straight off the roof and into the clouds. She was on top of the world.

Just goes to show, no matter how hard you tried, you could never predict the ups and downs of life. One day, you're a pathetic victim, crying on the dingy shoulder of a dinky hotel manager in Phuket. The next, you're in a suite at a five-star hotel in Bangkok with a massage scheduled after lunch.

She had only one person to thank for the incredible swing in her circumstances: herself. When Leandra lost everything, including her pride, her first thought was to go crying to her parents, like a little bitch. But she held off. They would have insisted she come home. Leandra couldn't quit after one bad day. She had to keep it going somehow. So she called the only person she sort of knew in the entire country, her mom's friend's son, Charlie Lemming. What a brilliant stroke that turned out to be.

She remembered him vaguely as a roly-poly mouthbreather from New York. She'd made a much better impression on him. "Leandra Hunting," he said, picking up the phone. "My mom told me you were coming to Thailand! I'm so glad you called. I really hoped you would."

She told him what had happened. He was so eager to help; it was like she did him a favor by letting him. Three days later, he'd arranged for her to get a replacement passport, and booked her a first-class ticket to Bangkok. Her only complaint: She was forced to stay at the same run-down shack of a hotel until the paperwork was sorted out. The manager bent over backward to make her as comfortable as possible, and he didn't charge her for the room or any of her meals. It was the least he could do! She ate as much food and drank as many mai tais as she could keep down. She left Karon Beach with a radiant tan and an extra five pounds. If she still had any of her old clothes, they wouldn't fit. She'd been living in voluminous sarongs and Thai fisherman pants that tied around the waist and made anyone look like a whale. Fine for the beach, but not in the city. The day before her flight to Bangkok, Charlie wired her some traveling cash. She spent it all on a few new outfits, some makeup, and a suitcase. For the flight, though, she slobbed out in her grubby fisherman pants, flip-flops, and a T-shirt.

At the airport in Bangkok, Leandra was pleasantly surprised to find a black-suited driver waiting to pick her up. The driver didn't speak English. All he could tell her, on repeat, was, "We go see Mr. Charlie." She could call Charlie and demand to know what was happening, or she could just settle into the buttery leather seats of the limo, have a glass of champagne, and stop worrying. It's not about the destination, she reminded herself, it's about the journey. She would sit back, and enjoy the ride.

Before long, she realized the limo was headed toward a white building that towered over all the others around it. Its roof was a golden, gleaming dome. She recognized the structure from *Hangover III* and her pretrip googling as the Tower Club, one of the architectural jewels of the city. The limo pulled to a stop at the hotel's curb. The driver said, "You go up. Mr. Charlie wait for you."

"Up there?" she asked.

He bowed and said, "Sky Bar."

She couldn't go to the most expensive club in Bangkok looking like cat puke. "I need to change." Her suitcase was in the limo trunk.

"Okay," said the driver, nodding, not moving.

"My lug-gage," she spoke slowly.

He smiled and bowed. "Okay."

She rolled her eyes and banged the trunk door with the palm of her hand, then pantomimed carrying a suitcase. Sometimes Leandra hated how entitled she should be, but if she didn't fend for herself no one else would. The driver finally got it, and opened the trunk. She rummaged through her new things for a no-label silk shirtdress in electric blue and strappy sandals—nowhere near her usual standards, but they'd have to do—and her new makeup kit. After half an hour in the backseat, she was presentable.

The driver liked her quick change. "Okay!" he said.

Idiot, she thought, turning on her heel and leaving him on the street. A woman in a traditional one-shoulder Thai red dress bowed at her as she entered the soft-lit lobby. "How do you get to the top floor?" she asked.

The woman took her to a private elevator, ushered her in, and used a key card to access the button that said "Sky Bar." Then she stepped out of the elevator backward, bowing. The door closed and Leandra was whisked sixty-eight stories up, to the top. As she exited the elevator, the golden dome loomed on the other side of the roof between her and a candlelit expanse of tables and chairs.

She walked through the restaurant, scanning the faces for a fat American banker. She got all the way to the end of the roof, where a circular bar glowed pink, then blue, then green, the three bartenders in the center mixing neon yellow and purple cocktails. Bangkok was a shimmering blanket of diamonds spread out below her. Three days at sea level were more than enough. She preferred to be here, at the apex of the Southeast Asian universe.

Sometimes, destination kicked journey's ass.

"Leandra?"

She turned and saw a slim, sexy, nattily dressed man in a gray suit at the bar, beaming at her with unabashed joy.

"Charlie?" Couldn't be.

He wrapped her in a hug. She melted into it. The guy's chest was hard as oak, and it'd been awhile since someone looked that happy to see her. "I'm so relieved you got here safely," he said.

"Thanks to you," she said, giving him her wide-eyed my-hero blink.

"Sit down," he said, gesturing to a stool at the bar. While he ordered them drinks, she checked out his bod. Excellent shoulders. Nice, hard ass. She could seriously chow down on it.

The bartender brought over her drink, a concoction called a Hangovertini. He raised his glass of what appeared to be orange juice, and said, "To your safe landing." They toasted and drank.

"Beautiful spot," she said. "We're so high up."

"It's a status thing in Bangkok. The higher the better. Whoever builds the highest hotel, with the highest bar, wins. The latest thing is the highest swimming pool."

"It is such a rush to look down on all the little people," she said, a mischievous, snotty glint in her eye. Charlie seemed confused. Oops. He didn't approve of classist humor. "I mean, they're just so small down there! Like ants."

"Yeah," he said.

"So," Leandra purred, "when did we last see each other? Five years ago?"

"Four," he said. "I'd just graduated from Columbia Business School. I didn't want to go to that party, but my mom insisted. And then you walked into the room. You were a high school senior, visiting New York with your parents. I stared at you all night. Hope I didn't seem threatening."

He'd been as threatening as a bowl of raw dough. "You look different," she observed.

"I was a bit heavier then," he said. "I transferred here two years ago for work, and got into Muay Thai."

"What's that?"

"It's like Thai karate. I started taking classes, and the pounds just fell off."

"You lost weight beating people up?"

"It's a discipline, lots of training and mental sharpness. I compete on the lowest amateur level. You fight with every body part, fists, shins, elbows. You should see the pros go at it; they're like killer spiders. It's brutal."

That sounded like something she'd pay *not* to see. But if this sport turned Charlie into a hottie, it couldn't be all bad. She sipped her drink and studied him over her glass, so glad she made the quick change in the limo before she came up. "Tell me more about how you use every body part," she said.

Three drinks later, Leandra was sitting on Charlie's lap, taking a selfie. "I'm sending this to my mom so she knows we hooked up. I mean, met up."

He tensed beneath her. "Or hooked up."

"The night *is* young, and so are we."

"And rich," he added, much to her delight. "Don't forget that."

How could Leandra forget that?

"So, when you battle some guy, do you just tear his head off? Is there blood? Do they mop up between rounds?"

"You amaze me," he said, gazing at her worshipfully (as he damn well should). "A lot of girls are turned off by the combat stuff."

"Are you kidding? It's only the coolest thing in the world!" Leandra had less than zero interest in contact sports. Sophia and Demi had dragged her to a few hockey games under duress. Boxing? She'd attend a match to sit in a VIP box with an open bar and free unlimited shrimp cocktail, and only if she were fucking the winner.

He turned serious for a second, and then confessed, "You were my inspiration to change, you know. I really wanted to talk to you at that party, but I was afraid you'd blow me off because of how I looked."

"Not true," she said. She would have blown him off for how he dressed, too.

"I thought of you a lot over the years as this gorgeous girl who got away. You're even more gorgeous tonight, by the way. Considering what you'd been through, I thought you'd show up in a T-shirt and flip-flops."

"I always try to look my best, even on the plane," she said. "It's just common courtesy."

"You probably look flawless when you wake up."

"Only one way to find out," she said.

Leandra did pause, briefly, to weigh her options. Jumping into bed with Nick was what got her into this mess in the first place. But Charlie wasn't a stranger. Their mothers were friends. She didn't owe him anything more than a hearty "thanks," some light flirtation, and a heartfelt promise to repay his kindness. Or, she could dig in a little deeper. He was hot and loaded, and he spoke Thai. She was in Bangkok and in need of a place to stay, some walk-around money, and a translator.

He asked, "Are you serious?"

"Tell me more about the highest pool in Bangkok. Is it part of a hotel, like this bar? Can anyone go see it?"

"No, not everyone," he said.

"Oh."

"But we can. My bank keeps a suite at the Rama Grand for international clients. Give me five minutes to see if it's occupied." He took out his phone.

"I'll run to the ladies'," she said, hopping off his lap.

In the bathroom, she took off her panties and threw them in the garbage. She could've pulled the classic move of walking back to Charlie and putting them in his hand. But her undies were cheap and awful, not fit for his eyes. Better to wear nothing and give Charlie a very pleasant surprise. Leandra guessed it'd take him approximately fifteen minutes—the length of time to get down the elevator and into the limo—to find out.

It actually took three. As soon as the elevator doors closed, he went for it, gasping when he touched bare skin. Between the sixty-eighth and fifty-third floors, she knew she had this guy in the palm of her hand.

Since then, Leandra had been living in a two-thousand-square-foot suite at the Rama Grand, pampering herself by day, and lavishing sexual goodies on Charlie by night. His boss was cool about letting Charlie's out-of-town guest stay for the first week of her time in town. But at the top of week two, Charlie came home with bad news.

"A British client arrives tomorrow," he told her while they snuggled in the afterglow. "We have to leave."

"But it's our home," she pouted. "This is where we first fell in . . ."

Charlie's eyes burned into hers. "In what?"

She blushed, embarrassed for him. "Fell in *love*," she whispered, and slowly lifted her eyes from his chest to his lips.

An hour later, Charlie put his AmEx Platinum card on file at the front desk, and Leandra moved her rapidly expanding wardrobe into the identical suite next door, where she'd been loving life, and "loving"

Charlie, for nine days. She wasn't exactly sure what it cost to stay in the suite. But price wasn't her concern. As long as she made Charlie happy, he'd keep her comfortable.

At noon, Leandra left the pool, and met her favorite masseuse for her daily Swedish rub. She tried a Thai massage, but it was like being twisted into a pretzel, not a sensual pleasure at all. When her rub was over, the masseuse bowed out of the room, and Leandra settled in for her afternoon nap. It'd be hours before the limo arrived to take her to whatever restaurant Charlie picked for them tonight.

Just as she was nodding off, the suite door opened, and Charlie appeared in the bedroom. Finding her naked in bed, he sighed and smiled dreamily at her. "This is what I want to see every day for the rest of my life when I come home," he said.

Let's not get ahead of ourselves, she thought. To distract him from sentimentality, she patted the bed. "Come on in," she said.

"I wish I could. But we have to check out in an hour."

She bolted upright. "What?"

"My AmEx is maxed out."

"It's Platinum!"

"The limit is thirty thousand per month."

Had she drained him of that much? In only two weeks? Oh, well. They'd just have to bridge the gap for the next two weeks until his AmEx was good again.

"Do you have another card?" she asked.

"I don't," he said. "But that doesn't matter. I've sorted it all out. The Thai people are pretty conservative, so they don't let unmarried people share rental apartments. So I bought us a house! A colleague at work was transferred back to New York, and he needed to sell quickly. Furniture, dishes, cooking and cleaning stuff, everything. We closed this morning and it's ready for us to move in."

Leandra blanched. Move into a house? With dishes and pots and pans, and act like some boring married couple? "Leave here? Where we fell in . . ."

"And move into our first real home, where we'll start the rest of our lives together." He jumped on the bed and gathered her up in his arms. "Are you as happy as I am?"

"Holy fuck," she said. Even people on *The Bachelor* didn't fall in love this quickly.

"I know! Our dreams are coming true."

Be careful
what you wish for.
You might just get what
you deserve.

7

what if i pretend
to give a shit?

Demi sat at their usual table at Opus, her back to the door, with her friends. Shortly after ordering their first round, Sarah's eyes got wide, and then she ducked low in her chair and hid her face with a hand over her eyes. "Don't look," she said. "James just walked in."

Demi's spine turned to ice. She froze in place, and didn't dare twist around. Eve and Jo snapped their heads to look, and then bent low over their wine.

Jo said, "He looks *good*. Who's that girl he's with? She's a fucking eleven." A strangled whimper nearly escaped Demi's lips, but she held it in.

"He's getting closer," whispered Eve.

"Like ten steps away," said Jo, her voice rising.

It was happening, *now*. Demi had been dreading her first post-breakup encounter with James. She'd been preparing for it, too, trying to build self-esteem via mirror selfie. Humiliating to admit. Demi also posted a hundred pictures on Instagram in the last month. In every one, she looked like she was having the time of her life, going out every night, closing the place, raising a glass. She posted pics of her pregame primping, with duck face, and artful shots of cocktail glasses lined up on the bar, group shots of all her pals with their heads pressed together, a pose Sarah called "The Lice Spreader." Demi did love a good head lilt. According to her social media postings, Demi was having the time of her life, and looking great doing it.

It might've come off as "trying too hard." Demi didn't give two shits. It made her feel better, for now.

The objective of her post-breakup social campaign was to make James see what he was missing. Her "I don't need you!" Instagram feed would show him that (1) she didn't miss him, (2) her life was more fun now than it ever was when they were together, and (3) if he hadn't been a cheating, lying douche, he would still be part of her fabulous life (that his parting gift was still funding). Demi posted nightly selfies with hot guys, including cryptic captions, subtle stuff like "You have my [heart emoticon]!" Should he feel jealous about them, good. Should she feel embarrassed about them? No. Eventually? Hell, yes.

Her secret objective (which she admitted only in her heart of hearts and would have denied if tortured) was to lure him back to her. She'd made it easy for him to find her, always going to the same place, at around the same time, enabling locations. She checked daily; James was defs still following her online. But he hadn't yet followed her in real life. Until now.

"He's right behind you," whispered Sarah, glancing at the space over Demi's head.

Demi took a big swallow of liquid courage, put on a smile, and turned around to face . . . no one. No James, no one at all. She turned back to her friends, who were now laughing hysterically.

"You got me," said Demi graciously, casually, of the group joke on her. Inside, she was livid.

"You should have seen your face!" said Sarah. "It was priceless. You nearly shit yourself."

"I nearly *bolted*!" she said. "He's the last person on Earth I'd want to walk in here tonight."

"Oh, *please*," said Jo.

Demi said, "Okay, you're right. He's the second to last."

"Who's the last?" asked Eve.

"My boss."

Maya had been furious with Demi about the permit thing. Demi couldn't blame her. Turned out, Maya had been such a nag about Demi getting the alcohol permit that day for a reason. To be valid, it had to be issued twenty-one days *prior* to the event. So when Demi showed up the next morning bright and early, crack o' dawn, to get it, it was a day too late. If Maya had made that painfully clear, Demi wouldn't have put it off. But she and Catherine had gotten to talking. One Bailey's and coffee turned into two, and then it was too late. Maya straightened it out, greasing a few wheels. She started triple check- ing Demi's call log, reading emails and counting expenses to the penny. It was humiliating.

After lunch today, Demi had come back to the office to find Maya sitting in her chair. "This has got to stop."

"I'll be on time from now on."

"You're making my job harder. I'm not going to pay you to screw things up anymore."

Demi should have seen it coming. The ice had been getting thin- ner, and thinner. Then *crackkkk*. It happened. She was getting fired.

Maya got on with it. "It's not *only* how hungover you are *every day*, or how slobby and lazy that makes you. You don't really care about First @ Second. You don't! It's obvious. Your apathy pisses me off, and anger is draining."

"What if I *pretend* to give a shit?" Demi asked, grinning.

It was supposed to be funny! A little jest to lighten the mood. But Maya's face turned to stone. There was no point in apologizing or begging for another chance. The horse had left the barn. Demi collected her personal things—not much, surprisingly, considering her years of service. Maya watching her like a hawk, like she'd swipe a precious stapler. It was unnecessary and insulting. Demi drove right home to the death trap, and baked a quiche with Catherine, so the day wasn't a total loss.

Maya was right about the constant hangovers. They were making Demi a bit slow on the uptake. With a margarita in her hand, she thought, *Tomorrow, I'm not drinking at all.* She had to detox, clean out her system of alcohol, negativity, and reunion fantasies about James. Enough with the heartbreak and grieving. She used it as an excuse to get wasted and suck at work. It wasn't James she grieved for, but the routine of their lives together. She'd organized her life and thoughts around him. With him gone, Demi didn't know what to do with herself. Without her job, such as it was, she lost the only thing that gave her life structure.

To Sarah, Demi corrected herself. "My *ex*-boss."

"You're really racking up the exes lately," said Eve.

It was true, but who the fuck was Eve to say that? The implication was that Demi's life was falling apart. It was fine for Demi to make jokes about it. But her friends should be trying to lift her spirits, not make her feel worse.

"I'm getting another drink," said Demi.

"Get me one, too," said Sarah.

"Fuck off. Get your own."

"We were just kidding."

"And I'm just leaving, no big deal." Demi pushed away from the table. She could tell Sarah was relieved to see her go. She was halfway to the bar, and she knew they were already talking behind her back, saying what a sensitive, prissy bitch she was being. They could talk about her all night. She had no intention of going back to their table.

Right there at the bar, Demi found new people to hang out with. Her old pal from high school, Warren, and a few of his friends from his year-round hockey league were holding forth about the best way to hip check without getting a penalty. Demi joined right in, and matched the guys glass for glass, and stat for stat. She knew hockey, and she liked how it felt to be surrounded by men. The shots kept flowing her way, and she kept drinking them.

Sarah was glaring at Demi with her resting bitch face, like Demi was too loud or having too much fun. The drunker Demi got, the less she gave a crap what Sarah thought of her. But it would be preferable to get out of her line of sight. Demi could just go home, but then she'd be alone with a serious buzz. What fun was that?

"Hey, let's go to my place," she said to Warren and the crew. "No one will bother us." It seemed like a wiser idea than staying here with Sarah and her stink face. "Who's in?"

Three of the guys were into it. This would be the night of a thousand selfies. When Demi left Opus with the guys, she made sure to give Sarah the finger on their way out. They headed to the Audi. After a quick assessment—fingers to nose, walking a straight line—it was determined that Demi was the most sober, so she got behind the wheel. Two of the guys, big, sexy, muscley guys, had to squeeze into the backseat.

Warren was copilot. "How far?" he asked, putting his hand high on her thigh.

Flutter in her chest, she said, "Close. Just a few miles."

"What're we waiting for?" he asked. Squeezing her leg, leaving his hand.

Demi pulled into traffic, driving slow, carefully. Warren's grip was distracting her, though. She said, "Move your hand."

"Okay," he said, and started rubbing her thigh.

"I didn't mean like that!" she said, laughing, swatting at him.

"Oh, shit," said Bill? Jim? from the backseat.

Red and blue lights flashed in her rearview mirror. A cop car was hugging her fender. Just in case she hadn't gotten the message, the bullhorn blasted, "Pull over."

Demi did as she was told. The Grace was only half a block away. She could see the building. Warren was putting his stash in his underwear. The guys in the backseat were cracking up, talking trash. "You're so busted, Demi. You're screwed."

The cop got out of his white-and-blue, and came up to her window. Demi knew his dash cam was running—it was the law. She felt tempted to wave at it. He was young with a few zits on his chin, around her age or a little older. For all she knew, it was his first day on the job. Dude was textbook. "License, registration, and insurance," he said.

She fished them out of the glove box, and handed them over. They were valid and up-to-date. Demi had let some things slip, but not the big stuff, like car, rent, and taxes. Her father had drummed that into her from birth.

"Were you aware that you rolled through a stop sign?"

"I should have come to a complete stop. I'm sorry about that." If she argued about it, he'd definitely write her a ticket. But if she was contrite, he might let her off with a warning.

He sniffed the air. "Have you been drinking tonight?"

"Only a tiny bit," she said, and brought her index and thumb together to made the teensy sign. "Like a cocktail for a cockroach."

Warren stifled a giggle, which made him snort. "Sorry," he said.

The cop was not amused. "Please stay in your vehicle."

Demi turned to Warren and said, "So smooth. I think he likes you."

"You better hope he likes *you*," said Bill? Jim? What the hell were their names?

"I've got nothing to worry about," she said. Demi had been with James a few times when he was pulled over for minor traffic hiccups. She'd tested her sobriety at their impromptu field test back at Opus. She was fine. Rolling through a stop sign was no big deal. She'd get a warning. Maybe a ticket. And then they'd go back to her place, and see if four people could fit on her mattress on the floor.

The cop came back with a Breathalyzer, and Demi got a little nervous. Vancouver had one of the toughest DUI laws in the world, and the lowest acceptable blood-alcohol limits. A reading of only 0.05 would qualify as drunk. She had to be under the limit. She didn't feel drunk, but would she measure that way?

"You can refuse," said Warren. "Don't do it."

"If you refuse, you will be arrested and taken into custody," said the cop. "You will be compelled to give a blood or urine sample."

"By then, it'll be out of your system."

"Clearly, you've been in this situation before."

"I'm in law school," he said, looking hotter than ever.

The cop said, "If you don't do it, we can take your license for a year."

"They can threaten, but without evidence, you can fight it."

"I'm not drunk," she said. Demi didn't want to argue or fight anything. She could see her house. It'd been awhile since her last drink and she was starting to feel kind of miserable about getting fired and everything else. The fastest way out of this was to take the test and be on their way.

Demi took the device from the cop and blew into the nozzle, stifling a little burp while she did. The digital readout flashed FAIL in big red letters.

"You're over," said the cop. "Exit the vehicle."

"Should have listened to me."

She got out. He gave her a field sobriety test. "You're swaying," he said as she walked a straight line.

She wasn't, at all. She felt very firm on her feet. "That's bullshit," she said, and immediately regretted it. It'd only make things worse.

The cop clicked his shoulder walkie-talkie gizmo and said, "I've got a DUI. I need a tow truck. Over. All of you, please step out of the vehicle."

"I can't believe this is happening," she muttered as she followed his instructions.

"Place your hands on the car," he said to her, which she did. He swept one of her arms around, and then the other to cuff her. Then he escorted her to the white-and-blue, and locked her in the backseat.

Warren talked to the cop and then came over to confer with Demi in the squad car. "He said we can go. What do you want us to do?"

A stand-up guy. He was willing to stay with her. But what would be the point? Why ruin their night as well as hers? "My apartment is right up the street. You guys can take my keys and I'll meet you back there."

"Are you sure?" he asked. "It might be awhile."

"Yeah, go ahead."

She gave him the address. Warren got permission from the cop to take Demi's keys, and they left, off to smoke and drink and eat her quiche without her.

"What now?" she asked the cop.

"We wait for the tow truck. Then we drive to the station. You're going to be formally charged with DUI."

"After that?"

He said, "I have no idea what's going to happen to you."

Join the club.

"Can I fix my hair?" Demi asked the matron before her mug shot.

The woman said, "You do realize you're under arrest, right?"

That shut her up. Wiseass was her defense mechanism. Maybe not the smartest strategy in jail. The reality settled in during her hourlong wait in the back of the squad car. She was going to lose her license. Vancouver was a driving town. How was she going to get around (not that she had anywhere in particular to go . . .)? It'd be humiliating to have to call friends for rides. And it could be a lot worse: She might do jail time. She didn't love the idea of sleeping on a bench or sharing an open toilet with twenty junkies, but she could handle it for a night or two. It would never come to that. *Or would it?* Demi started to feel a little scared.

After she was fingerprinted and photographed, Demi was cuffed again and escorted into a large room with about a dozen desks, each manned by a uniformed cop. She was taken to one of them and pushed down into the chair next to it. The matron gave a folder to the cop and removed the cuffs.

The officer was her father's age, with the same brusque no-bullshit manner. He was white, tending to fat rather than lean, with slicked-back salt-and-pepper hair. In a cop show, he'd play the untalented slob who never made it off desk duty and was content to work for the pension. He opened her folder, and started logging info into the computer without really looking at her.

"Orange is not my color," she said.

"You will be arraigned in court fourteen days from today," he said by rote. "Will you be able to appear before the judge on this date?"

He'd printed out a sheet, and showed her a date at the end of July. Ironically, it was the opening day of First @ Second. So even if she wanted to attend the festival, she had a really great excuse not to, if Maya cared, which she probably didn't.

"I think I can squeeze it into my schedule," she said.

He glanced at her then, and frowned. "Sign here to confirm you've agreed to appear in court on this date." She signed. "If you fail to appear for arraignment, a bench warrant will be issued for your arrest. A bench warrant is a public record. If you try to get a job, rent an apartment, or apply for a loan, your potential employer, landlord, or banker will see that you've been arrested and failed to appear in court. Do you understand what I'm saying?"

"If I don't show up, I'm screwed for life."

"Sign here," he said.

"You have the right to hire an attorney to come to court with you," he said. "Otherwise, you can consult with a public defender five minutes before your scheduled arraignment. Sign here."

On and on it went. Demi had to sign off on every single detail of what was happening to her. They went in one ear, and threatened to come out her asshole. She simply couldn't concentrate. "Is there a handout I can take with me?" she asked. "In case I forget something? That would be bad, right?"

The guy took pity on her, and went off script. "Says here you're twenty-one. If you were nineteen, I could write off the attitude as youthful ignorance. Twenty-one means you're an adult. You have to take this seriously. Get a lawyer. Have him argue the margin of error in the borderline reading. You might get the charge expunged, do community service, and get your license back sooner. Or stick with the attitude, and never drive again."

"Well, when you put it like that . . ."

"If I were you, I'd reconsider who you are surrounding yourself with or your lifestyle. I've seen smart pretty girls throw it all away for their lowlife friends. You're damn lucky you didn't kill anyone tonight. This could have gotten real ugly, *fast*."

That stopped her cold. He was right. What if she had hit someone?

The officer went back on script. "I'm giving you a copy of what you signed today, and have set up email and cell phone alerts about your court date. Sign one more time. And you're free to go."

Free to go fuck up your life, he didn't need to say. It was all over his face.

She was directed to another desk, where she collected her personal effects—her bag, which had been searched, her phone, and a receipt for her impounded car. Then she left the building and stood on the front steps, absolutely gobsmacked about the entire night.

She texted Warren. He replied that they left her key in the planter out front hours ago and hoped she was okay. If she ever heard from him again, she'd be shocked.

What now? Call a cab, go home, and cry herself to sleep?

She could call Sophia and unfairly ask her to absorb another load of Demi drama. But that was just too much to ask, even of her best friend.

She could call James and beg him to take her back, swear to him that she didn't care what he did with other women as long as he made her feel halfway human right now.

Demi dialed the phone. He picked up after one ring. "Hello, Dad? It's me."

Richard Michaels pulled up to the station steps in his Mercedes. He didn't speak at first, just let her settle in and fasten her seat belt. She had a flashback to when he taught her how to drive. "Listen for the click!" She let the silence hang a bit. He gripped the steering wheel with white knuckles, and tried to appear calm.

"Are you pissed at me, or at the cops for railroading me?" she asked.

"I'm furious at *him!*" he said. "You never got into any trouble before James." *None you knew about, anyway.* "I don't know why or how, but I'd bet my house this is all his fault."

Demi considered it. She could twist the situation around to blame James. He drove her to drink, etc. "James has nothing to do with it," she said. "And now, I'm going to say something that will shock and amaze you. James and I broke up a month ago. He cheated on me. I found out and left him. I moved into God's waiting room by myself and I've been living there for three weeks. What else? I got fired today. Plus this situation here, which is probably the worst of all of it. Basically, it's been a very bad month. Before you jump down my throat, I didn't tell you about James before because I didn't want to hear you gloat, or start issuing life instructions. So don't bother doing that now. I'll get out of this car and walk home."

The wheels in Dad's brain were spinning so fast, smoke might come out his ears. If Mom or Demi's stepparents were here right now, they'd pulled her into a hug. Dad would do the same, but in crisis, his fallback position was problem solver. First he'd yell. Then he'd solve. He used to make Demi take notes while he lectured, and then read them back for his approval.

Right now, though, Dad looked like he was trying to crush the steering wheel into powder with his bare hands. He didn't say a word for a full minute. She might have short-circuited his brain.

"Are we just going to sit here? Because I'm starving. I thought they had to feed prisoners every three hours. Don't believe the hype."

"Did you actually get locked up?" *He speaks!*

"If I say 'yes,' will you buy me a burger?"

"Take me to this apartment," he said. "Now."

She gave him directions. While he drove the fifteen minutes to the Grace, she described what had happened with the arrest, and how long it took for the damn tow truck to arrive, the humiliation of walking into the station in handcuffs. "The digital fingerprint machine at the station was way cool," she admitted. "No ink. Just press onto a tablet, and *bam*! You're in the system. Left here. It's the building on the right."

The Mercedes rolled to a stop. "That building? It looks okay." He looked around. "Nice flower boxes."

"That's Wally's work. He loves a project. Ohh, you thought that when I said 'death trap,' it'd be a junkie squat with broken glass and needles. No, Dad. I'm not an idiot, contrary to popular opinion." She explained the apartment's unique history, and brought him up to see her place.

Catherine heard them coming up the stairs, and opened her door to say hello. Demi made the introductions, but Catherine didn't start up a conversation or invite them in (not that there was much room for guests in there; Catherine, it turned out, was a collector and her apartment was packed with stuff, which was why she described her place as "messy"). Her neighbor sensed something major was up. "You had some visitors before," she said.

"Friends," said Demi. "They were okay, right?"

"Lovely boys. Well, nice meeting you," she said to Richard, and closed her door.

After a brief tour of Demi's one-bedroom apartment—he seemed to dig it, and grunted approvingly a few times—he asked, "How can you afford this place? Even with the death discount."

"I saved up a ton living with James," she said. "I've got fifteen thousand."

He sat down on her brand-new couch, just delivered this week. "Good. You're going to need it. Lawyers aren't cheap. I'll help you find someone."

"Thank you."

"Don't thank me yet. I have conditions," he said. "Relax, I'm not going to read you the riot act tonight. I'm sickened by all this, and that you moved without telling me. Does your mother know?"

"No."

He seemed relieved. "I understand why you did it. You're an adult, and you want to live your life your way. I completely agree. That includes fixing your own mistakes. So you're going to pay for your lawyer, and all the fines. That fifteen thousand isn't going to last long, especially without an income. You should download a bus schedule. Write that down. There's probably an app."

She just smiled at him. "I'll remember. I don't really have anywhere to go. Job interviews, eventually, and I'll take a cab."

"You do have somewhere to go," he said. "In exchange for finding you a good lawyer, you're going to come work for me. Thirty hours a week. You have to show up at my office every morning, and prove to me that you're okay."

"I'm twenty-one. You have no legal right to tell me what to do. You can't say, on the one hand, I'm an adult and I can make my own mistakes. And then, on the other hand, boss me around."

"You got arrested tonight for drunk driving!" he yelled. "You're *lucky* you got pulled over! You could have killed someone, or yourself. I can't believe I'm about to say this, but when you have kids one day, you'll understand. I reserve the right to boss you around until you get your shit together, which seems to be a long way off. Tomorrow morning, nine o'clock. Take the bus, not a cab. You need to reel in the spending. And quit lying to everyone about what's going on with you."

He left soon after that. What else was there to say? If she refused to agree to his terms, her parents (all four of them) would stage an intervention, or put her under twenty-four-hour surveillance (they could do it; there were four of them, after all). She also knew he was right.

She took a long, hot shower, after which Demi fell onto her mattress. The train wreck of her life was just too mangled to contemplate any more tonight. She closed her eyes and expressed gratitude to the universe for keeping her safe and having people who loved her.

Ten hours later, at eight A.M., she was up and dressed, ready to take the bus to her dad's office. She opened her apartment door. Propped up against the wall was an old bicycle with a red ribbon. An envelope was taped to the seat with her name on it.

Demi opened the envelope and read the note: "I couldn't help overhearing last night. Your father has a very loud indoor voice. Please use this in good health. I know it's a bit rusty, and it has only three gears. But it works, and I'd hate for you to have to take the bus, which often smells like urine. Love, Catherine."

She folded the note, put it back in the envelope, and burst into tears. It was just so kind. Demi hadn't been on the receiving end of much kindness lately. It felt so good, it hurt.

~ SOMETIMES ~
THE MOST IMPORTANT
LIFE LESSONS
ARE THE ONES WE
HAVE TO LEARN THE
HARD WAY

how to be perky

The California trip cost $2,500 and Sophia had nothing—*nothing*—to show for it. Besides the financial hit, she had to quit her job, too. She just couldn't go back to CRUSH. If daily degradation was character-building, then her character was the Sears Tower. The thought of putting on her black mini-dress and high-heeled boots and dancing around like an escaped mental patient whenever a creep waved around a credit card just . . . no. She'd dodged enough hairy man hands for one lifetime.

Plus, Renee.

She hoped Renee's Hot Link ads inspired a million horny chats, and kept her so busy in LA that she never came back to Toronto again. In the nightmare version, Renee's career hawking toe fungus cream went bust, and she returned to Canada in humiliating defeat.

A shell of a woman, bitter, haunted, she would pick up where she left off, taping sparklers to overpriced bottles of vodka and hating every one who came near.

Sophia would not stick around to see that. It was just too depressing. Her first call after touching down in Toronto was to Vinnie. Thank god, she got voice mail.

"Hi, Vin. It's Sophia. I just wanted to thank you for being a great boss. I learned a lot and . . ."

"Sophia," he said, picking up. She forgot he had an old-fashioned landline answering machine. "You can stop right there. I know a kiss-off when I hear one. So you got a job in Lalaland?"

"Don't think so. It was eye opening, definitely. I'm not sure about my next steps," she said. "But I can't come back to CRUSH."

"Say no more. I don't blame you. You lasted longer than most."

"Can you give me a reference?"

"Tell you what. I'll even make a few calls, see what's out there. You'll have a job in three days, tops."

"Thanks, Vin."

"Just stop by once in a while, say hello."

Within two hours, restaurant managers and bar owners were calling *her*. Not the maître d' at the Canoe Club—Vinnie's reach didn't go that high—but the breadth of his connections was impressive. She set up interviews at a few well-known places. Cocktail waitressing would be better than bottle service in terms of money, hours, and dignity.

She took the offer at a high-end lounge called Bar 111. It wasn't the coolest place or the most expensive (which would have meant bigger tips). What appealed to her were the customers: old rich geezers who smoked cigars, sipped scotch, talked about foreign exchange rates, and complained that "the Internets" made the younger generation fat, lazy, and stupid. Stuffed shirts vs. sleazebags? No contest.

On her first night, Sophia arrived early, eager to make some money. She had to replenish her coffers after the LA trip ASAP if she were going to get new head shots (a common request from casting agents), or move out of her studio apartment, which she'd been thinking about for a while. Which upgrade first? A year ago, she wouldn't have hesitated to say "head shots." But now she wavered. That said a lot.

Her new boss, Josie, a kittenish redhead with a vine tattoo winding around her neck and collarbone (and probably lower), had her fill out the necessary forms before handing over her new uniform: a maroon minidress, super tight on top with a flouncy skirt that made Sophia think *slutty figure skater*. It was a big step up from slutty biker chick. Progress!

"Hey, doll face, come on over here!" said a gray-haired dinosaur with a silk tie as she walked by his table. He wore a smoking jacket (he kept it in the coat room to slip into for his "toddy").

New place, same old shit.

"Can I get you something?" she asked, dodging a wrinkly hand as it reached for her hip. The old men moved in slow motion, which made avoiding the pinch-'n'-slap a snap.

"What're you doing here, honey? You should let some man take care of you, buy you chocolates and cars. Not too much candy, though. Don't want to get fat!"

Could he have delivered that speech to a man—any man, anywhere, anytime—and expect to get away with it? Even a gay sugar baby wouldn't tolerate it. But Sophia was supposed to act flattered, as if she wanted to listen to this. As if she enjoyed serving cheese plates and martinis to a higher order of asshole.

"Thanks for the advice. What can I get you?"

"Another round." He winked. She must have looked repulsed. "You're a lot prettier when you smile," he said, an edge to it.

Bar 111 opened at lunchtime and closed at ten P.M., when the silvers were poured into cabs and sent home to their long- (long) suffering wives who had the good sense to drink at home where they wouldn't embarrass themselves. After closing, Josie paid out the credit card tips, and gave Sophia a tip of her own. "Just roll with it," she said. "They're harmless."

Excuses like that perpetuated sexism. It wasn't harmless to be de-humanized for a living. But Sophia kept her mouth shut. If she was too obviously annoyed, she'd get fired. They weren't paying her to be psychologically aware or to stand up for herself.

"Sorry, I was just in a weird mood today. I'll be perky as shit to-morrow."

"Perky as shit, I like that," said Josie, nodding. "We should make T-shirts."

Sophia sat down at the bar to count her money. She'd clear around $250 tonight. It was enough to keep her going, but not to lift her up. Still, it felt good to hold the cash in her hand. A fist full of dollars. She fanned herself with it.

A text ping. She checked her phone, hoping it'd be Demi. They hadn't talked in a week, just a few texts here and there. It seemed like Demi was avoiding her, but then again, her new boss was a real ballbuster. He never let Demi out of his sight, and monitored her phones and emails. Why would Demi take this job when she and Maya got along so well? Sophia would love to hear Demi's reason-ing, if she could get her on Skype for five minutes.

The text was from Agnes, her agent. "Wide-net casting call for female actors ages eighteen to twenty-five for a network pilot. Audi-tion in Los Angeles day after tomorrow."

She replied, "I thought pilot casting was over."

"Not quite."

"Can't do it," she typed back. Sophia couldn't afford to go back to LA with her old, crappy head shots and thin patience. "No $$$." A last-minute flight would be over a thousand.

"I'm sending the sides. Just read them. If you love, you can make a self-tape and email it."

"How much would that cost?"

"Seventy-five dollars."

Why spend any amount to audition for a part she wouldn't get? "I don't know," she typed. Was there really any point to this? Scott had made friends, and seemed content to hang on to the outer fringe of the entertainment business. That wouldn't be enough for Sophia. She wouldn't settle for less than being a star.

"Just read the sides," typed Agnes. "Then call me."

The document arrived. Sophia didn't open the attachment. She knew if she read a single word, she'd start imagining how to play it, the backstory, the nuance, all the stuff she loved about acting. She'd get excited about it, feel the pieces falling into place, and believe in the deepest fiber of her being that this part was meant for her alone. She'd burrow into the character, express all her emotions, and make the audience feel them, too. That was the ideal, to connect her heart and soul with theirs. It'd be like plugging into the freakin' universe.

At this point, anything less wouldn't be worth the pain. It was just too soon after LA to put her head on the chopping block again.

Or was it? Sophia called Scott, and asked for his advice. "More punishment?" he asked. "Make a life for yourself that's not dependent on the approval of strangers." He must be in a bad mood.

She called her mom. "It's been four years," she said. "You gave it a shot. Now come home and start your life for real. It's not too late to get an education. Go to college and business school, and get a secure job to support yourself." The same speech, word for word, she'd heard since high school graduation, only the opening line changed. "It's been six months," "it's been a year," etc. Both her parents worked in finance. They respected her striking out on her own and pursuing her dream. As Dad said, "We love you. We want what's best for you," with the heavy subtext of "enough is enough." Sophia was starting to see their point.

Why did she feel like she needed permission from her friends to give up? The vow they made at Lighthouse Park wasn't written in blood. If following her bliss led to disaster, they'd beg her to turn around. She tried to reach Demi, but her phone was offline, again. She texted Leandra. "You up?"

"Hi! It's morning in Bangkok," she replied instantly. "I'm having congee with my sexy boyfriend, Charlie." She included a photo of

Charlie, shirtless and sexy indeed, in what appeared to be a back-yard garden with exotic flowers spilling over a trellis, a teapot, soup terrine, and pastries on a table in front of him.

"Beautiful," Sophia texted back. Then she got to the point, and asked Leandra what she should do. Do the audition tape or rethink her entire life?

"You're so so sosososo talented," typed Leandra. "But, from what I've seen, the acting life doesn't make you happy. Do you want to be happy? If you do, then stop doing the thing that you know makes you unhappy. Look at me. I know exactly what I want, I go out and get it, and I'm the happiest person I know."

She included a selfie of herself, complete with a shit-eating grin, sitting on sexy Charlie's lap.

Sophia had gone looking for someone to convince her to keep going, and had come up empty. The consensus—minus Demi's opinion—was to trash her dreams and move on. She sent back a sarcastic smile selfie.

The next night, Sophia was a lot more relaxed at work, and the crust-ies weren't being as obnoxious. The only annoyance was Agnes. Her agent would not stop texting. A long string of "Call me. Call me. Call me" appeared on her notification screen. During a break, Sophia slipped into the bathroom and called her back.

"Did you memorize the sides?" asked Agnes.

"No, I . . ."

"Good. I have updates. Forget the last set, and memorize the pages I'm sending now."

"Agnes, I really appreciate all the hard work you've . . ."

"Stop. Right. There. I haven't been working for you out of char-ity. This is my *job*. It's how I earn a living and feed my kids. If I didn't believe in you, I'd have dumped you a long time ago."

"I know that," she said. "I owe you a lot . . ."

"Read the sides!"

Sophia sighed. "What's the name of the show?"

"Come to Jesus."

"Is it, uh, a Bible story?"

"Not the show. You. I've been doing this for a long time, and I hear what's going on in your voice. You're on the edge. Think of this audition as your last shot, and I will, too. I care about you. I believe in you. But I'm not going to go back and forth with you. I need to know, either way. So call me back when you decide." Then she hung up.

Sophia heard the implied message loud and clear. If she didn't follow through with this audition, Agnes would no longer be her agent. It was perfectly understandable. She'd put in a lot of time and energy into Sophia's career and hadn't made a dime. It was a miracle Agnes had stuck with her so long.

Ping. The email arrived with the new sides. Sophia opened the attachment. The name of the show was *Hipsters*. The premise: three girls in Brooklyn living the aesthetic life and falling in and out of relationships. The sides were for the part of "Valerie, 22, a writer."

The scene was Valerie and Steve, her boyfriend, at a dive bar.

Steve: "I'd say, 'It's not you, it's me.' But it is you. I wrote a poem that explains my feelings, and I'm performing it tonight at the Cutting Room. You can come, but I can't get you in for free."

Valerie: "Just record it and send me the voice memo instead."

Steve: "Yeah, okay."

Valerie: "I mean it! I want to study it. I take getting dumped very seriously. It's like my special skill. I'm really good at it. Guess how many times I've been dumped since I was ten years old."

Steve: "I don't . . . whatever. Five? Six?"

Valerie: "Twenty-three times. And each time, I get a little bit smarter. I figure, I've got about twenty more disasters before I become a genius at love. Thanks for getting me one step closer to figuring it all out. I'm thinking of writing my own poem about it, called 'How to Fake an Orgasm,' and dedicate it to you."

Okay, this was a *Girls* rip-off, but whatever. Last year's winner was always copied by the mainstream. But the words resonated with her anyway. It was supposed to be funny, but the emotional truth was dead on. Throughout her humbling experience in LA, and her umpteen botched auditions in Toronto, she believed down deep that each rejection was a victory of the spirit. Doubt could be twisted into confidence. Losing could be winning if you saw it through the right lens, namely, whichever one you chose for yourself. And Sophia chose to see through that rose-colored glasses. She always had. After this little slip, she had them back on.

No one else could tell Sophia what do to with her life. Life didn't work that way. She could hear out her family and friends. But the choice to take their advice or ignore it was up to her. She was in charge of her destiny. She would, absolutely, fuck up royally at times and make mistakes she couldn't avoid or anticipate. But the messes would be her own and, therefore, gratifying to clean up.

Objectively, it might be wrong or stupid or insane to keep bashing her head against a wall. That was how her parents and friends saw it. But Sophia was going to do it anyway. She had (time check) . . . twelve hours to memorize the sides, get someone to make a professional recording of her audition, and email the video to the *Hipsters* producers.

A knock on the bathroom door. "Sophia? Did you fall in?"

"One second!" She left the bathroom and quickly took orders from her customers. After she fetched their drinks and served a few charcuterie platters, she ducked into the cloakroom to memorize one line at a time. Then she'd rush back into the bar to take orders.

Josie caught her crouched between the hanging trench coats. "What the hell are you doing down there?"

"Winning!" said Sophia.

"How about Serving? Like, now?"

Whatever, nothing could deflate her. She had this.

Sophia arrived at Casting Central at eight o'clock in the morning. Along with hosting live auditions, the facility had a recording studio for making high-quality audiotapes and videos. A staff of videographers ran the studio, charging for the space and their services. It was booked solid every day, with a waiting list. There was no chance she could talk her way in during regular business hours and convince a professional to do her shoot for $100 in tips, which was all she had to spare. But if she arrived early, she could maybe get in there, line up the equipment, and do it herself or ask a certain someone for help.

Harriet the receptionist always showed up early to open the offices. Sophia knew this because whenever she had a morning audition, Harriet would say, "You think this is early? I've already been here for hours." Sure enough, Harriet was wiping chairs in the waiting room with Windex. "Hi, Harriet," said Sophia. "I brought you coffee."

"Now I'm nervous," she said.

"I need a favor." She explained the situation. All she needed was for Harriet to open the studio, point the camera, push record, and let her do her thing for five minutes. "I have a flash drive. We can record directly into it. No one will ever find out."

"I've always liked you, Sophia. Most of the actors treat me like a piece of the furniture. I'm not saying 'no' right off the bat. But. When actors ask me for a favor, I give them a litmus test. Hope you're smarter than you look."

"Okay," said Sophia. *Please let it be trivia about the provinces in Canada.* Sophia had that down cold.

"What are the names of my kids?"

"Er, you don't have any kids."

"Ding, ding, we have a winner. I knew I liked you for a reason. You actually listen. Most actors, they just talk, talk, talk. Makes me sick. Come on, let's do this before anyone shows up."

Sophia followed Harriet down the hall to the studio. "I can pay you."

"Forget it. Just give me your autograph when you're famous."

"I can give it to you right now."

They entered the recording studio. "Go stand on the mark in the center of the room," said Harriet. "Are we doing close up or full body?"

"Full body," she said.

Harriet set up the camera, already in position on a tripod, and adjusted the boom mike on a swing stand overhead. "I'll start recording remotely when I get in the control room."

"Got it," said Sophia, shaking herself out, running a hand through her hair. She wore light makeup, a dark green Urban Outfitters V-neck, her favorite JBrand jeans, and Converse sneakers, a stripped-down girl, confident enough to show her real face. A few producers in LA said that the heavy makeup in her head shot made her look older. When the photos were taken, she had been eighteen, and purposefully aged herself up. Now she wanted to look exactly like herself.

From the control room, Harriet turned on the overheads and a spotlight. She flicked a few buttons and the red light on the camera started flashing. "You look great," said Harriet through the control room mike. "Ready?"

Sophia was ready.

"Here we go."

LIFE IS **NOT** A
dress rehearsal.
THE CURTAIN IS UP
and you are **on**,
SO GET OUT THERE
and give it your
BEST SHOT.

my brain is a dirty sponge

Afterward, as the sweat dried, Leandra asked Charlie, "How many women have you been with before me?"

They were in their queen-size bed in their small but comfortable house in the fashionable Bang Rak district. Ninety-nine percent of the citizens of Bangkok would consider it the lap of luxury. By Leandra's standards, it was okay. Only six rooms, and two bathrooms. The ceilings were only ten feet high. They were living with the former resident's furniture, which Charlie didn't mind, but kind of grossed Leandra out. She was sleeping and fucking on a used mattress. It was a Tempur-Pedic and less than a year old. But still.

"Why do you want to know?"

Sensitive subject for the former tubby? She assumed he wasn't all that experienced. Sexually, she was the *sensei*, and Charlie was the *senpai*. But, Jesus, had he been a *virgin*? It wasn't possible, was it? She had to play this right, or he'd feel awkward and ashamed, the first step down the road to romantic ruin. "Forget it. I don't really want to know," she said. "I'll get jealous."

He turned it around, and asked, "How many men have you been with?"

She had lost count after twenty. "It's embarrassing."

"Wow, that many?"

"Three," she lied. "See? You *are* embarrassed for me." She buried her head under the sheets.

"You learned a lot from three guys," he said. "I should thank them."

"I did not! They would just, like, roll on top, and then roll off. Not a lot of imagination. I've learned more from magazines and movies—and from you. Being with you puts crazy ideas in my head. Dirty, filthy ideas that make me wonder about myself. But you make me feel so safe, I just go for it."

"So you've never done . . . that thing with your tongue . . . before?"

Eyes wide, she was convincingly offended. "Of course not! I wouldn't do *that* with someone else! Oh, my god. You think I'm a total *whore*." She pretended to throw the covers back, like she was about to storm off in a huff.

Charlie held on tight. "You are the opposite of a whore."

She pouted. "I'm a nun?"

"You're a good person. A dream come true," he said. "Before you, I've only been with one other woman. We met in business school. She was willing and I was grateful. We stuck it out for a year. She's a good person, too, and is still a friend, but I never got all that excited about our sex life. I figured sex just didn't live up to the hype, and that was that. When I got into Muay Thai, I put all my energy into it, until the night you walked into Sky Bar. Heaven cracked open. The oceans rose up. You've shown me a world I didn't think existed for me. I can't thank you enough."

Still pouting, she said, "I'm willing and you're grateful?"

"I'm worshipfully, madly in love with you," he said, cupping her cheeks and staring into her eyes.

Leandra gazed back, a bit warily at first, then softening and reflecting back the same emotion he poured into her. Voice trembling, she said, "I love you, too."

He pressed his lips to her forehead, and, to her horror, started weeping, rocking, repeating, "Thank you, thank you, thank you . . ."

Leandra was tempted to say, "You're welcome, you're welcome, you're welcome," but he probably wouldn't think it was funny. Instead, she said, "Oh, baby," and stroked his back like the emotional infant he was. *He'd only slept with two women?* She assumed his number was low, but she had no idea it was *that* bad. Leandra's ovaries shriveled at his soft, interminable whimpering. She breathed into her own discomfort, flooding her cringing impulses with calm and oxygen. She took the Zen approach, knowing that, at some point in the very near future, this mortifying moment would end.

And it did. Eventually, she shifted him onto his side, and rubbed his back until he snuffled into sleep.

Leandra got out of bed, wandered through their house toward the desk where Charlie kept the laptop. She booted it up. It was midnight in Bangkok. She sent an email to her parents, assuring them she was fine. (They were over the moon about the match, her mom taking full credit.) Then Leandra did her nightly perusal of Charlie's bookmarked pages, his bank accounts and investment portfolios, just keeping track of where they stood. It wasn't snooping, or devious. She wasn't secretly transferring money into a Swiss bank account, not that she had any idea how one would go about doing such a thing; although it seemed like an important life skill to learn, like playing tennis or riding a horse. She was just peeking behind the curtain.

A text chimed in from Sophia. "Miss you," it said.

A lump formed in Leandra's throat. Two words of longing from her old friend hit her a hundred times deeper than Charlie's weepy confession.

"I miss you, too," she texted back.

"Toronto just isn't the same without you."

Leandra pictured Sophia thumbing the text, her hair dipping down her shoulder, dark eyes focused on the screen. Not for the first time, Leandra wondered if she were gay for Sophia. She'd toyed with the idea many times over the years, but always came back to the same conclusion. She loved Sophia, was jealous of her other friends (especially Demi), found her breathtaking, could easily imagine kissing her. But the fantasy screeched to a halt when she got to one part of Sophia that left her cold: vagina. Leandra just wasn't into girl bits. She was barely interested in her own. Men had described her cooch as magical, mysterious, and "alive, so alive" (a film student boyfriend in college). Did she delve into the magic, the mystery herself when she was alone? Meh. Leandra would rather keep her hands clean.

"I might be heading west," she typed, although, until that second, she hadn't thought about leaving Asia.

"What about Charlie?"

"He's okay, but the world is full of big fish."

Sophia wrote, "Sounds like true love. Got to go. Stuff to do before work." She tacked on the winking face with a tongue-out emoji. Not the declaration of undying love Leandra had hoped for, but it would do. She felt a lot less alone just knowing that Sophia was thinking about her. Charlie loved her, had never loved like this before, and would never love like this again, etc. The truth was, he didn't even know her. During his waking hours, Leandra became exactly what he wanted her to be, a good person, his dream come true. When Charlie finally fell asleep? Leandra lay awake or padded through the house, letting herself breathe. There was little comfort in being herself. She just felt empty.

"Tell me the truth," said Leandra, watching Charlie eat a bowl of shrimp pad thai she'd made from scratch at her cooking class today.

He took a bite, and smiled. "It's perfect. I love it!"

She'd cajoled him into eating a quart-size portion to prove it. Charlie was so whipped by her magical pussy, she could shit on a plate and he'd slurp it up and ask for seconds. "I'm glad you like it."

"Yeah, keep at it," he said. It was meant to be encouraging, but it struck her as an insult. Why did he insist she take a cooking class anyway? They could just go to restaurants—something other than Thai food, please. Noodles and curry every night for weeks on end? She was sick of it. And now, she was being asked to cook it, too. What Leandra wouldn't give for a big bowl of poutine (French fries smothered in cheese curds and gravy; it's a Canada thing).

"I have a special surprise planned for tonight," he said, rising from his chair.

Tonight? She'd spent hours over a hot stove, and she still had dishes to do. *Whoa. Did I just really think that? My brain is a dirty dish sponge.* Charlie got excited watching her cook (fun . . . for ten minutes) and clean (hate), but he couldn't possibly like the nagging and insecurity that were part of the wifey package.

She had to snap out of this mood. Charlie wouldn't lavish jewelry and designer goodies on a dirty dish sponge. She would shine like a diamond, because that's how precious she was to him.

"I love surprises!" she said. "What should I wear?"

"What you're wearing is fine."

She was in a halter dress, dotted with food stains. Was he taking her to a Laundromat? "I'll just shower and throw on . . ."

"Double quick. The car arrives in five minutes."

Half an hour later, Leandra looked sexy and elegant in a black Armani minidress, diamond earrings and bracelet from Cartier, and strappy Stuart Weitzman heels. Their limo pulled up to the temple complex called Wat Pho. They'd been there before to see the Emerald Buddha and the Reclining Buddha (the statue was the length of a football field with feet as tall as she was), immediately followed by a trip to another Wat to see the Golden Buddha (solid gold, but not *that* huge).

"Here again?" she asked, trying to sound excited about it.

He said, "Remember that Ram Thai dance concert you loved at the Grand Palace?"

"Of course!" Leandra wasn't such a dance fan, actually. It was the most absurd of all art forms, people prancing and leaping around while the audience stared at their crotches. Meanwhile, why did everything in Thailand have to tack on the word "thai" to it? Pad thai, thai tea, Muay Thai, Ram Thai. It was like saying Canadian bacon, but for everything.

The driver parked and they walked toward the temple entrance. A guard at the gate thrust a folded-up few yards of fabric at her. Charlie said, "Oh, I forgot. You have to cover your legs. Just wind this around your waist and tuck it in like a skirt."

"My outfit," she said. Last time they'd come, she wore pants.

"It's a sign of respect," he said.

Now in a yellow print maxi skirt, Leandra followed Charlie as they walked between gold-shingled A-line structures with scary sharp spindles jutting heavenward from the roof corners. If one of those spires cracked off and fell, it could slice you in half.

"Why are there two thousand statues of Buddha in every temple?" she asked Charlie. "Sitting, standing, lying down, one hand up, hands together, hands on knees. Pick a position already. Can you imagine a church back home with a thousand statues of Jesus—eating, drinking, anointing, playing golf?"

"Keep your voice down," he snapped. Jeez, she was just making a joke.

Charlie guided her to their assigned folding chairs set up in the courtyard of the complex. The chairs were on cobblestones, so every movement caused rocking. He seemed distracted, so she brought his hand to her lips and kissed his knuckles. Charlie snatched his hand away. He'd corrected her a few times about being affectionate in public—a major no-no in Bangkok—but she felt entitled to sulk anyway.

The dance was nearly identical to the last one they went to, girls with white face makeup and pointy hats, doing the twisty wrist movements and lifted-knee poses that anyone who'd seen *The King and I* would recognize as Siamese. A small band plunked on sitars and xylophones for an hour. Then there was the meet and greet. Charlie chatting away in Thai while Leandra smiled and nodded in a thick fog of ennui.

In the limo home, Charlie said, "You seem upset."

"I'm not upset," she said. "It's just . . . I've reached my Wat limit. If I see one more Buddha or one more girl in a pointy hat, I'll scream."

Charlie looked at her like she'd grown a third head. It'd taken eight weeks for her mask to slip, which was a good long time for anyone to pretend, even a pro like her. She backpedaled. "I don't mean that. It's just that"—she groped for a phrase that would trigger an emotional response in him—"I miss you."

"We live together," he said.

"You work all day, and then you go to the dojo after dinner. When we go out, we can't touch or talk in public. I love that you have Thai friends and speak the language, but I feel left out."

He seemed irritated. "So what do you expect me to do?"

"We're in Bangkok! Sin City. I want to go to the Patpong, and do shots with ladyboys. Or ride an elephant while feeding a monkey. I want excitement."

"I thought I was exciting."

Christ, was he a woman? "You are!" she said. "You're all I need!"

"Me, and a monkey."

"And an elephant."

He laughed and hugged her, forgiving her momentary lapse of decorum. She was able to readjust her perfect girlfriend mask. It chafed, though. One day, Leandra would have an honest relationship with someone and not have to wear a mask at all. She'd had that with Stacy. Born a year apart, they might as well have been twins. They could read each other's thoughts, without judgment. When Leandra lost that, she always felt off when relating to other people, like she couldn't completely trust anyone. Even with Sophia and Demi, she felt compelled to put on an act. One day she'd be able to say to a man, "Let's just have great sex, eat the world until we can't stand the sight of each other, and then go our separate ways."

Until then, Leandra would play the part as best she could, for as long as she could. Charlie bought a house so they could live together. She did feel some moral obligation to be the woman he wanted her to be, for a while.

As they pulled up to their house, Charlie said, "I'm sorry, Leandra. I didn't realize how isolated you are here. I was dreading bringing this up, but now I think it's good news."

"What news?"

"My boss wants me to go to London next week. Why don't you come with me? A change might do you good."

"I love London!" she said, although she'd never been. "Yes, let's do it! You're a genius, Charlie! You know me so well. We'll have so much fun."

"I'm going to be working a lot," he warned her.

"Don't worry about me," she said.

Two days later, Charlie and Leandra flew to London aboard an Emirates Airbus. She packed every item she possessed. When Charlie asked why she had five suitcases for a five-night trip, she said, "A girl has to be prepared for any situation."

The bank paid for Charlie's first-class ticket, and he paid $10,000 for hers. In just two months, Leandra upgraded her seat and her life from economy to first class. She gazed out the plane window from her catbird seat, and wondered where she could possibly go from here.

travel
is the
only thing
you buy
that makes
★ you ★
richer.

10

the world's
wimpiest biker gang

For two weeks, Demi prepared for her day in court.

First, she hired a lawyer. A Google search for "DUI lawyer Vancouver" netted a surprising number of specialists. Demi set up consultations with three of them based on their websites. Dad was her legal eagle wingman, going to the appointments with her. The last meeting was with John Dooey, Esq. He wore a Vancouver Canucks team jacket and jeans. Dad didn't like his casual Friday on Monday look. Demi found it kind of charming, besides . . . Go, Canucks!

"My defense will center around the infallibility of the Breathalyzer result," he said. "Since you tested over by just a hair, your case should be a slam dunk. One," he counted off on his fingers, "we have the margin of error with the test itself, which puts you in the gray zone. Second, some gastric issues, like burping, while doing the test gives it a higher reading."

"I did burp!"

"Three, there's a discrepancy of the swaying issue. In your favor, it wasn't shown on the dash cam. Although saying a police officer lied won't necessarily help you."

Dad said, "So you're going to get her off on a technicality."

"Not exactly. Technically, legally, she was drunk," he said, making Demi flinch. "But the technology itself is fundamentally flawed. The strategy works. I've gotten off eighty percent of my clients with borderline readings like Demi's."

"Sounds good to me," she said. The Breathalyzer result really stuck in her craw. A one hundredth of a decimal point was going to decide whether she was a criminal, and it seemed wrong. If she were anywhere else in the world, her Breathalyzer test would have gotten her a dirty look and a pass. Instead, she had to pay Dooey his minimum retainer of $4,000, which was the going rate.

Dooey would do his part, and he told Demi she'd have to do hers. "One," he said, "show up at court on time looking like a Catholic preschool teacher. Two, for the next two weeks, you will bike to work at your father's office. You will bike home and have dinner with your elderly neighbor. You will not go to a bar, or see your friends, or post a photo of yourself partying on Instagram."

"What's Instagram got to do with . . ."

"I guarantee you, the judge will have done a lap of your social media to see what you've been up to since your arrest. To be safe, don't post *anything*. You're off Facebook, Twitter, and Instagram for the next two weeks."

"Okay," she said. Jesus, this guy was strict. "What else?"

"No drinking, smoking weed, snorting blow, at all. When you appear in court, you will probably be asked to give a urine sample. Your urine has to be squeaky clean. So clean, you'd drink it."

Demi gulped. "What do you think will happen?"

He shrugged, making the Canuck jacket bunch up around his neck. "Worst-case scenario: You're convicted, pay a fine, probation, community service. You'll lose your license for good. Every potential employer, landlord, bank loan officer, cop, paranoid boyfriend for the rest of your life can find your conviction in court records with a few clicks of a mouse," he said. "Best-case scenario: You're exonerated. What's likely to happen is something in between."

Her DUI had cost her $8,000 so far. Half went to Dooey, and the other four grand went to the city of Vancouver to regain possession of her car, which she couldn't do until a city-approved mechanic made all necessary repairs to it (including a semi-detached muffler, caused the night she stalked James's apartment at three A.M.).

When all was said and done, she'd be broke by the end of this, regardless of the outcome of her court appearance. Convicted, exonerated, it didn't make a difference to her bottom line. She'd saved for years, and lost it all in weeks. Sometimes it was hard not to take bad luck personally, like God had it in for her. Was it punishment for being an atheist? No matter what her beliefs, Demi was getting tired of having to learn things the hard way.

Dooey sent her the occasional email, but otherwise, Demi didn't speak to him again until her court appearance. Dad and her step-mom, Mary, came to lend moral support. He was noticeably relieved that her lawyer wore a suit to court. He brought an assistant, first-year-law-student niece named Tracy. Tracy was Demi's age, but she acted a lot older, the picture of responsibility, efficiency, and competence. She was cute, too, in a soft gray suit and heels. When she and Demi were introduced, Demi sensed that all the adults in their group were comparing the two of them. Tracy's parents were probably proud of her, and felt confident she'd find her way in the world. Dad and Mary? They'd be thrilled if Demi wasn't sent to prison.

The court proceedings lasted only twenty minutes. Demi had dressed exactly as her lawyer advised, in a cardigan and trousers she borrowed from her stepmom, flats, next to no makeup, and her hair in a tight pony. She sat and stood when instructed by her lawyer. She'd followed his instructions and was ready to pee in a cup and present it to the judge. "My piss, your honor, nice and warm," she'd say with a wink that might get her thrown in the clink.

But it didn't come to that. No one asked for her precious fluids, or her testimony. Dooey did his thing, and gave a speech he'd probably done a thousand times. She hoped he'd stage a dramatic courtroom stunt of having a random person from the gallery burp into the Breathalyzer, maybe even the judge herself. But no, he just recited the defense, plus a lot of puffery about Demi's promising career in marketing, her upstanding place in the community, and the tragedy of such a promising life being marred by a technological flaw.

Dooey wasn't finished when Judge Klavan, a matronly, big-breasted, thin-haired grandmotherly type, interrupted him. "I've heard enough," she said. "We can go to trial, or I can give you a judgment right now."

They huddled at the defense table. "If we go to trial, you'll probably win," said Dooey.

"Let's go to trial."

"It'll cost another five thousand dollars."

"Let's get a judgment right now. Your success rate is eighty percent, right?"

"It's a risk."

"No risk, no reward."

"There is no reward," he said. "The only outcomes are varying degrees of punishment."

Despite hearing his warning, Demi believed it would all go away with the drop of the gavel. Call it willful delusion or unbridled optimism. "We have a solid defense, and the judge doesn't seem like a hard-ass."

"Okay," said Dooey. To the bench, he gave their decision. "We waive the right to a trial."

Judge Klavan said, "Demi Michaels, you are guilty of driving under the influence. Your driver's license is suspended for twelve months. You're ordered to pay the fine of two thousand dollars. You will do fifty hours of community service. The record of this arrest will be expunged. If you're arrested again for DUI, you will serve jail time. Next case!"

That was it. Dooey and the law student each took an elbow and guided Demi out of the courtroom. Her parents met them in the hall-way. Mary dabbed tears of joy from her eyes. Dad slapped Dooey on the back and said, "I knew you were the right choice all along!"

"Guys!" said Demi, breaking up their victory party. "We lost. I got the book thrown right at my forehead."

The adults all seemed surprised. Dad said, "The record is expunged."

"I lost my license and all my savings!"

Mary, usually sympathetic, said, "You drove drunk, and you paid the price. You should be *thrilled* your stupid mistake won't destroy your future. I never want to hear you complain about this outcome again."

The drive back to Dad's was tense, to say the least. If Demi were in grade school, Dad would teach her a lesson by making her write a thank-you note to the judge. It took Mary a minute to calm down and find some compassion, and even longer to stop feeling guilty about crossing the nonbirth-parent line. She hadn't. No one else could have broken through Demi's selfish first reaction to the judgment. But after Mary's brutal honesty, she rethought it. Her parents were right. She should be as relieved as they were.

She really should. One day, she would. But right now, she saw a year on two wheels, picking up trash, and depending on her dad for a paycheck.

That Sunday afternoon, Demi and Catherine set up lawn chairs in the front yard with a pitcher of lemonade and a platter of jerk chicken. She baked a pan of corn bread, too, and gave out squares to all the residents. Wally took one, and asked, "With whole corn? Because that'll give me the runs."

"No whole corn," Demi assured him, and he went back to trimming the hedges.

"Why don't you call a friend?" asked Catherine. "You lost your license, but you're not dead."

"It's only a matter of time."

"That's true for all of us. I just don't get why you want to sit around with me on this beautiful day."

"I like hanging with you." With Catherine, she could relax. She didn't feel pressure to be funny, or a hard drinker, or talk about "her future" (Dad's favorite subject). Sarah had checked in a few times since the arrest, trolling for gossip. Demi texted back that she was laying low until it was all sorted out. Now that it was, Demi didn't feel inclined to get back in touch with her. She was still bruised and battered, not in a party mood. Plus she was broke, and had to rely on pedal power to get anywhere.

"Do your friends even know what happened in court?" asked Catherine.

"I told them it was a close call, but I won't be joining the cast of *Orange Is the New Black* and won't get a cool prison nickname, like Squeaks or Sliver."

"Most of the women in prison are there because of some man, you know."

"Makes sense."

"If my husband hadn't run off to Australia, I would have killed him."

"Wait . . . *what?*"

"He deserved it. I woke up one morning, and he was gone. He left a note, though, thanking me for twenty years of support, my jewelry, and all the cash in our bank accounts."

"Are you bullshitting me? You're making this up."

She laughed, and said, "I'm not! I went to sleep a happy housewife, and woke up penniless and alone. This was forty years ago. I look back in disbelief that it actually happened to me. But it did. I lost everything. My shrink says it's why I grew up to be such a collector. I cling out of fear."

"How do you recover from something like that?"

"I just did," she said. "I moved into my parents' house. The timing turned out to be good. I was there when they needed me at the end of their lives. After they died, I spent months cataloging the furniture and the art—they were collectors. I researched the providence of some of the pieces, and realized I enjoyed doing it. My parents hoped I'd share their passion, but it wasn't until they were gone that I got into it, and eventually became an early-American-furniture appraiser at Sotheby's. I had boyfriends—historians, collectors, and curators. I traveled all over the world. But I never fell in love again after Rufus."

"Rufus?"

"I know, silly name. Like a shaggy dog or something. He did have shaggy hair—he was a bit of a beatnik. So was I! I rebelled against my parents, ran off with a poet. And then he ran off with a stewardess."

Demi couldn't believe what she was hearing. "You let me whine about James for months, while you've been sitting on all this amazing stuff?"

"I like your stories! I know mine already, and I get so tired talking about myself. My theory is that, when you're born, you're an egomaniacal narcissist. Every day you're alive, you care less and less about yourself. If you live long enough, you get so sick of yourself that you're relieved when you die."

"Where do you think I am, on the egomaniacal narcissist scale?"

"You're exactly where you should be," said Catherine, with a sly smile. "Tell me again about your day in court, but this time, add *Law and Order* theme music and *ka-chung* sound effects."

The sound of bells drew their attention to the street. A dozen bike riders pulled up to the curb at the Grace. The rider in front removed her helmet.

"Sarah?" asked Demi, standing up. The other riders took off their helmets, too. Eve, Jo, and a bunch of their other friends.

Sarah laid her bike down on the grass, and came over to give Demi a tight hug. "We heard what happened. I still feel like it's my fault. If we hadn't made that joke about James, you wouldn't have gone off with Warren, and the cop wouldn't have pulled you over."

"It's not your fault! It's mine. I shouldn't have been driving." That night, or any other night. In a way, she was glad she lost her license so she'd never do it again. Mary's honesty had gotten under her skin. *You should be thrilled.* After meditating on it for a couple of days, she agreed wholeheartedly. To Sarah, she asked, "What's all this? Hey, guys!" She waved at the other riders.

"We're heading down to First @ Second. It's the last day, and we thought you'd want to check it out."

Her heart grew two sizes. Her friends rounded up a bunch of bikes so they could ride to the festival with her, a show of solidarity she never expected. "We'll be the world's wimpiest biker gang."

Catherine said, "Go ahead, Demi. Wally and I can polish off the chicken."

Demi ran upstairs to get her helmet and bike. Then they were off, riding in rows of two on the streets, ringing their bells and intimidating no one all the way to the beach.

The food festival was crowded and hot with rows upon rows of brightly, post-ironically painted food trucks and carts catering to every conceivable taste, from French truffle grilled cheese to bowls of Vietnamese pho. You had to stand on line for an hour to get a soggy breakfast burrito or a few measly pot stickers. But as an event, First @ Second was a massive success, well attended and well organized. When Demi ran into Maya, she told her so. She also apologized for being a punk, and wished Maya all the success in the world. Maya was grateful and relieved to clear the air with Demi, but she didn't offer her her old job back. Just as well. They hugged it out by the Asian pizza truck, but then Maya had to go put out a fire. Literally. The Oinkwich barbecue was going up in flames.

Demi and her posse spent a couple of hours at the festival, eating, not drinking, and making fun of the foodies and their gusty, precious, and snotty descriptions of every dish's ingredient and preparation. Demi loved food. Cooking was her passion. But foodies? Meh.

Sarah said, "James is walking toward you."

"Fool me once, bitch."

"Seriously. He's five paces away."

"Yup, and he's got Barack Obama and Jennifer Lawrence with him."

"He's one step away. He's here. It's happening."

"Bullshi . . ."

A tap on her shoulder, and the voice she knew all too well in her ear. "Have you tried the churros?"

Demi turned around. There he was, the man who'd been the epicenter of her universe for three years. The man who stomped on her heart and had no right to look as groin-achingly sexy on such a hot sweaty day in the J.Crew navy shorts and striped shirt she bought for him a while back. Demi reached up to touch her hair, which was a tangled mess from riding. She wasn't wearing a lick of makeup. Her shorts and T-shirt were baggy and food-stained. In her daydreams about this moment, she wasn't such a slob.

"Hello" was all she could muster.

"Hello, yourself." He leaned down and kissed her cheek. An electric current raced from her neck straight to her crotch. "I was hoping I'd see you here."

She looked around, trying to find someone. "Where's your bimbo?"

"I'm alone," he said. "I've been alone since you left."

That might be true. On her Instagram, she'd been trying to give the impression that she was living it up. His feeds included likes and links, but nothing personal. Not even a photo of a nice plate of food or a cute dog. If he were hitting some hot girl, James would want his followers to know.

He said, "You must have been busy lately. You haven't posted any pictures. I was worried something happened. Or someone."

Did she tell him she'd been off the grid on the advice of her attorney? It wasn't any of James's business. She caught Sarah's eye. Her friend mimed dragging her away. Demi shook her head. She'd sobered up in more ways than one over the last couple of weeks, and Demi was no longer vulnerable to James's dubious charms. But it would still be nice to get some closure.

"I have questions," she said bluntly. "And I deserve answers."

"I need to talk to you, too." James bowed his head slightly, as if he were ashamed of himself for the way he behaved. If he were so contrite, why hadn't he sought her out before?

"Okay, let's talk."

"It's kind of hectic here."

"So where?" she asked.

"Our place?"

"*Your* place." His apartment was closer. Besides, she didn't want him to know where she lived.

"Let's go."

Sarah stopped her. "Are you sure?"

"It's not like I'm going to sleep with him," said Demi.

Her friend didn't look convinced.

demi's jerk chicken

ingredients

1 tbsp ground allspice

1 tbsp dried thyme

1 tbsp sage

zest of 1 lemon

1 tbsp cumin

1 tbsp salt

½ tbsp red chilli flakes

2 tbsp agave

1 tbsp cayenne pepper

½ tsp ground cinnamon

2 tsps ground nutmeg

8 garlic cloves, peeled

2 bunches scallions, chopped

two 1-inch cubes fresh ginger

1 bunch fresh cilantro, leaves only

1 cup fresh lime juice

¼ cup tamari sauce

¼ cup sesame oil

3 packages organic free-range chicken thighs (or breasts)

instructions

1. In a good blender, add all of the ingredients (minus the chicken) and blend until smooth.

2. Place the chicken in a plastic container with an air-proof lid, then cover with the marinade. Toss around the chicken and make sure all of it is coated evenly.

3. Cover the container with a lid and leave in the fridge for 24 to 48 hours—yes that's 1 to 2 days.

4. Once the chicken has successfully marinated, pop the chicken on the grill 6 to 8 minutes each side or bake at 375 degrees for 35 minutes.

Enjoy with some steamed rice and veggies and get carried away to Jamaica, mon!

11

i'm not here to make friends

"Are you Sophia?" asked the flight attendant.

"Yes."

"I have a meal for you."

"I didn't buy one." She'd glanced at the plane food menu, and decided against it. She'd rather eat peanuts and pretzels for free than pay twenty dollars for the "meat plate." Although it did look appetizing.

The flight attendant checked her tablet. "It's already been paid for by M. King Studios."

"Oh. Yeah, thanks." *They bought me lunch?* She didn't want to let on that she was surprised. *Play it cool! Sit like a star.*

The flight attendant handed her a cardboard box. She opened it and found a ham and cheese sandwich.

Sophia was on her way to Los Angeles for the second time in a month. Her *Hipsters* audition tape, shot by Harriet and emailed to the production team with five minutes to spare, did not, apparently, suck. An hour after she sent it in, Agnes called. In a hysterical, hyperventilating lather, she told Sophia that she'd been invited to "test" for the part of Valerie, which was the next level of hoop jumping. A callback! In all her years of auditioning, Sophia had never been tested for *anything*, which was itself a test of her endurance and commitment.

As she happily snacked, Sophia had a déjà vu. A few rows back, the flight attendant said, "It's been paid for by M. King Studios." Sophia leaned over the seat to look down the center aisle in coach. The flight attendant handed a box to someone. A slender brown arm with multiple bangles reached to take it.

Sophia faced forward again. She wrapped her sandwich for the time being, unbuckled her seat belt, and walked down the aisle to the bathroom. She had to size up the owner of that arm. The girl was her age, also multiethnic, gorgeous, with a similar girly personal style. Just like Sophia, she seemed amazed by the good fortune to get a free lunch.

This girl was her competition, and possibly the only other ethnically ambiguous young, pretty female actor in all of Toronto. Did the producers have a thing for Canadians? Or maybe there were dozens of girls all over North America eating ham sandwiches right now, and winging to LA to test for the same part.

Locking the bathroom door, Sophia focused on her eyes in the mirror. Men had told her often enough that her eyes were a dark bottomless mystery. She stared at them, and into herself, to find calm and strength. "You got this," she said.

The statement felt real and true. It would have been more appropriate if the rush of confidence came, say, after climbing a mountain and not in a cramped airplane bathroom. The setting was irrelevant. She met herself in her reflection. The girl staring back at her showed steely resolve. She might not get the part, but it wouldn't be because she psyched herself out of it with fear. Sophia went back to her seat, grinning with her purpose. *Relax. Walk like a star. Know the part is already yours.* They could bring in ten girls, a hundred. It didn't matter. She had this.

The plane landed at LAX. Sophia, along with the rest of the passengers, headed toward baggage claim, past Burger King and Starbucks, and then to the airport exits. A row of drivers in black suits, white shirts, and ties stood by the doors holding up signs or tablets with names on them, including hers. Sophia approached her driver, giddy. The car and driver, like the sandwich, had been unexpected. She handed her overnight bag to her driver, and noticed out of the corner of her eye the girl with the 'fro doing the same exact thing to her driver. Sophia quickly read the name on his sign—Leslie Abbott.

Sophia and her driver headed out to the parking lot. Leslie and hers followed only a few steps behind. They got in their respective cars, and drove, caravan style, from the airport to the hotel, The Sheraton in Studio City. With comic precision, Sophia and Leslie exited the cars at the same moment, and walked toward the concierge desk on a parallel course.

Should she say something? It was kind of obvious what was happening here. Sophia glanced at Leslie, who very pointedly did not look at Sophia. *Okay then.* Message received. By tacit agreement, the rivals would not acknowledge each other or speak at all. Maybe Leslie was superstitious about talking to the competition, or she was soaking up the tension to put into her test? Sophia was fine with the silent treatment. *I'm not here to make friends*, she thought. It was so cold-blooded, so reality TV, that she burst out laughing. Her tension evaporated. It didn't matter what Leslie thought or how she used the emotion of this experience. Sophia's only job was to breathe it all in, and love it all out.

After she checked in, she went up to her room (Leslie waited for a different elevator; superstitious, or obnoxious?). It was nice, clean, nothing to write home about. A basket of fruit waited for her there, and a note from Stella Rosen, casting agent, welcoming her to LA and inviting her to order room service for dinner and breakfast. A call sheet was attached, with all the important info for her test tomorrow. At nine A.M., the driver was scheduled to pick her up. At noon, a driver would drive her directly to LAX to catch her return flight to Toronto.

Since Sophia had only one night in LA and only twelve hours until her screen test, she decided to put on a sexy dress, take a cab into West Hollywood, find the biggest, baddest club, do shots, dance, hook up with a male model, and get a tattoo of the Hollywood sign on her neck.

Fuck, no.

But that would make a great story for her future memoir, of how she got wasted the night before the test that changed her life. Instead, Sophia ordered a pizza from room service (it seemed the safest choice), and then took a bubble bath. After a quick call to her mom ("I can't believe how calm I am," she said), Sophia settled down to a Wayne Dyer guided meditation CD she had on her computer until she fell asleep.

Rise and shine to the siren sound of her alarm. She made it extra loud so she wouldn't oversleep. Some nerves arrived with breakfast. Sophia crushed them and psyched herself up by repeating things that Demi always told her. "You're a star!" she said, and took selfies of herself all over the room. "You got this!" she yelled while videotaping herself jumping on the bed. As always, she wanted to document everything, and to remember what it felt like to go from "before" to "after." Today was the great divide. Life was full of hairpin turns. But usually, you didn't see them coming. Even if the outcome wasn't what she hoped it would be, she knew she'd never feel quite the same again. It was such an enormous relief to finally get acknowledgment. She was just so grateful to be here, to have this chance.

When the time came, she took the elevator down to the lobby. The doors shushed open and she stepped out. Leslie emerged from her elevator a second later, like they'd timed it. Wearing the same green shirt from her self-tape, Sophia smiled, not letting her competition kill her positive vibe. They walked awkwardly side by side to the curb, where their drivers and separate cars were waiting. Caravan style, they rode to the studio only a few miles away.

A couple of production assistants were waiting for them, One went right up to Leslie, and took her to a room on the left. The other, a girl around Sophia's age, guided her to the door to her right.

"I thought Stella Rosen would be here," said Sophia.

"Right this way." The PA handed her the sides, the same pages she'd already memorized for the audition tape, which was a relief, and ushered her into a room with a U-shaped table. Seated at the table were a dozen people. They quickly introduced themselves as the writers, producers, and casting directors on *Hipsters*. One woman who seemed to be in charge—Julie? Julia?—asked Sophia to stand in the front of the room and do the lines. As she got in place, she had a five-second flashback to that frightening audition at Casting Central when she blanked her lines. But that wasn't an issue today. She was in the Zone today. Sophia could have read the phone book and nailed it. After reading the lines twice, the head woman said, "Thank you."

And that was it. The PA showed her out of the room and said, "Your car is waiting to take you to the airport."

She was shown to her car, which was exactly where she'd left it on the circular driveway of the office building. Leslie's car was also idling at the curb. Would it give her an edge, going second? Who knows.

On the ride back to LAX, Sophia called Agnes, who picked up on the first ring. "I crushed it," she said.

"I expect nothing less," said Agnes.

"I was only in the room for ten minutes, max. Is that a good sign or a bad sign?"

"Impossible to say. They might have loved what they saw, and one bite of perfect was enough."

"It just seemed really short." Now that it was all over and she couldn't do anything to change the test, she slammed the door on doubt. It wasn't welcomed.

"I've already emailed the producer to say thanks and that you felt really positive about it. All we can do now is wait."

"What's your vibe? If you were a witch and you pulled a 'yes' or 'no' out of thin air?" Sophia asked, grasping for anything.

Agnes laughed. "I wish I were a witch! All I've got are the chin hairs. Just hang in there, Sophia. We might get some feedback before you land."

Sophia was at the gate for her flight with plenty of time to sit and stew. About a half hour into her wait, she spotted Leslie in line at the Starbucks. She shrank down in her chair and raised her magazine to hide her face. Now that the test was over, Leslie might want to call truce and talk about it. Sophia would rather die. It'd be awkward and strained, like chatting the morning after a one-night stand when all you wanted was to put on your pants and get the hell out of there.

Following her rival's movements, Sophia tried to suss out Leslie's mood, elated, deflated, what? She seemed normal, wandering through the newsstand, sipping her coffee, looking at her phone every thirty seconds, just like Sophia. Agnes hadn't called or texted yet, but, judging from Leslie's constant screen check, neither had her agent.

They were probably on the same flight. When the call to board was announced, Leslie didn't seem to care and barely looked up from her phone. Sophia sprang out of her seat like she'd been jolted with a cattle prod. Agnes said they might have an answer by the time she got off the plane, so Sophia couldn't get on it fast enough. Hovering at the rope line, she shifted from foot to foot until her row was called.

The stewardess took her boarding pass and put it under the scanner. Sophia had already started down the ramp.

"One moment, Ms. Marcus," said the flight attendant.

"Something wrong?" she asked.

The woman beamed at her. "Not at all. You've been upgraded to first class. Here's your new boarding pass."

What the fuck? An upgrade? What was going on here? It had to be a mistake, but she wasn't about to protest. She took her new paper, and walked down the ramp, convinced they were going to change their minds.

The stewardess checked her pass, and directed her to her seat in row two. This wasn't a seat. It was a pod with side panels for privacy, a table, a cabinet with noise-canceling headphones, bottles of water, a snack assortment, and a leather tote bag stuffed with amenities. The TV screen was twice as big as in coach. Playing with the controls, she discovered she could make the seat recline flat, like a bed.

She'd never flown first class before. She'd never done *anything* first class before.

A bit embarrassed by her good fortune, she watched the economy passengers file past her seat, looked enviously at her, just as she always did on her way back to coach. She tried to shrink into her pod, make herself a bit invisible, convinced that, at any second, the stewardess was going to come and send her back there, where she really belonged.

"You," said a voice over her. Oh, shit, that was fast!

She looked up. It was Leslie.

"Hi," said Sophia.

Leslie stared at her, her pretty mouth in an O. She looked at her boarding pass, and then back at Sophia. Her features hardened. She said, "Shit," and then trudged on down the aisle toward the back of the plane.

Sophia immediately started texting Agnes. "I got an upgrade. The other girl didn't. WHAT DOES IT MEAN??"

Right as she hit send, her phone pinged. A text came in from Agnes. It was only three words, the most beautiful words in the English (or any) language: "You got it!!"

Hands shaking, heart thundering, Sophia buzzed all over, like her blood was electrified.

"Excuse me, you have to put your phone in airport mode now," said a roving stewardess with a silver tray. "Would you like a glass of champagne?"

"Yes, please," Sophia croaked, taking a glass and downing it in a gulp.

"Thirsty!" said the woman. "If you'd like, I can bring you a bottle."

"Yes, please!"

"Would you prefer lobster or filet mignon for your dinner? Or, if you're hungry, you can have both."

"Both please!"

The stewardess just laughed. "You got it," she said, repeating the three most glorious words in any language. Sophia wanted to scream and run up and down the plane aisle! That would probably get her arrested. *FUCKING PINCH ME!!!* she screamed in her head.

From a sandwich in a box to champagne and lobster on a silver tray. This was her life now, at least for the next five hours, and possibly a lot longer.

Sophia couldn't help feeling a bit sorry for Leslie. But then they brought around warm cookies fresh out of the oven, and she thought about chocolate instead.

WINNERS
NEVER QUIT
AND
QUITTERS
NEVER WIN

12

**nothing looks
pretty on a bitch**

Leandra kissed Charlie on the
side of his neck and purred, "You are the sexiest man I've ever met."

He returned it with a cheek peck. "The driver might see us."

Improper. That was the implication. Leandra leaned back on the leather limo seat, but held tightly to his hand. "You're exactly right, Charles. A time and a place for everything."

She'd taken to calling him Charles—with a British accent—while they were in London. That was the only change in the dynamic of their relationship. Charlie worked all day, and usually had dinner with clients. When he got back to their suite at the Connaught Hotel in Mayfair, he expected Leandra to be waiting for him, warm and toasty, ready to bounce around their king-size bed for an hour and then stroke his manly chest hair while chanting "I love you" until he drifted off to dreamland.

Barf.

Truly. Leandra bit her lip, and never complained. Charlie's affection seemed real. He'd fallen in love with the devoted, selfless wifey she pretended to be. She spent her afternoons in London shopping for banker's wife outfits, and having her hair and nails tended to. She'd let herself get coarse in Thailand. For the London look, she needed an overhaul. Mildred, her English stylist, gave her a brow shaping that literally changed her life. "Eyebrows should be sisters, not twins," said Mildred. She plucked one arch slightly higher than the other, and it had completely altered Leandra's face, like adding a secret ingredient to a stew. Her strawberry blond hair was brightened to platinum, and straightened permanently using a Brazilian treatment that, she read, was part formaldehyde. She'd soaked her head in embalming fluid. Worth it! She looked as sleek and sophisticated as all the gorgeous specimens she saw walking around Soho.

In the limo, Charles checked his Rolex. "Where are we going, exactly?"

"Raffles," she said. "A club in Chelsea. Some girls told me about a party there tonight."

"What girls?"

She shrugged. "Just some people I met while shopping."

Actually, she'd overheard—one might say *eavesdropped*—Blinky and Shaggy (seriously, that was what they called each other) talking about it in the fitting rooms at Yves St. Laurent on Sloane Street. They were shiny and sparkling human jewels, poreless pale skin and gleaming long, skinny baby giraffe legs.

"I thought you went to the Tower of London today," he asked. "Didn't Beatrice set you up with a private Beefeater tour?"

Beatrice was Charles's assistant at the bank. He'd been asking her to arrange tours and expeditions for Leandra all week, but she had no intention of being dragged through medieval piles with some banger-breathed old man, no matter how cool his hat was. "I over-slept," she said. "I'm going to do some sightseeing tomorrow. Maybe you can get away, and come with me?"

"I'd love to," he said. "But Mr. Yamamoto . . ."

His client, the man he'd been called to London to see, was a Japa-nese master of the universe. He kept Charles at his beck and call. Leandra would have loved to complain and whine about it, but she reminded herself that nothing looked pretty on a bitch.

"I'm just worried about your health," she said sweetly. "You work so hard."

"I'm exhausted," he agreed. Her rules—no nagging, no whining— did not apply to him. "Let's have an early night, okay?"

It was their third night in London, and the first time they'd actu-ally gone out together. She intended to party until dawn, even if Charles was fagged (meaning tired; Blinky and Shaggy's dressing room conversation had been quite an education) in the morning.

Leandra's look tonight was classy-cum-trashy, aka *clashy*: a super-short lamé dress with a high neckline—Joan of Arc on top; a Playboy Bunny below. Given the choice of highlighting her ass or her boobs (both splendid), Leandra always chose butt. Most men, including Charles, gravitated to the ass like a rat to cheese. Boobs could be mes-merizing. But a butt gave men Big Ben boners.

"I'm serious, Lee," he said, using his hateful nickname for her. "I have a meeting at eight."

If one put a gun to her head, Leandra could not tell you what Charles did all day at work, or what these millions of meetings were about. The details—his job title, his responsibilities—were irrele-vant to her. All she needed to know was that their expenses were covered—including the room at the Connaught, all their meals, and the car and driver. Her walking-around money, which she was burn-ing through like the Great Fire of 1666, was out of (his) pocket. One night, when she wanted a double helping of pounds, she licked his hands like a cat, and he went crazy on her in bed. Men were so pre-dictably perverted.

The limo rolled to a stop in front of a black awning with the word "Raffles" on it. The club was the watering hole for young London's titled entitled upper class. If you weren't stunning and superrich, you couldn't get in. Leandra had been worried about being turned away at the door, but she was prepared. The limo would help. So did her dress, and the faux fur shawl and Louboutins. Charles's Tom Ford suit and bratty expression put the icing on the scone. It all added up to give them a "don't you know who I am?" wealthy American image. The bouncer would have to let them in, or live in fear that he'd turned away VIPs.

He wasn't much of a bouncer. In Canada, the bigger the bouncer the better. But the Raffles gatekeeper was a slim fop in a skinny suit with a Union Jack pattern. He preened like a cat, running his slender fingers through shoulder-length brown hair. "Hello, luvs," he said as Leandra and Charlie walked up to the velvet rope.

"Hi," said Leandra, on the edge of friendly and frosty.

"Can I help you?" asked the bouncer. "Do you need directions or something?"

Charles sighed. "We'd like to go inside." He pointed at the club door impatiently.

"So sorry! We're having a private party tonight."

Shit. "Yes, we know. It's Wubby Trumell's twenty-first birthday," she said. "Blinky invited us."

"Did she?"

"We're friends of hers from New York."

He smiled. "Welcome, friends from New York. Blinky's already inside. Cheers!"

In they went. Charles leaned down to mutter in Leandra's ear. "We're crashing a party? Really? We could be back at the Connaught in bed."

Yes, well, Leandra had had enough of rolling around in bed with Charles. He was still making up for all his quasi-virginal years of masturbating to her memory. The sex was fine. But he insisted on talking about it during the act. "Does this feel good? Tell me it feels good," over and over again, like, every thrust. Once, when a little tipsy, she said, "It'll feel better if you *shut up*," and he went as soft as a rotten banana.

The Raffles entrance was dark except for blue and green tube lights embedded on the black hallway floor and walls, like walking down a tunnel into a spaceship. The hallway opened into a cavernous open room, with flashing green and blue lights, pulsing along the walls and up columns in the middle of the dance floor to the beat of the music. Only a few people were standing on the dance floor—beautifully turned out, with six-inch stilettos and halter dresses—but none were dancing. Most of the party people were congregating around the bar or in small cliques in the sunken couch pits. For a club this size, it was strange to see so few people inside. She'd hoped to slip in and then be obscured in the crowd. The gathering was too small, with no place to hide.

"What now? Do we introduce ourselves to the host and say, 'Allo! We're crashing your party!'" asked Charles.

"Watch me," she said.

Leandra clicked over to the nearest sunken couch pit with about a dozen Harry Styles and Ellie Gouldings seated poshly in it. A few of the men watched her coming, their puffy red lips (in striking contrast to their pale-as-paste skin) turned into curious grins. She said, "Happy birthday, Wubby!"

The Brits stared. The girls tittered rudely. Leandra wasn't overdressed, but she didn't quite fit in. Even she could tell she came off as someone trying to match their style, but missing the mark by a hair. She was a poser. They knew it. She knew it. At least her eyebrows were above reproach.

"Wubby's not here yet," said a man, white blond hair swept across his forehead in an artful and haphazard wave. "But he'll be so glad to meet you when he arrives." He held out his hand. "I'm Oliver Bracknell the Third, nineteenth Earl of Grayson."

A fucking earl? Was that higher in rank than a baron or a duke? "Leandra Hunting, of the Malibu Huntings. And this is Charles Lemming, of the Park Avenue Lemmings." She took his hand, and Oliver kissed her knuckles.

The girls howled, definitely making fun of her.

Charlie shook Oliver's hand, too. Side-mouth, he whispered, "Malibu?"

Leandra shrugged. Like this crowd would be impressed if she said, "I'm a car salesman's daughter from Bumblefuck, Canada"? No. If she were going to impress the affected royals, she'd have to fudge her background a bit. Charlie *was* from Park Avenue. Not the ritzy part, though. His parents' place was at the corner of Park and Thirty-third Street, a mid-market Midtown address. He might as well be from Queens.

Oliver said, "You look a bit parched," and handed them glasses of champagne. "Join us. Introductions. Everyone, this is Leandra and Charles." The crew recited their names as Oliver went around the couches: Bruno, Cosimo, Hugo, Jaime (boy), James (girl), Spanky, Spotty, Swanky, and ('allo again!) Blinky and Shaggy.

They made room for Leandra and Charlie on the red leather couch between Spotty and Spanky. The conversation picked up where it left off.

"I have a major, major announcement," said Shaggy.

"What?" they asked, which sounded like *hwaut*.

"I'm going to cut off my 'air."

Her friends went ballistic. "No!" they cried in shock and horror, as if she announced she was joining a convent. Fifteen minutes went by, with each person weighing in on the upcoming sheering of Shaggy. It did seem like a questionable call. Her 'air really was stunning, long, thick, and shiny like an overgrown mink.

"I really need to make a major change in my life," she said.

"You just got back from four months in Saint-Tropez," said Hugo, who looked exactly like Liam from One Direction.

"Precisely, darling," said Shaggy. "We go there every yeah."

By *yeah*, she meant *year*? Probably. Or it could be like, "We go there every YEAH, BABY!" Shaggy went on to describe her different wardrobes for Saint-Tropez, Capri, and Cannes, because she wouldn't be caught dead wearing white linen in Cannes or a silk print in Capri.

"So, Charles," drawled Spotty, a glamorous ginger with blue glitter eye shadow over ice azure eyes. "How's New York?"

"I'd have to ask my mother," he said. "I've been living in Bangkok for the last two years."

And they were off and running. Spotty "absolutely madly deeply" *loved* Thailand—especially Phuket. Leandra squeezed Charlie's leg to say, "Do *not* tell the story!" and he got the message.

Just hearing the name of that hideous hellhole gave Leandra a minor panic attack. Charlie started discussing Bangkok banking stuff with Bruno, which went on and on. The Brits listened closely to him, and seemed to accept Charles into their fold. Meanwhile, she sat there, invisible, completely frozen out. She tried to get a word in, but the girls spoke over her, deaf to her voice. After about twenty minutes of being ignored, Leandra had reached her limit. She excused herself and headed for the ladies' (not that anyone seemed to notice). A few glamour girls were bent over the vanity table in the bathroom antechamber, rolled hundred-pound notes up their noses. They barely glanced at her as she walked by.

She went into a water closet and tried to calm down. Charlie fit in with the posh people, which should have made her proud of him. Instead, she resented it. He was a real international jet-setter. She was a fake. They saw through her like a pane of glass. She felt uncomfortably exposed. Her dress cost $2,000, but she might as well be wearing a burlap sack. Her hair, makeup, and outfit screamed "Look at me!" They had taken a look and written her off as a wannabe. Well, they could fuck off. She didn't have to stand around being judged. She'd grab Charles—

"There she is," said Oliver. He was leaning against the wall in lanky handsomeness when she came out of the ladies'. "I was waiting for you."

"Me?"

"I consider myself the ambassador for our little group," he said. "It's my job to make newcomers feel welcomed." He led her toward the bar, which was more crowded than before. "Wubby is the bloke at the end of the bar."

She thought he'd be chubby with a name like Wubby, but the birthday boy was another elegant Cumberbatch with an asymmetrical haircut. "Do you think he'll mind that we're crashing his party?" she asked.

"Of course not! Well, he might not warm to Charles, who's holding forth on foreign exchange rates, because we all care *so much* about them. I'm being ironic, darling. I'm sure Wubby will adore you. He turns to pudding around California blondes. I'd watch out for Blinky, though. She doesn't like it when people lie about being her friend."

"Got it."

"I have to ask you a question. Is Charles your boyfriend?"

She started to say "maybe," but why be coy? "He's just a friend."

"I happen to turn to pudding around California blondes as well," he said, blue eyes twinkling. "I can't help picturing you in a bikini, riding a white horse on the beach, sand and ocean water kicking up. You're like the summer dream of America, fresh and tan. Tell me, do you eat tofu often?"

Leandra had never been to California. Helpfully, Oliver's vision of the Golden State matched her own. All she had to do was live up to the stereotype, and she could wrap Oliver around her fingers. *Okay, then. Here we go. Organic, health-conscious, bodacious, airheaded, sexually adventurous, all teeth and boobs.* Leandra morphed from the doting proper lady of Charlie's fantasy into the bubble-brained ditz of Oliver's. She took off her shawl to show her tan shoulders, arched her back so her chest jutted out, smiled bright as the Pacific sun, and eyes wide open and vapid.

"Believe it or not, I've never eaten tofu," she said, her voice pitched higher, bordering on babyish. "But I'm open to trying anything— and I do mean anything—at least once."

Oliver stared, twinkling at her à la vintage Hugh Grant, and said, "Let me introduce you to the birthday boy. Just promise me one thing. No matter how deeply Wubby falls in love with you, you must stay by my side, all right?"

Dapper Oliver put his arm around Leandra's shoulder and held her against him. He was so skinny. No American buff on his skin and bones. She tried to soften against him, let herself relax. With Oliver, her key words were soft, warm, and stupid.

One hour later, Charles found Leandra at the center of a circle of blokes, describing each man's respective aura color and vibration.

"I'm ready to go," he said, glaring at Oliver in particular.

She said, "I'll take a taxi back to the hotel. Don't wait up."

He left, reluctantly. Leandra didn't make it back to the Connaught that night. She returned to the hotel midmorning when she knew Charlie would be in his meeting. She packed her suitcases quickly. A couple of bellboys and the nineteenth Earl of Grayson's valet piled her luggage into Oliver's Bentley and drove Leandra and all of her possessions to his five-story town house on King's Road.

Leandra had successfully swung on the monkey bars, grabbing a firm hold of her new boyfriend before letting go of the old one. And what a swing in the right direction! Oliver was a peer (whatever that meant). He had a castle in Scotland, and family money and treasure going back hundreds of years. It wouldn't have worked out with Charlie anyway. He was just too damn needy.

Leandra wasn't completely heartless. She left him a note.

Dear Charlie,
    I've decided to stay in London. Thank you for being such a generous host in Thailand. It was great catching up after so many years.
    Your friend,
    Leandra

P.S. I cashed in my Emirates return ticket. Since I won't be using it, I just thought, why the fuck not?

Don't ever change yourself to impress someone. They should be impressed that you don't change to please others.

13

the art of
pissing people off

Demi could spot Sophia in a crowd of thousands. For one thing, at six feet in heels, she was taller than most women, way taller than her costars (actors tended to fall on the short side of the spectrum). For another, she knew her friend's walk and gestures better than her own. She'd been watching Sophia since they were young. And now, the whole world was going to be watching Sophia, too.

The pilot episode of *Hipsters* was being shot in Vancouver. The *Sun* and the *Courier* tweeted locations each morning, and posted pictures from readers and staff photographers throughout the day. It wasn't such a big deal that a TV series was shooting here. Vancouver had been pseudo–New York in TV and movies many times before. But this wasn't just *any* series. It was starring Vancouver's own

Sophia Marcus. The story of a local girl makes good—even if the "local" was a city of 600,000 people—resonated. It gave dreamers hope that shooting for the moon was a viable life plan.

Demi stood behind the spectator blockade. Her spot sucked; the crowd pushed her right behind the camera setup. If she leaned to the left, she could see seventy-five percent of Sophia's head, which was enough. She didn't need to see more. When the shoot was over, Demi was meeting Sophia in her trailer. It'd be the first time in over a year that the best friends were in the same place at the same time. They'd talked last night, a quickie, but Sophia couldn't linger on the phone. Her mom and dad were having a party to celebrate her return home, and her success. Demi was invited, but she didn't want to have to fight through the Marcuses' friends and neighbors to grab a few minutes with the returning champion. She wanted Sophia's undivided attention. They had a lot to talk about. Things had been such a whirlwind in Sophia's life, she hadn't been able to give her the blow-by-blow story of landing the part. Demi hadn't mentioned a word to Sophia about her DUI, and everything that happened afterward, including her encounter with James. She wasn't sure what she was going to tell Sophia about it, if anything.

The excitement of watching the shoot turned to restless boredom among the spectators before long. The crowd thinned, and Demi moved closer for a better view. The scene appeared to be the three stars of the show exiting a coffee shop, waving good-bye to one another, and going their separate ways—clearly, a pivotal moment in the script. The scene took an hour and a half to shoot and would account for fifteen seconds of airtime.

When the cameraman started to dismantle his setup and move the equipment inside the coffee shop, Demi received a text from Sophia.

"Lunch break! Come to my trailer."

Demi left the blockade, and rode her bike the four blocks over to where all the trailers were parked. She could've left her bike chained by the blockade, but Demi had become paranoid about taking care of it. She was determined to give it back to Catherine in better shape than when she received it—and that meant, first and foremost, locking it up so it wasn't stolen.

Three whole city blocks were lined with trailers, equipment trucks, and portable tents with craft food service tables laden with bagels, sandwiches, and sodas, food choices the actors wouldn't touch with a ten-foot pole. Demi pushed her bike on the sidewalk until she found the trailer with the name "Valerie" written on a strip of tape on the door. Demi chained her bike to a parking meter. A dude in a flannel shirt and headset rushed over to her, saying, "This is a restricted area. You can't leave your bike here."

"I'm meeting a friend," she said. "I'll only be a few minutes."

"Move your bike, or I'll have to call security."

"Fuck off, little man."

He snarled into his headset, "Security! Bravo, bravo!"

Oh, for Christ's sake. Did Demi look like a terrorist in her bike shorts and T-shirt? What was it about her that struck fear in the heart of low-level authority figures? She was a bona fide magnet for officious assholes.

Demi ignored the PA and knocked on the trailer door. That act made him hyperventilate into his walkie-talkie. Sophia answered the door twenty seconds later, just in time to see two beefy giants bearing down on Demi.

Sophia shook her head at Demi. "She's with me," she told the security guys. To Demi: "What is it with you?"

"Pissing people off is my art," said Demi.

They let her go. She smirked at the PA and climbed the short steps to go inside. The two friends giggled and hugged tight. It'd been so long since they'd touched each other, since Demi hugged anyone with unconflicted happiness, she almost cried with relief. She thought, *This is my friend! My friend is here!*

When they broke apart, both of them had tears in their eyes. They took each other in. Skype was awesome, but it was no substitute for breathing the same oxygen, and laying hands and eyes on a person.

Demi noticed subtle changes in Sophia. Her hair was parted in the middle, not on the side as usual. Her makeup was heavy. She was thinner, not alarmingly so, but noticeably. Instead of her usual flirty, girly style, she was hipstered out, with a beanie and flannel, even.

"What going on?" asked Demi.

"What's going on with *you*?" asked Sophia.

With a start, Demi realized that Sophia was examining her, too, and found her appearance . . . lacking? Okay, yes, Demi wasn't exactly shimmering from the inside out with joy lately. But she thought she looked okay.

"Something amiss?"

"You look great," said Sophia. "Just different."

"I've been replaced by my evil twin," said Demi. "Actually, I'm a Stepford Daughter. My dad is the best boss ever! I love doing redundant website bullshit all day! Desk lunches on the clock are fun!"

Sophia laughed. "Your robot body got skinny."

She had lost weight. The combination of not pounding shots and biking to work every day had done the trick. In the month since her arrest, Demi had dropped ten pounds. Her legs were rippling, and her ass had never been harder.

"It's excellent to see what's left of you!" said Sophia.

"You, too, TV star!"

They hugged again. The second time felt even more solid and grounding than the first.

"What's with the bike?" asked Sophia. "I thought we could drive to Rodneys for lunch." Their favorite seafood spot in Yalestown.

What to say? The whole truth and nothing but? "I'm saving money on gas," she said instead. "We could just grab sandwiches from the craft table and stay here." Saving money was Demi's prime directive, along with staying sober.

"Okay. But I'll do it. You wait here or they'll arrest you for stealing food."

Sophia was laughing and giving Demi a hard time. Little did she know that her friend had recently been arrested. After she left, Demi gave herself the five-second tour of the trailer. Not much to see. A chair and mirror with a makeup kit and products on the table nearby. A scratchy fabric couch with a couple of rips and stains. The floor was a dark gray weather carpet, also stained in a few places. A dressing screen with a rack of clothes behind it. The trailer had some miles on it, like it'd been used by a thousand other actors. And now, it was Sophia's. She was the star of a network pilot. Demi had known it would happen for Sophia, but she was still amazed that it did.

Sophia returned, and they spread out their lunch on the couch between them and started eating.

"What are the chances that the show will film in Vancouver for the whole year?" asked Demi.

"One step at a time. First, the pilot. Then we wait to hear if we get picked up for a half or full season. They want me to get a place in LA, though, as soon as possible. I'm just thanking God the pilot is shooting here, or I would have been fucked."

"Do you have your work visa yet?"

"Not for another two weeks, which is almost to the day I'll have to be in LA."

"Cutting it close."

"After all this time, to lose my chance because I didn't have the right paperwork? If my visa doesn't come in time, we're going to have to forge the documents. Or you can drive me to California in the Audi's trunk."

The Audi. Right now, it was in her dad's garage. She couldn't drive it. She could sell it, but then she'd be without wheels when she got her license back.

"Okay, seriously, what's going on with you?" asked Sophia. "You have this insane look on your face right now."

"Forget it," said Demi. "Let's talk about how famous and rich you're going to get, and how you're going to thank me when you win your first major award. I wrote your speech already, if you'd like to hear it. 'I'd like to thank the Academy, and Demi Michaels . . .'"

"Quit stalling. Just tell me. I know there's something you're dying to get out."

"Oh, believe me, there isn't."

"You *are* keeping something from me! Out with it! You didn't fuck James, did you?" She laughed at the very idea.

It was laughable. Only a self-destructive schmuck would get back into bed with a liar and a cheater, no matter how hot he looked that day at the food festival.

"Do I look like a self-destructive schmuck to you?"

Two weeks earlier . . .

James ushered her into the apartment that used to be hers. She thought it would look different now. Dirtier. Smellier. But the apartment looked pretty much the same. Obviously he couldn't do anything on his own, so he must have hired someone to do his laundry and clean.

"I've got a box of your stuff in the bedroom," he said.

Like she'd follow him in there? "I'll wait here," she said, sitting on the couch.

He brought the box out and dropped it on the coffee table. There wasn't much in it. A few pairs of socks, a few books, a nail clipper, a mug. If it'd been his stuff, she would have thrown it in the garbage weeks ago.

"Thanks," she said. "I've been looking everywhere for this clipper. I haven't trimmed my nails since we broke up."

He actually looked at her hands. "I didn't ask you here just to give you this," he said, sitting next to her.

"You're going to kill me?"

"I owe you an apology. I really am sorry how it worked out."

"Are you begging my forgiveness?" Finally! She'd been waiting for this. In her fantasies, he sniveled and groveled at her feet. In reality, he was a bit detached, like testifying in court. Did the defendant show adequate remorse?

James said, "You can forgive me or not. That's up to you. I hope you do. I don't like the idea of someone out there hating me."

Someone out there? Okay, now it made sense. The impromptu closure session had a purpose—to absolve him of his guilt.

"I accept your apology," she said. "But I'm not going to forgive you. I love grudges. They're like golden nuggets I can hold in my hand and rub for good luck. It gives me joy to hate you. I'm sorry, but it's true."

He smiled (huh?). "I can live with that. I guess there's a thin line between love and hate. If you hate me, you still love me."

"So you don't mind the idea of someone out there *loving* you?"

"What?"

Jesus, was he always so slow on the uptake? Without sex to distract her, Demi could see James more plainly. "I'm going to go," she said.

"Okay, yeah, good idea."

"What do you mean by that?"

"We don't want anything to happen," he said.

She scoffed. "Nothing is going to happen."

"Right. Because you're leaving. Otherwise, it'd be only too easy to just . . ." He touched her hair, twirling a lock around his finger like he used to. She would have pushed him away, but it felt good, familiar. "I haven't been with anyone since you left," he said.

The door was now wide open. Demi had the choice: Leave now with her pride and dignity intact, with memories of self-control to last a lifetime, or take him up on his sad offer of hollow sex, erode her self-esteem, and regret it forever.

How would she choose?

It had been an awfully long time since a man touched her.

His hand moved from her hair to her shoulder, rubbing. When he used to give her massages, she would say, "You knead me. You really knead me." He knew exactly how to do it, good and hard. If nothing more, she knew exactly what she'd get out of a libidinous encounter—and, more important, what she wouldn't get. Sex with James would not be a reconciliation. There was no going back to living a lie.

Demi leaned into his hand and closed her eyes. She realized that sensation was enough. She didn't want any more from him emotionally or romantically. But sexually? She could have him, and then leave without a backward glance.

She made her move, locking lips before he knew what was happening. Their bodies fell on the couch, Demi taking off her clothes and his unhurried, not caring about being seductive. She was wearing old panties and she didn't care what he thought of them, or her leg stubble. She was amazed that he didn't seem turned off by it—not that she cared what he thought anyway. Instead of letting him lead, Demi took control. Freed from caring how she looked, Demi could concentrate on her own bliss only. At the finish, she released it all: the doubt, stress, resentment, everything she'd kept corked since the breakup. It was a revelation. All that time, she had thought their sex life was about her pleasure. But now she realized, it had been about feeding his ego.

Demi looked at James, a bit surprised he was there. Her experience was so inwardly focused, she'd nearly forgotten about him. But he looked up at her, enthralled, amazed, a bit afraid.

"Why weren't you like this when we were together?" he asked, gasping for breath.

"Would you have been faithful?"

He knew not to answer that. She got off him. "Thanks again for the stuff"—a phrase that had new meaning. She dressed quickly, picked up the box, and headed for the door.

In the trailer, Sophia said, "I didn't say you were a self-destructive . . ."

"It was empowering!" said Demi. "If I hadn't slept with him, I might still care about him. I'm telling you, just FYI, the best way to stop obsessing about your ex is to have sex with him and not care."

Demi told Sophia the whole story. "The only problem was that I had to bike home with the box balanced on the handle bars," she said. "I'm lucky I wasn't arrested again . . . oh, yeah. So. A few other things happened."

Sophia didn't seem to breathe while Demi updated her on recent events—getting fired, the arrest, the verdict. "I know I should have told you, but I had to lay low, and then you got the part and I didn't want to bring you down. I know it sounds bad, but I've got my bike. I'm over James. It sucks working for my dad, but I'm making money. It's all good."

Sophia shook her head. "It's not good. It's awful. DUI? Sex with James? If you said you did it because you were horny, or lonely, or wanted to screw him for screwing you, *that* I'd believe. But to empower yourself? Here's an orgasm, James, thanks for the dose of girl power? He'd have to *pay* a hooker to fuck and leave. You did it for free. What's next? Having James's baby to prove you're over him? And I don't trust Sarah. She did a nice thing that one day, but she's got a mean streak. You're right back under your dad's thumb. I love him like my own, but Richard is a control freak. You have *got* to get out of Vancouver, and away from all these people! If the show gets picked up, you're coming to LA with me. We've been talking about living together since we were fourteen years old. This is our chance. You could get a driver's license, too, and start over with a clean slate."

Demi had dual citizenship. Her parents had been living in Seattle when they had her. Unlike Sophia, she didn't need a work visa or any paperwork to move to California. All she had to do was pack up and go—and find the cash to do it.

"If we move in together, are you going to be as blunt as you are right now? Because forget it," said Demi.

"Did you tell Sarah you slept with James?"

"No." But she had, and Sarah thought the story was hilarious.

A knock on the trailer door. Sophia opened it. It was the flannel-shirted PA. "Ready on set," he said, and glared at Demi.

"I'm mad at you," said Sophia. "And I'm probably going to stay mad for the next hour. But after that, we're going to talk about this move so I can keep an eye on you."

She left, and Demi sat for a few minutes thinking about it. She had to admit, it felt pretty sweet to be yelled at by Sophia. Like old times.

————

"So what do you think?" Demi asked Catherine that night.

Catherine tried Demi's stew, just out of the oven. "Too hot," she said.

"I meant California," said Demi. "I don't think I could leave the only place I've ever known. Saying adios to my parents and siblings? I'm happy for Sophia, and it'd be fun to have a front-row seat when she becomes a star. But that's *her* life. What am I going to do in LA? Mope around an empty apartment while she's off being fabulous? I could look for a job, but my résumé is as thin as a mint. I'll get bored and start drinking again, I know it."

Catherine nodded as Demi explained her rationale. "Why do you think Vancouver is safe and secure for you? I've only known you for a couple of months, and you've been in quite a lot of trouble. I understand why you're afraid to let it go. But if you stay, you won't grow. If I were you, I'd be packing already."

"And leave all this?" she asked, arms sweeping around the lobby of death.

"The last six people left this apartment feet first."

"I thought five."

"I lied so you wouldn't feel frightened."

"Because five is so much less scary than six?" asked Demi. She tasted the stew. It was too hot. "Move and grow, I agree with you. I'm not staying in Vancouver forever. It's just until things settle down."

"You say that now. And then fifty years will go by."

"Oh, please."

"Five years. Ten years. Even one year is too long."

"Okay, okay. Jesus Christ. You're going to nag me to death. That's probably how Miriam bought it. Now shut up and eat the stew."

"I will miss your food when you leave," said Catherine.

"I'm not leaving," muttered Demi.

demi's beef bourguignon

SERVES 8

ingredients

MARINADE
2 cups red wine

3 lbs lean beef cut into 1-inch cubes

½ tsp celtic sea salt

¼ tsp cayenne pepper

1 tbsp minced fresh thyme leaves

2 bay leaves

1 carrot

2 cloves garlic

2 celery stalks

2 tbsps olive oil

STEW
2 zucchinis

2 white or yellow onions

2 cloves garlic

3 tbsps olive oil

1½ cups pearl onions, parboiled

1½ cups quartered button mushrooms

3–5 tbsps tomato paste (or dr. bo's tomato alternative)

1 cup beef broth

¼ tsp celtic sea salt

instructions

1. In a bowl, pour the wine over the beef. Add salt, cayenne, thyme, and bay leaves to the bowl. Slice one carrot, two cloves garlic, and celery, and add to the bowl with the wine and beef. Marinate beef in this mixture for at least 2 hours

and up to 24 hours. Turn occasionally. *Note: Alcohol will burn off during cooking.*

2. Remove meat and pat it dry using paper towels.

3. Strain marinade, reserving the liquid.

4. Heat 2 or 3 tablespoons olive oil in heavy skillet. Brown the meat quickly on all sides. Remove meat and add to a two-quart baking dish.

5. Deglaze skillet with 2 cups reserved marinade and add to baking dish.

6. Chop zucchinis (I like these to be small pieces but still identifiable), 2 onions, and 2 cloves of garlic. Heat 2 tbsps olive oil in skillet and sauté zucchini, onions, and garlic until lightly browned (about 5 minutes).

7. Cover and cook at 375 degrees for 2 hours.

8. Thirty minutes before the 2 hours are up, heat the remaining tablespoon of olive oil in a skillet, and sauté the pearl onions, mushrooms, tomato paste, and beef broth for about 7 minutes. Remove the beef from the oven carefully, add the pearl onions and mushrooms to the baking dish. Continue to bake for 30 more minutes.

Boil some new potatoes and serve on the side for a healthy, hearty, and waist-friendly meal . . . voilà!

14

i run, you chase

"How's Bangkok?" asked Sophia, smiling at the image of Leandra, now a platinum blonde, on her phone.

"Darling! I'm in London now," said Leandra.

"Sounds like you've been there since birth."

"It's quite amazing how quickly you pick up the accent."

"How long has it been?"

"Two weeks, luv."

"That is fast," said Sophia. Should she tell her how fake the accent sounded? *And spoil her fun? Not that it would,* she thought. If she liked doing it, more power to her.

"Can you see my new town house?" Leandra turned her phone around to show Sophia. "My new friend Ollie Bracknell is letting me stay in his flat. He's an earl, darling! A royal. He's got gobs of money, a Bentley, a castle. His family owns a plane. We might fly to Ibiza this weekend."

She'd said wee-*kend*, emphasis on the second syllable, just like the stars of the BBC reality show *Made in Chelsea*. In Toronto, they used to binge-watch episodes on YouTube and imitate the accents. From the look of it, Leandra had managed to wriggle her way into that world. Sophia gawked and made appropriate gushing noises as Leandra took her on a FaceTime tour of her new gilded digs, the marble lobby and regal staircase, the oil portraits on the walls and "important" furniture.

"What happened to Charlie?" asked Sophia.

"It wasn't a healthy relationship. I didn't tell you, but he used to make me crawl around on all fours."

"Did he really?" Sophia had her doubts. Leandra tended to exaggerate every tiny thing. Sophia found it hysterical. If Leandra said he made her crawl on all fours, it probably meant he asked her to pour the tea.

"I know, right? Very degrading and not good for my self-esteem. But Ollie loves me for who I am. And he's obsessed with me."

"And who are you, as far as he's concerned?"

"Why, darling, I'm myself! We met at a club, and have been inseparable ever since. It's like one of those romance novels, truly. *How to Seduce an Earl*, or whatever."

"How did you seduce him?" asked Sophia. She took a sip of her morning smoothie. The question might have sounded judgey, but she didn't mean it to be. She was curious. Leandra had more tricks than a circus clown.

"I sucked his dick like I was mad at it," said Leandra.

Sophia spit green drink halfway across the pool patio. "I hope you didn't put him in the hospital!"

"Oh, no. He's perfectly safe. Just needed a nap after," said Leandra. "We're madly in love and I feel content and fulfilled for the first time in my entire life."

"And you say that to me with complete sincerity—with a fake British accent." Sophia was beginning to wonder if Leandra should be the actor. Demi called her a phony, and she was. Sophia could see through the mask because she understood why it was there in the first place. After Stacy got cancer at nine, Leandra acted like nothing happened. During the course of Stacy's treatments, Leandra pretended that nothing was wrong. After she died, Leandra refused to talk about it. It probably wasn't the healthiest way to grieve, but Sophia wasn't in the position to judge. She hadn't lost a sister. One night, in high school, Sophia drunkenly brought it up, and promised Leandra that she would be her friend forever. Leandra replied, "You don't know that." Sophia had done her best to uphold her promise. Even though Demi and Leandra had their issues, Sophia knew that Demi would have Leandra's back, too.

"Where are you?" asked Leandra.

"I'm in LA. This is my new building." She turned the phone around to show Leandra the white stucco two-story, U-shaped complex called Rosewood Mews in West Hollywood. It reminded Sophia of *Melrose Place*. She found it thanks to one of her *Hipsters* costars, Paula Rosa, a twenty-five-year-old originally from Chicago, already a veteran of three TV series. She had lived here when she first arrived in LA, and still had friends in the complex. The third costar, nineteen-year-old Cassie Lambert, came from a Hollywood family and was still living at home in Brentwood.

Sophia signed the lease electronically, sight unseen, and was relieved that the building, with a swimming pool, was exactly like the photos. The rent for the two-bedroom was a lot: $3,000 a month, but split two ways with Demi, she could swing it. If the show got picked up, she'd decorate it nicely with real—"important"?—furniture. (If the show tanked, she had no idea what she'd do.) The other residents were all Hollywood wannabe actors and models like herself. As she sat by the pool, she watched one stunning specimen after another walk in and out of their apartments, waving and smiling, as was the California way.

"You got my email about the change of address, right?" Sophia asked Leandra, just checking. She'd been rushing around, under a logistical ton of bricks, and hadn't had a minute to double-check that her mass email didn't wind up in spam folders.

"Yes, and the announcement about your show! A million congrats! I can't wait to see it. Do you think it'll be available in London?"

"No clue. I'm not a hundred percent convinced it'll be available here."

"I've got to run, luv. Ollie wants to take me shopping in Mayfair. Cheers!"

Sophia waved good-bye, but Leandra was already gone. She sent a quick text to Demi: "Get your ass out here now, bitch!" Then she settled back on her plastic slatted lounge and closed her eyes. Moving hadn't been as awful as she thought—she had so few possessions worth keeping—but it had been a schlep. She deserved a day in the sun.

"Hey," said a male voice. "You're the new girl?"

She opened her eyes. Standing across the pool from her—a respectful distance, which she appreciated—the guy was around her age, aviator sunglasses, short hair, a ratty T-shirt, and a pair of worn jeans that telegraphed slacker, but then again, in LA, anyone could be a billionaire.

"You live here?" she asked.

He said, "I'm David, one-C."

Okay, not a billionaire. "Sophia," she said, but stopped short of giving her apartment number. He looked harmless, but you can't be too careful.

"Nice to meet you," he said. "I just thought you should know: Don't go in the pool. It's not safe."

Really? So much for her *Melrose Place* fantasies of a dozen hotties frolicking in the pool while plotting to steal each other's boyfriends and babies. "It looks all right."

"It's like a giant petri dish of body fluids."

"Gross!"

"Yeah, I know. That's why I don't go in there."

Sophia took a photo of the pool. David bombed into the frame.

He was determined to keep the conversation going, fine. Sophia should get to know her neighbors. It was only polite.

"So, are you an actor?" she asked.

"God, no. I'm a writer."

A writer? Sophia's character on *Hipsters* was a writer. She could pick his brain. His body was worth a closer look, too, actually. For a guy who sat in front of a computer for work, he had nice legs, a slim waist. The ass remained to be seen. Was he successful, or did he have a dozen screenplays in a drawer? And how to ask without being a bitch?

"Any luck?"

"I'm on staff at *Sex & Murder: LA*."

"Wow! That's impressive. Do you actually see the seedy underbelly of LA or just make it all up?"

"Where are you from?" he asked. "I can't place your accent."

"Canada," she said. "It's my second day in LA."

"Really? Second day, and you haven't been asked to pose nude yet? That might be a record. Unless you have . . ."

She laughed. He wasn't the most handsome guy in the world, but he had a hamsterish charm. "Are you from LA?"

"I was born and raised in Brooklyn, New York, but I've been out here for five years. I'll never feel like a native, but I know West Hollywood pretty well. I could show you around WeHo if you want."

"WeHo?"

"Only too appropriate, given the population of starving actors, writers, musicians, comics, and models who live here and would do *anything* for a gig."

She laughed out loud, which gave David the go ahead to walk around to her side of the pool. She tuned into her internal alarm system. Code red? Orange? She wasn't getting a whiff of weird. He seemed like a normal, friendly person who wanted to get in her bikini, as opposed to an aggressive asshole who wanted to get in her bikini. Also, he passed her ass test. Just bubbly enough.

He sat on the lounge next to hers. "Nice day. Again. All this constant sunshine makes me miss New York."

"The show I'm in is set in Brooklyn," she said.

"Is it called *Girls*, or *2 Broke Girls*, or *One Artisanal Cheese Monger Who Is Also a Girl*?"

"It's called *Hipsters*."

"Oh, god, I'm sorry," he said. "Hipsters fall in love, drink coffee, and murder each other?"

"Yes to the love and coffee. Remains to be scene about the murder."

"Mark my words, by episode three, the writers will throw in a murder. The brick-oven pizza case, or the ukulele caper."

"I hope my character survives," said Sophia, "or I'll have to go back to VaCa."

"VaCa. No, don't tell me. Let me guess. Vancouver, Canada. VaCa went from really sexy to so *not* in like five seconds."

Sophia said, "Okay."

"Okay what?" He looked scared.

"You can give me a tour of the neighborhood."

"Great! But you might want to put on some clothes first. Just a suggestion. If Lady Gaga can rock a bikini on the Sunset Strip, you definitely can, but you might not want to."

Sophia gathered up her stuff. "Give me five minutes."

Six minutes later . . .

Sophia emerged from her apartment in a red Alice+Olivia dress, Tory Burch sandals, and a big Balenciaga bag (all items bought on sale after stalking them for months; just because she was financially challenged didn't mean she couldn't look good), and found David right where she left him. "I don't have a car," she said. "We'll have to take yours."

"I don't have a car either," he said. "I never learned how to drive— no one did where I grew up. The kids with licenses were total losers."

"What then? Uber?"

"We walk," he said. "WeHo is the only neighborhood in LA that you can walk around in, like a real tourist. I'm going to show you all the sights."

For the next few hours, David was the ideal guide. He took her to the Grove, where they walked around the mall through throngs of tourists and stopped for short ribs at the homey restaurant Jones, with red-and-white-checked tablecloths and beer in mason jars. Then David made her trek up to the Sunset Strip, where they passed Chateau Marmont. A photo of that legendary hotel had been on Sophia's vision board since inception, and here she was, taking a dozen more photos of it in person. (Manifesting worked!) They headed west down the Strip, and ended up at the Sunset Towner for a cold crisp Moscow Mule on the private patio, flowers and interesting and attractive people everywhere she looked. She was *here*, on Sunset Boulevard, hanging out with a funny, sexy guy. Sophia paused for a second to snap a photo of David and take it all in.

After walking for miles, they got hungry again, and made the spontaneous decision to take an Uber to Venice for "the best tacos in LA," as David described them, from James' Beach. But dinner would have to wait. When Sophia got her first look at the powder sand beach, she kicked off her flats, threw them in her bag, and ran all the way from the street entrance to the Pacific Ocean.

"So this is how it's going to be for us?" asked David when he caught up to her. "You run, I chase?"

That was how it usually worked.

They sat down on the sand and watched the whackos and crackos. Sophia loved the diversity and constant stimulation. It was almost sundown, and the surfers were taking their last ride for the day. Moms were packing up umbrellas and portable chairs and rounding up their kids. Groups of friends swigging the last of their beers. Bodybuilders and sun worshippers gathered up their detritus for the night. So much was going on, but the pace was lazy and calm. Sophia felt profoundly at peace on the water's edge. It might very well be her spiritual home, and why California had always tugged so hard on her consciousness.

Obviously, she would have found the ocean on her own. But David brought her here, to this spot, and it was so much sweeter to share the moment with a new friend.

Sophia was not going to let this moment, or any moment, pass without making it as perfect as it could possibly be. She smiled at David, and leaned against his warm arm. When he didn't do anything, she rested her head on his shoulder. Green light, dude.

He said, "Can you move your head a second?"

Oh, shit. She lifted it off his shoulder, thinking she'd been shot down (that was *not* how it usually worked). But David then took her head in his hands, and brought her lips to meet his. His lips were soft and sweet, but the angle wasn't the most comfortable. David put his hand on her back, and gently eased her back onto the sand.

Sophia was a little afraid he was going to be soft and gentle all night.

She worried for nothing. David lay down next to her, and pulled her toward him with both arms—stronger than they looked—pressed against her before coming in for another kiss. This time, he was insistent, an explorer, entering her mouth with his tongue, neatly, firmly, in a way that made her go a little crazy.

They touched and tasted as the sun went down, as people walked by and whistled, their mingling bodies nestling into a pocket of cooling sand. When Sophia looked up, the beach was empty. Had they been making out for hours?

"You're a really good kisser," she breathed while his lips drew a line down her throat and across her collarbone.

"So are you," he said.

"That's all we're going to do," she said. "Today."

"No problem. I could probably do just this for the next ten years," he said. "Hoping for more, don't get me wrong!"

She wasn't getting anything wrong tonight. The cosmic spheres were all spinning in the right direction.

Be Crazy.
Be stupid.
Be weird.
Because life
is too short
to be anything
but happy.

15

so much blood and bleeding with the english

Leandra put on her most vapid, idiotic smile, and asked, "Do they wear polo shirts in matching team colors? Is that why they're called 'matches'?" She didn't dare do her faux-British accent with Oliver. He praised her for being "different from all the other girls," and wouldn't have appreciated her mimicking Blinky or Shaggy in the slightest. He liked her to look American, so she had to go return to Oxford Street to shop for a brand-new wardrobe, trading the Charlie-approved trustifarian wifey style for Oliver-preferred blousy bimbo. Also, her eyebrows were back to being twins, so long sisters.

She sat on Oliver's lap in the backseat of the Bentley as they were chauffeured to the Ham Polo Club in Richmond, England, just outside of London. Oliver stabled his ponies there, as did the Duke of Ellington. The duke was expected to helicopter in for a Pimm's Cup before luncheon in the Chukka Club.

Leandra had no idea what was in a Pimm's Cup or what a Chukka was. "Is it a frat boy who pukes on himself?" she asked Oliver.

"You are delightful," he replied. "Just so bloody charming! The duke is going to eat his bleeding heart out when he gets a look at you."

So much blood and bleeding with the English.

Oliver was her life now, and she'd made the necessary personality adjustments. As long as she acted the part of a shallow-yet-spiritual Valley Girl, Oliver was enthralled. When she rambled about chakras, auras, meditation, anything she could think of that sounded like Malibu wackadoo shite, it was like Oliver fell under a Harry Potter drooling spell. *Expecto expecterato!* He loved it all. His crowd, he told her, "didn't care about inner growth." They were too busy designing jewelry, up-Chukka-ing over the sides of yachts, and Gulfstreaming to Majorca whenever the craving for fried anchovies struck. It sounded like heaven to Leandra. But Oliver was a searcher. He had questions about the universe, and thought the answers could be found in between the ears and legs of his American girlfriend. The poor deluded (bloody, bleeding) bastard.

He nibbled Leandra's ear (avoiding the twenty-four-karat gold ankh-shaped earring he'd given her last night), and said, "I have a surprise for you."

More gold? "I love surprises!! Yay!! What is it? Tell me! I hate waiting!"

"Now, now, darling. You have to learn to be patient. Before I tell you, let's do it again."

"Of course, baby."

"You start."

"Okay." She closed her eye and put her hands in prayer position at the heart chakra. "Breathe in," she said, and inhaled deeply. On the exhale, she sang "Ommmm," and he joined in. When Oliver got it in his head she was some kind of Zen master (ironic, considering her complete rejection of Buddhism in Thailand), she remembered omming in unison from the one and only yoga class Sophia dragged her to. She introduced him to sharing the vibration of the chant. It did nothing for her, but he went berserk.

Their voices faded, and then Oliver bent her over the backseat and slipped his tackle into her. Leandra bit her lip when they had sex to keep herself from asking "Is it in yet?" and "Are you kidding me with that tiny thing?" As usual, he was finished quickly. When he came, he hit a high note; she believed it was an A flat. She joined in—just like "omm," except "ahhhh"—which he seemed to believe was evidence of their mutual, shattering orgasms. He fell back on the seat to right his trousers. She straightened herself and applied another coat of lipstick right as the Bentley pulled up to the polo grounds.

If Leandra had a shred of self-consciousness, she might be worried about the driver. Oliver didn't give "his man" a second's thought. So she didn't either, even though there was only a thin panel of glass separating their compartment from his.

Leandra put on a wide-brimmed hat for the polo match. It was the one classic English concession Oliver allowed her, and only because her Malibu Barbie hair spilled out in waves underneath it. Oliver escorted her through the clubhouse to the fields, along a white picket fence and into the grandstand to the VIP box at the top of a small tower. Oliver introduced her around. He kept one arm around her waist, kissing her, licking her neck, rubbing her backside. It was the opposite of Charlie, who kept her at arm's length in public.

Before long, the Duke of Ellington's helicopter touched down, and he jogged with his entourage to the grandstand. His arrival was met with much fanfare. The crowd whistled and applauded as he climbed up to the grandstand and then, leaning over the bunted railing, he waved at them, queen style (all in the wrist). The goodwill business done, the duke addressed the VIP group.

"Who's this?" he asked when his watery blue eyes landed on Leandra. "Your new friend, Grayson?"

"Allow me to introduce Leandra Hunting, my spiritual advisor," said Oliver.

The duke, only about twenty-five years old, whiter than the picket fence and just as stiff, said, "Indeed. I'm always pleased to meet a woman who goes deep."

On cue, Leandra said, "I love to go deep!" inspiring Oliver to kiss her full on the mouth, knocking her hat off.

At certain moments, pretending to be a blithering idiot bothered her, like an itch she couldn't scratch. But the discomfort faded in the bright sunshine as she looked down from her perch at the plebes in the grandstand below. She felt smug, superior, and all melty inside with condescension.

Oliver excused himself to go suit up for the match. He was playing today, for her entertainment. She settled into her seat next to the duke, beaming with self-importance. A server in a tux and white gloves brought around drinks. A Pimm's Cup turned out to be fruit juice with gin. Then a trumpet blared, the PA system crackled to life, and the players trotted out onto the field, only four riders per team. They *were* wearing matching polo shirts.

"Grayson rides with Equus, in red, on Fergus, his chestnut stallion," said the duke helpfully.

An earl was fine. A duke would be better, Leandra couldn't help thinking. "Do you ride . . . horses?" she asked, and put a hand on his knee.

"Oh, no, darling. That was very clumsy," he said. "It won't work on me, I'm afraid. Unlike my dear friend Grayson, I'm not susceptible to obvious, common women."

He said it loud enough for a few others to overhear. Leandra turned bright red under her spray tan. "I'm not . . ."

He leaned in close to whisper in her ear. "But you are. You grew up in some suburb, with a patch of lawn and a one-car garage, correct? A special night out was to an Italian restaurant for spaghetti and meatballs. There are millions of girls exactly like you all over the world. But there is only one Earl of Grayson. He's so smitten that he's fallen for your act. But I see you. And do keep your hands to yourself."

He leaned back, and said loudly, "What a fine afternoon!"

The conversation in the box turned to the weather. Leandra sat completely still, struggling for breath. She didn't move or speak for the rest of the match, but was all too aware of the primping antics of the duke as he drank Pimm's and sent barbs around the grandstand at his mates. They laughed at his insults. Maybe they were obliged by societal contract. That was the English way, a throwback from the feudal past, to worship another human being like a god because of an accident of birth. Everyone knew the duke was an entitled prick who got off on humiliating friends and strangers alike, but they just sat there and took it.

Leandra was devastated by his private remarks to her. Except for the one-car garage part (the Huntings' garage fit *two*), he nailed her background to a T. Sophia would comfort her by saying, "Fuck him. My parents are good people. They've dealt with a lot of heartache and come out of it in one piece. I've got nothing to be ashamed of." But he'd dug his blade right into Leandra's soft spot. Her deepest fear was that she was ordinary, nothing special. It was her life goal *not* to be common. She intended to be one in a million, and to be loved like she was one in a million.

The polo match wasn't much of a distraction. The horses thundered up and down the field. The players swung their mallets. The ball got thwacked. The game was like soccer, she supposed, but she couldn't keep track of what was happening. At one point, a rider fell off his horse and was nearly trampled. Everyone gasped, except for Leandra. She was just too gutted to react. The match ended and the riders cantered around the field like a parade. The duke stood up, waved at the crowd again, and left the VIP box with his entourage. Once the duke was safely gone, Leandra could breathe again. She waited for Oliver in the box, ignoring the other people who remained to finish off the tea sandwiches.

He arrived soon after, still in his togs. He kissed her passionately, flushed from sport. "Did you enjoy that?" he asked.

"Yes, very exciting."

"Are you ready for your surprise?"

Oh, yeah. She forgot about that. Her spirits rose slightly. "Yes, of course."

Eyes twinkling, he said, "We're taking the duke's helicopter on a short ride . . . to Scotland!!"

"Is the duke coming?"

"No, no, he's on his way to the House of Lords," said Oliver.

In that case, Leandra could show some enthusiasm. "Yay! Yippee! A helicopter ride! Hooray!!" and so on.

"All finished with your drink? Wonderful. Grimly packed a bag for you. It's in the chopper. We're ready to go."

Grimly, the valet, had pawed through her panties? "How does he know what to pack?"

"It's just a few things. You won't need much where we're going."

"Your family seat in Loch Lorrain?" Paintings of Castle Grayson lined the London town house walls, along with centuries-old portraits of the previous eighteen earls in Oliver's line.

"You'll find out," he said, grinning. "It's another surprise."

Leandra decided she hated surprises. But anything that got her away from the duke and Oliver's snotty friends was probably an improvement.

Two hours later, Oliver and Leandra's borrowed chopper landed on a tiny island off the coast of southwest Scotland. Loch Lorrain and Grayson Castle were hundreds of miles north. Looking out the windows, Leandra couldn't make out much of anything on this green, craggy dot in the North Sea.

They ducked low as they jogged away from the still spinning helicopter blades toward a man waiting with a pickup truck. He wore a saffron orange robe, sandals, and glasses.

"Welcome to Holy Isle!" he said, bowing his shaved white head.

Holy Isle? Make that *holy shit*. She turned to Oliver. "What're we doing here?"

"You haven't heard of Holy Isle? I thought you must have. It's world famous. I've asked my mates to come here too many times to count, but they begged off. I knew you'd be chuffed about it, and as luck would have it, we got the last two spots for the final meditation retreat of the year!"

"Meditation retreat?"

Saffron piped in. "A week of silence, contemplation, rock painting, flower arrangement, and shadow watching. We also have morning yoga and sheep-shearing seminars."

Oliver introduced himself and Leandra. Saffron said, "I'm Lama Winterfield." Instead of shaking hands, they bowed to each other.

"Silence? Like, no talking? For a *week*?"

Saffron nodded. "Mr. Bracknell told me you two are vegetarians. It should be an easy transition to our raw vegan diet."

His Scottish accent was quite thick. She must have misunderstood. "I'm sorry, did you say raw vegan?"

"Yes! Mostly locally foraged grasses and leaves."

Leandra felt faint from hunger just hearing about it. She'd starve to death!

Lama Winterfield directed them to climb into the back of the truck with their luggage. Grimly had packed a small shoulder bag for her. She took a quick look inside and found only toiletries and her wallet. She had no makeup, no clothes, no jewelry. Was she expected to meditate and be silent *in the nude*?

"It's just a few minutes to the compound, but it can get a little bumpy," said Lama Winterfield.

They were thrown around the truck like socks in a dryer. Oliver had the nerve to say, "Isn't this fun?" She wanted to kill him. Along the way, they swerved to avoid hitting some wild goats grazing on the side of the road. She'd be on the same diet as they were for a week.

Bruised and exhausted, Leandra limped after Oliver and the Lama into a barnlike structure the Lama described as "the dormitory complex."

"The men's dorm is over there. This is the women's dorm," he said. "Right this way. I'll show you your room, Ms. Hunting."

The Four Seasons, it wasn't. Leandra's rooms would have been considered Spartan in Sparta. A bed with a scratchy blanket ("Made from indigenous Soay sheep wool!" he said), and a dresser already full of clothes. She held up a pair of enormous drawstring pajama bottoms, and a tunic. "Made with indigenous cotton?" she asked.

"Yes, in fact!"

"I'm supposed to wear this all week? I only have the bra and panties I've got on."

"We don't wear undergarments here," he said. "No clothing that binds."

Leandra and Oliver both looked at Lama's robes at crotch level.

"It's our policy not to use any electronics during your stay. Since we don't have electricity in the dorms or wireless technology, your devices are useless anyway. I'll take you to your room now, Mr. Bracknell. You should say good-bye to each other. You won't see each other again until breakfast tomorrow morning at six A.M."

"What about dinner?" asked Leandra.

"We've already eaten. I can ask someone to bring you a tray, but just this once. It's an early morning, so after you eat, please go right to sleep. From this moment on, there will be no talking."

Lama zipped his mouth closed, and threw away the key, then urged them both to do the same. Leandra did so ironically, but Oliver beamed at her, way into the spirit of spirituality. After they left, she flung herself on her cot and cried, full drama. She'd been airdropped into her personal version of hell. She'd wail if she wanted to.

Dinner arrived, brought in by a woman in saffron robes. It was a plate of greens, a biscuit made of rock (tasted like it), and a glass of water. She ate every bite, wishing she hadn't been so rocked by the duke's nastiness that she didn't chow down on the smoked salmon and watercress sandwiches at the polo match.

She was almost too hungry to sleep. But exhaustion and emotional upheaval got the better of her, and she crashed hard. She awoke before dawn to a tinkling of bells, put on her organic daytime PJs and slippers, and followed the line of sleepy seekers into the dining room. Oliver waved at her from the men's section. He looked overjoyed with his lumpy plain oatmeal.

The day was strictly structured. The men and women were led like Soay sheep from one area and activity to the next. A watercolor workshop in the art studio, yoga class in the dojo. The last activity before lunch: meditation.

A woman sat cross-legged on a pillow at the front of a white-walled room. She was skinny with a long gray braid down to her waist. Leandra envied her all-black robe and leggings ensemble. "Good morning," she said. "Find a pillow and sit in the lotus position."

Leandra held up her hand. "I thought there was no talking."

The instructor said, "I'll be leading the meditation with as few verbal cues as possible. Let's begin with deep pranayama breathing. I'll ask you to place one hand on your heart, and one on your belly."

Leandra's pillow was thin and her anklebones hurt on the hard, wood floor. She raised her hand again. "Can I get a few extra pillows?"

"It's not supposed to be comfortable. We meditate to learn to sit with discomfort." Insane. Why would anyone choose to be uncomfortable? The instructor continued. "Let's begin our breathing practice. Deep breath in, belly rises . . . what is it now?"

"We're practicing breathing? I can't speak for everyone here, but I kind of do that pretty well already. Like, thousands of times a day."

"I'll ask you to remain silent and follow instructions."

Leandra did her best. Really she did. But after five minutes of breathing, sitting, counting backward and forward from one to ten, she'd had enough. "Excuse me again. Is this it? If it is, then meditation does not work for me, at all."

"I'll ask you to leave the room."

"You're throwing me out?" Meanwhile, what was with the "I'll ask you to . . ." verbal tick? *I'll ask you to fuck off*, she thought.

The instructor just pointed to the door.

She was ejected from her first meditation session, after only five minutes! And she'd be stuck here for another six days without clothes, food, or the Internet? It was unthinkable. She would surely go crazy.

Not knowing what to do or where to go, Leandra stormed away from the meditation room, picking her way through the hallways until she found the front door. Fresh air would help. She exited the building into a cloud of cigarette smoke. A man in beige PJs and slippers stood there smoking, which was one thousand percent against policy. He was around thirty, dark brown hair and olive Mediterranean complexion. He was slim, but not a toned yoga skinny, just naturally lean. When she saw the cigarette, her heart leapt. She wasn't a smoker, but to find someone here with such an unhealthy habit? He probably ate meat, too. They were going to be new best friends.

"Hey," he said.

"You talked."

"Sue me."

American, and about as happy to be there as she was. They got to talking (with their voices), and she learned Harris Belsky was a movie producer from Los Angeles. He'd come to Glasgow to meet and woo a Scottish actress to appear in his next movie. "She said she'd consider it if I brought her here," he said while snuffing out his cigarette in the mud with his slipper. "I've spent two days eating dirt and drinking my own piss, trying to get her alone to talk, but she won't even look at me."

"Drinking your own piss, really?" asked Leandra.

"I exaggerate a little."

He handed her a smoke. While she enjoyed the tobacco product, she told him her story, about being brought here against her will by a man she'd only just met (she exaggerated a little, too). She felt just as suckered and trapped as Harris did.

"So let's get out of here," he said.

"How?"

"The ferry. It comes in every day at noon with supplies and returns to a harbor town on the mainland. From there, you can go back to London, and I can get to Glasgow and then fly to LA."

"I don't have any money," she said.

"I do." Harris arched his eyebrows conspiratorially. "So we're making a break for it?"

She considered her options. Stay here, starving, free boobing, sitting and breathing, or go on a madcap adventure with a smoking hot, rich American?

"I'm in," she said, her heart speeding up. "I have to go to my dorm room and change into my real clothes."

"The ferry leaves in half an hour and it'll take about that long to get there."

She had to get her wallet and her phone. "I'll be super quick."

He had stuff to grab, too, so they ran to the dorm complex and separated to get their stuff. In five minutes, they were on the road, in their PJs and slippers, to the ferry landing.

"I can kick your ass if you try anything. I know Muay Thai," she lied as they hoofed along, past the goats and the sheep.

"Whatever that is. But, yeah. Noted."

Their great escape went off without a hitch. First, they walked double time to the ferry at Brodick on the Holy Isle. It was freezing on the boat, even after they put on their regular clothes. She and Harris had no choice but to huddle together for warmth. Being forced to cleave to a complete stranger had a way of breaking down barriers. By the end of the hour-long ferry ride, she and Harris were as cozy as kittens in a basket. The ride ended at Ardrossan Harbour, where they found the general store. Harris whipped out a platinum card, and they bought

Scottish sweaters, dry jeans, and fleece-lined wellies. The logical choice would be to taxi to Glasgow and then go their separate ways, but Harris had another idea.

"Let's drive to London together," he said. "It's only five hundred miles from here. We can see the countryside and be not silent the entire way."

That did sound tempting. "How do I know you won't rape and murder me, and leave my corpse on the moors for some Sherlock in a deerstalker hat to find?"

"I'm not forcing you to go with me. You can do whatever you want. I can do whatever I want. He"—Harris pointed at Shane Mac-Creedle, the ferry master, who waved—"can do whatever he wants. It's simple. I want to drive to London, smell heather, see Shetland ponies and Guernsey cows, eat greasy pub food and drink stout in every town along the way, maybe spend the night in a village inn called The Bucket of Haggis or The Swan with Three Heads. I want you to come with me. We'll have fun. Promise."

He really was cute when he referenced *The Notebook*, his thick, brown hair wafting in the wind, his dark eyes beaming certainty. This man knew exactly who he was, what he wanted, and where he was going. His confidence was hard to resist. He offered Leandra an adventure, which was what she'd set out to have. Plus, he had a platinum card, and all she had in her wallet was a rolled-up hundred-pound note she'd swiped off Oliver's dresser one night.

They walked to Discount Car Hire, the only rental place in town. Harris prowled the lot, looking for a decent ride, and chose a vintage Jaguar convertible. She snapped a photo of Harris leaning against it, debonair and scruffy in his oversized sweater. The rental office had WiFi, incredibly. "What's your Insta handle?"

He told her.

She posted, "Driving from Scotland to London with @actionHarris!" on Instagram. Now, if she disappeared, the authorities would know where to look and whom to question.

If Harris wasn't a rapist/murderer, he had *serious* boyfriend potential. He seemed to know her from the first moment, tapping into her sense of adventure and hunger for food she could tear into with her teeth.

They hopped in the Jag and headed south with nothing but miles and moments ahead.

Do not dwell
in the past, do not
dream of the future.
Concentrate the mind
on the present
moment.

—Buddha

16

love is the elixir of life

Demi took a sip from her cock-
tail. It was her first taste of alcohol since the night of the arrest two
months ago. The smell alone sent her into rapture. God, how she'd
missed the first swallow.

"How is it?" asked Sophia.

"It's divine."

The Los Angeles night was clear, dry, starry, and seventy-six degrees. Although Sophia thought their two-bedroom at the Rosewood
Mews was small, Demi's bedroom was the same size as the one at
the Grace, and the kitchen/living room/dining room might be larger.
Their apartment could be the size of a matchbox, Demi didn't care.
They were finally fulfilling their dream of living together. The chant
from childhood ("no parents, no teachers, no rules") didn't resonate

the way it had at fifteen, but Demi felt a teenage rush of excitement. California represented a rebirth for her, a chance to start over and really find out who she was and what she could do. She could become anyone here, and she couldn't wait to find out how her new life would unfold. The Rosewood Mews pulsed with promise. She was sad to leave Catherine at the Grace. But she proudly broke the chain, and left the lobby of death alive and kicking.

Two months of biking and sunshine had lightened her hair and darkened her skin, so she looked almost like a native. Having swept out the last remaining cobwebs in her psyche, she could assess her life with clear eyes. The move was so obviously right, her parents didn't object. Her family all cried and said they would miss her, though deep down she didn't think they would as much as she'd miss them. As the black sheep, she often felt isolated in a family where *alone* was impossible. Her dad asked for two-weeks' notice, which she gave. During off hours, Demi completed her community service hours by scanning old books to digitize them for the main branch of the Vancouver Library. While meeting her obligations to her family and the city, she sold the Audi and her furniture to collect funds. Then she packed what meager possessions she had left, and jetted to LAX.

To celebrate Demi's arrival, she and Sophia went out in West Hollywood. At the suggestion of Sophia's friend David, they went to Bar Marmont at the Chateau Marmont, a hotel Demi had seen in movies and read about but never thought she'd ever hang out in.

"So what's the deal with you and David?" she asked Sophia. She met the writer this afternoon and liked him, but found his chumminess with Sophia confusing.

Sophia said, "Just friends. So far."

"He's not your usual type."

"I don't have a type! I haven't had a real boyfriend since Jesse."

Demi bit her lip. She hated talking about Jesse. The guilt! It was awful, even after all these years.

Sophia said, "I semi-stalk Jesse on Instagram. He's getting married. I hope he and his horrible wife will be very happy."

"Is she really horrible?"

"No," said Sophia. "She looks nothing like me so I guess Jesse doesn't have a type either. Whatever. Water under the bridge."

"To old love, and new ones," said Demi, trying to keep the conversation in the present.

"To living the dream!" said Sophia, only half ironically.

The tragically hip bartender placed two fresh drinks in front of them. He pointed to a group of guys in LA-casual blazers and open shirts at the other end of the bar. "On them," he said.

"Really?" asked Demi. "I mean, look at us. And look at *them*. No offense, Soph, but in this room, even you look average."

By "them," Demi was referring to the throngs of stunning young women in various stages of undressed or overdressed. On one side of the room, a few women were in formal gowns. On the other side, a few were in sheer body stockings. Others wore leather pants and camisoles with lots of makeup and tortured hair. Still others went for the starlet-on-meds style—beanie, sunglasses, matted hair, billowy blouse, and boyfriend jeans. Every few minutes, another crew of beautiful people pushed into the bar. Demi and Sophia were seated directly under hanging red fringe lanterns. They cast a flattering pink glow on their faces and outfits. Sophia was wearing her usual leather pants with a black Louboutin silk blouse she got on sale, and accessorized with cool chunky jewelry. Demi wore black Paige jeans, Topshop wedges, a cotton tank, and a silk Tibi blazer that looked like Joseph's Technicolor dreamcoat.

Sophia eyed the donated drinks. "We're pacing ourselves, right?"

"Of course," said Demi.

The plan was dashed quickly. By the time they'd finished the first round, three cocktails were lined up and waiting for them, care of the open-shirt dudes and a pair of lesbians. They invited the lesbians—Stacy and Paulina—to join them, and the four girls managed to polish off their stockpile of beverages.

From that point on, the night got a bit blurry for Demi.

David showed up at one point. Sophia was pretty gone by then, too, and she threw her arms about him and said, "You're here!"

Before the writer had any idea what was happening, Sophia planted her wet lips on his mouth. When Sophia broke for air, David made a show of tasting his lips. "Okay, now I'm drunk," he said, which made them all laugh. Any joke, however lame, would have been hilarious.

Demi clinked her new friends' glasses, and said, "Ah, sweet elixir of life."

"Love is the elixir of life," said Sophia, who reliably went all Buddha.

They cheered and drank.

"I can't believe I'm fucking here!" said Demi.

They seized any excuse to laugh, throw their arms around each other, sing, shout, make out. The night had a magical tint, shimmering around the edges.

"Isn't life amazing?" she slurred to Sophia. "Everything was going wrong, wrong, wrong. And then, overnight, things just started to go right. How does that even happen?"

"You have to knock wood, right now."

"To knocking wood!" said David.

Demi had no idea when or how she started talking to the Aussie. He just became part of their party within a party at some point. She wasn't complaining. He was big and burly, bearded, a proper grown-ass adult man.

He'd told them his name, but they just called him Aussie, and he was okay with it. Around two A.M., he asked, "Who's hungry?" and proceeded to order one of everything on the bar menu, including oxtail bruschetta, crab and corn fritters, Taleggio mac 'n' cheese, and two-dozen oysters. Sophia, Demi, David, Stacy, and Paulina fell on the food like flies on shit. She noticed that the Aussie took his time chewing, savoring the flavor of each dish.

Around three, Sophia and David were making out in a dark corner of the bar. The lesbians went home. Demi and the Aussie sat in a booth together, talking. His accent got thicker as the hour got smaller. Demi missed about thirty percent of what he said, but she liked what she understood. Their one topic of conversation: food.

"I have two restaurants in Sydney," he said.

"What kind?"

"I'm embarrassed to say."

"Shrimp on the barbie?"

"We say 'prawns,' by the way," he said, grinning. "But yeah, we do prawns and other fish dishes. Our signature dish is fried John Dory. That's the name of the place."

"Prawns?"

"John Dory," he said.

"Your name isn't John." Or was it?

"It's Aiden. Aiden Bushwhacker."

Demi snorted. "You are so full of shit."

"Aiden Archer," he said, holding out his hand. "I've told you that three times already, Ms. Demi Elizabeth Michaels."

They talked more about food, and the dishes they'd tried tonight. Demi could have eaten a bucket of the oysters in shallot vinaigrette. So fresh, they tasted like the sea. "If I had to order one thing again, it'd be the calamari. Great batter. You can tell they use seltzer instead of beer, which works for this crowd. Even when they eat fried food, it's gotta be healthy."

"Good tip," he said. "I'll have to tell my chef when I get to hiring one. I'm opening a John Dory in LA in a month."

"Not with that name," she said.

"No?"

"John Dory sounds like some cheap seafood place where the waiters dress up like pirates and serve fried shit on a plate. So unless you want people to think you're serving fried shit, you have to change the name. Call it Dory. Lose the John."

"*Finding Nemo* flashback," he said, shaking his head.

"So? This is Hollywood. People live and breathe movies here, and *Finding Nemo* was a massive hit. They'll have warm, fuzzy feelings associated with the name. It says 'fish.' It says 'fun on the beach.' Or, you could go in another direction, and call the place *Jaws*."

He rewarded her with a hearty laugh, big as the outback. "Okay, okay. I'm sold. Dory it is."

"You know, back in Canada, I worked for a marketing company that launched restaurants. That was all I did, every day, for three years. There're a lot more golden nuggets where that came from." Huh? Her booze-addled brain might not be making complete sense.

"Are your nuggets for free?" he asked.

"Absolutely not," she said. "I value myself and my skills. So if you want my help, you're going to have to pay through the nose for it." Could she have made that speech if she weren't drunk? Doubtful. Alcohol was an excellent negotiating tool. She should drink before every job interview.

"Through the nose? That's disgusting."

"You don't say that in Australia?" she asked. "It means *I ain't cheap.*"

"I knew that already," he said. "I just spent three hundred dollars feeding you and your friends."

"So? How 'bout it? I've got five other offers on the table."

He looked a little too intently into her eyes. Demi's stomach flopped with nerves and excitement. Before it got awkward, Aiden picked up her iPhone, and input his contact info.

"If you can remember my name in the morning," he said, "you're hired."

demi's new york sour

SERVES 1

ingredients

2 ozs bourbon or rye
1 oz fresh lemon juice
¾ oz simple syrup
1 egg white (optional)
½ oz red wine

instructions

1. Add all the ingredients except the wine to a cocktail shaker and fill with ice.

2. Shake, then strain into an Old-Fashioned glass filled with fresh ice.

3. Slowly pour the wine over the back of a spoon so that it floats on top of the drink.

17

when the wheel of fortune turns, it rolls right over you

Hipsters had gone through a downtime transformation. It began its gestation as a half-hour single-camera Brooklyn-set comedy about relationships. The network overlords concluded that *Hipsters* wasn't as witty and raw as *Girls* nor as broad and vulgar as *2 Broke Girls*. Would the audience tolerate another show about this demographic in the same location? The decision was "no." *But* the network brass were gaga for the sexy young cast—a multiethnic brunette, a redheaded Latina, and a WASPy blonde—and decided that they could be the *Charlie's Angels* for the millennial generation. So the premise and format were changed. Now it was an hour-long three-camera Los Angeles–set drama about relationships . . . *and murder* . . . called *The Den*.

David predicted the murder bit weeks ago. He gloated when

Sophia told him. He also pitied the writers who had to scrap ten finished scripts and start from scratch in an entirely new genre. He told her this kind of do-over wasn't unheard of, although it was unusual. Any writer worth his or her salt should be able to make this one-eighty-degree turn on a dime. "That's what we get paid for," he said.

Sophia's character was still named Valerie. However, she was no longer an aspiring novelist. She and her costars' characters were bloggers for a hard-hitting news site called *The Den*. They chased down ripped-from-the-headlines stories about sexism and violence against women, while going on dates and trying to square the men they investigated—dirtbags and assholes—with the men they hooked up with romantically. Naturally, there would be some crossover.

At the meeting at M. King Studios to discuss the changes, Paula, the redhead Latina, said, "If you make us go undercover as models to expose sexual harassment in the fashion world, I fucking quit."

Cassie said, "Roofie rape on college campuses is relevant. Let's do that."

Sophia added, "We could do bottle-service girls getting molested in the VIP section at nightclubs."

The writers and show runners weren't enthusiastic about Sophia's idea, finding it "too narrow." She didn't need to relive the experience anyway. Although it was a bit harrowing to hear that the show was in jeopardy, only to be snatched out of the jaws of disaster, she welcomed the change. Her biggest success on stage in school had been in dramatic roles. She'd still get to deliver wisecracks, but she would not have to act endearingly klutzy, or get a cupcake in the face, or mug through an aw-shucks "I love you guys!" group hug. Not that there was anything wrong with group hugs. She welcomed them in her real life. But on TV, it always read as emotionally manipulative. Always.

So. Every aspect of the show—except the talent—had to be overhauled, including the shooting schedule, the scripts, wardrobe and makeup, locations, publicity stills, marketing, and network positioning. *Variety* and *Hollywood Reporter* chronicled the evolution, and predicted too much change could mean one thing: *The Den* would suck.

For weeks, the cast and crew were crazy busy doing the thousands of things required to create a TV drama before shooting a single frame. If *The Den* were to get a fall debut, it would be late in the season, and only if the network canceled another debut show. Their success depended on the failure of others, or as David put it, "That's entertainment!"

Episode 101's premise: a revenge porn plot about a high school girl, her jilted boyfriend, and a soulless troll. Sophia's character had two juicy scenes: In Act One, she comforted the suicidal girl whose naked pics were posted all over the Internet. In Act Three, she confronted the revenge porn site's creator in his basement lair and trashed his computer setup in a fury. She rehearsed her scenes with Demi and David every night until the first day of shooting in mid-September.

The night before, Sophia and Demi sat on their couch eating ice cream. Sophia could never decide on a flavor so they ended up getting three: Neopolitan (Sophia's fave), chocolate chip mint (Demi ate around the mints), and cookie dough. They were watching the reality show *The Harem*, mocking it. Demi said, "Ohh, she's crying again!" of one of the harem contestants. "Listen for it, she's going to say, 'My heart hurts.'" On screen, sure enough, the girl said, "I feel betrayed! I really fell in love with the Sultan, but he gave the orchid to Shasanna. My heart hurts."

They howled, and threw pillows at the TV. Sophia said, "Good thing she's not 'there to make friends.' Or she'd be totally fucked." Then she put her foot on Demi's thighs, and started rolling her ankles. She'd been doing it to Demi or anyone in close proximity since she was a kid. All the little pops and crunches loosened in her bones and joints, and she relaxed.

"So Leandra's in London now," said Sophia. "Burning her way across Asia and Europe."

"Let's hope she stays there."

"Just tell me! Why do you hate her? What did she ever do to you?"

Demi took a huge bite of ice cream and mumbled, "I can't talk. My mouth is full."

A text popped up on Sophia's phone, from, of all people, Renee.

"Renee? Last time I saw her, she called me a no-talent princess on the verge of losing my looks," she said.

Demi said, "Did she change her mind?"

"It says, 'Heard about @theden! Congrats!! Would love to buy you a drink to celebrate.'"

"I bet she would!" said Demi.

Sophia said, "I'm texting 'Thanks. Busy now, but I'll be in touch.'"

Renee replied, "The truth is, I need your help/advice. The party line ad didn't happen. Skyy scrapped my shoot. Could you introduce me to your agent?"

"When the wheel of fortune turns, it rolls right over you," said Demi.

"I have to help her," said Sophia. "If I don't, the wheel of fortune will turn and roll over me."

"You can't possibly believe that," said Demi.

Sophia wasn't generally superstitious. But with the show's upheaval, she left nothing to chance, especially her good karma. "I did push her into a swimming pool by-accident-on-purpose. I owe her. What if I invite her to the First Night party?" she said, referring to the planned celebration after the first shoot day wrapped. "You'll be working at Dory. David is on deadline. I can do one lap around the room with her, log the good deed, and then I can wipe my hands clean of her."

"I wouldn't cross the street to spit at her," said Demi. "Waste of my precious saliva. But I applaud your kindness to the bitch."

Sophia sent the text with mixed feelings. It was going to be a long day, and then, with Renee at her side, a longer night.

The first day of shooting was a thrill. She loved it all, the makeup, cameras, soundstage. She even loved the waiting around, and made good use of the time making a video of every inch of her dressing room to send to Demi and Leandra, and taking random shots around the set of her costars, the makeup tables, the wardrobe closets.

For the party that night, Sophia wore a slinky black cocktail dress from BCBG and jeweled sandals from Zara. She knew she'd over-dressed as soon as she walked into the Supperclub on Hollywood Boulevard. Despite the swank location, the other Denizens (as everyone on the show called themselves) were dressed down, casual.

"I should have told you," said Paula, the veteran. "First off, you get why we party the first night? In most of our contracts, you don't get the big check until after the first day of shooting. That's done, so now we all get paid. Yay, let's drink. But, because we're all exhausted from everything that got us here, the tradition is to dress casually, and make it an early night. The crew guys will stay until closing. I'm out of here in an hour."

"I might as well be wearing a sign that says 'Virgin.'"

"Don't worry about it. Just have a drink and relax. It's a party, re-member?"

Renee arrived soon after Sophia. She was dressed up, too, and seemed happy to stand out. "Hey," she said, kissing Sophia on the cheek. "Thanks for leaving my name at the door."

"No problem."

Silence. Renee broke it by being honest. "We don't have to hash over recent history. By my count, you owe me one. Put me in front of the right people tonight, and we're even."

Just get it out of the way, she thought. "Come on." Sophia brought her over to the power cluster of the showrunner, two of the writers, and one of the directors. They were having an intense conversation in a booth with serious drinks (scotches, neat) in front of them.

"It's our star," said Julie Chapman, the runner, aka the most im-portant person on the show. Her husband, Henry, was the director. They'd done a few hit shows together over the years, a bona fide dynamic duo. Along with the cast, the Chapmans were the show's backbone, and the real reason the network had faith in *The Den*. "Great scene today, Sophia."

"Thanks," she said, genuinely grateful to hear it. Now, on to her karmic labors. "I wanted to introduce you guys to a friend of mine from Toronto. This is Renee Quint. She's an actor, too, and has done a bunch of commercials."

The Chapmans smiled and then returned to their conversation. Cue to leave, *now*. Sophia got the message loud and clear. Logrolling would not be tolerated. Another rookie mistake Sophia would never make again. Her nerves jangling, she backed away from the booth, pulling Renee along with her.

Renee shook her off. "Wait a minute. I didn't get to talk to them."

"You did see their reaction, right?" said Sophia. "They couldn't have been less into it."

"You could have pushed it."

"I have to work with these people. I'm not going out of my way to piss them off on Day One. Even you must understand that."

"Even me?" Renee asked.

Even a mean, selfish bitch like you. "Time and place," said Sophia. "This isn't it. I'm sorry, I thought it would be, but it's not."

"Well, I'm here and I'm dressed, so I'm staying."

By now, the Supperclub bar area was crowded with people who worked on the show, their friends, and others who knew about the party and came to hook up or be seen. The idea that a civilian couldn't gain access to a private Hollywood party turned out to be a myth. If you were a friend of a friend, or a friend of the bartender, or a friend of the bouncer, you could get in anywhere. The non-Denizens looked a lot like the roving packs of models and actors who turned up all over LA, in every bar, lounge, and club, every night of the week and twice on Saturday.

"Flashback to CRUSH," said Renee.

"Don't remind me," said Sophia.

They shared a companionable cringe. Renee smiled warmly at her, and said, "I'll buy you a drink." They pushed through three-deep hotties to get to the bar. Renee ordered, and then handed Sophia a glass of red wine. "No hard feelings."

Sophia accepted it. In a few minutes, the tension dissolved, and they shifted back in time to their Toronto dynamic, just two girls with high hopes and low-cut outfits. Renee brought up a few classic Vinnie moments, and Sophia found herself laughing at the memories and warming to her old friend. Sophia wasn't one to hold a grudge.

There was no point in clinging to the negativity. Renee was Renee. Right now she was being pretty cool. They took a couple selfies together and then started talking to a few guys at the bar. Sophia recognized one of them from some TV show, but she wasn't sure which. She let him buy her a shot. Paola came over to kiss her good-bye. Cassie left soon after with her parents in tow. Before long, most of the other Denizens filed out. Someone put another drink into Sophia's hand. Renee kissed a model boy. Farther down the bar, a girl stood up on a chair, and started singing off-key. Her lips were bright red, lipstick smeared.

That was the last thing Sophia remembered, the smear.

Cold feet. A sour taste in her mouth. Sore shoulders. Sensations registered in Sophia's body, but her mind lagged behind. She came to consciousness gradually, and then all of the sudden, like swimming upward in slow motion, and then breaking through the surface. She opened her eyes. Her vision was blurry.

She rolled to her left for the glass of water on her night table, but it wasn't her night table. An abstract color-block painting hung on the wall where her vision board should be. Someone else's art. Someone else's bedroom.

She bolted upright, making her head throb so painfully that she had to lie back down. The sheet slipped off her body, and she realized she was naked. Next to her, a man lay on his stomach, his bare legs and back visible on top of the sheet. The pillow obscured his face. She could see only a beard and curly brown hair.

He didn't seem to be breathing.

Sophia scrambled off the bed, in a panic about where she was, who he was, what they'd done. Her movement dragged the sheet off the rest of his nude body. He flinched suddenly, making her scream. He wasn't dead. But relief was quickly replaced with rising fury. He wasn't dead, but he should be.

He turned over, exposing his junk to harsh morning light. She gagged and looked around frantically for a bathroom. She ran for an open door, and found the toilet. After unloading into it, she saw a mound of puke on the white-tiled floor near her dress. She put it on quickly. It was torn and damp. Her hair felt stringy and damp, too. She looked behind the shower curtain. Her underwear and bra were soaking wet on the tub floor.

When she came out of the bathroom, the man was sitting in bed, cross-legged, the sheet gathered around his waist. "Good morning," he said.

"Where am I?"

"My place."

"Who are you?"

"What do you mean?"

"*Who the fuck are you?* What happened last night?"

He looked at her like she'd woken up crazy. "We had a great time, that's what happened."

She dug into her memory but found only a hole. A sob seeped from her lips. *Did I have sex with him?* Vague images surfaced from the Supperclub. Paula saying good-bye. Model boys at the bar. Renee laughing, making out with an actor she sort of recognized. This guy was a friend of his? She could not remember meeting him or talking to him.

The saddest part was that Sophia had always been so careful to the point of paranoia. Her mom had trained her since junior high to buy her own drinks, cover her glass with her hand, and never leave a beverage on the bar unattended. How did this happen? She'd kept her palm over her wine. That actor handed her a shot. Had that been it? She should never have taken it.

Sophia had been going to bars, and worked at bars, for years. One slip, and she woke up into a nightmare.

Run. Run. Run. Panic and adrenaline raced through her blood. She had to get out of there. "Where's my stuff?" she screamed, frantic to find what belonged to her, to remove any trace of her from this place. She stumbled around the room, but couldn't find her bag, her phone, her shoes.

He said, "Chill out. Come back to bed."

Sophia vomited again.

"My carpet!"

She found her way to the living room and searched to no avail for her belongings. Had she left her bag at the bar? And her shoes? Her stomach flopped at the idea of putting on wet underwear. *Leave it. Just go. Go.*

Sophia bolted through the front door, and ran into the street in bare feet. She looked at the street signs as if that would help her figure out her location. It was just a random block, an apartment complex like hers, across the street from a gas station and a Taco Bell. She had no phone, no money, no shoes, and no idea where she was. Was she still in LA? Which part? For all she knew, she could be in another state.

Crossing the street, Sophia went into the gas station. The clock on the wall said it was after ten A.M. She was supposed to be on set an hour ago. The woman behind the counter acted nonplussed by the sight of a frantic shoeless girl in a torn dress stumbling into the Quik Mart. Maybe it happened every day. Sophia begged to borrow her phone for just a second. She logged onto her Uber account and dropped a pin to order a car. Then she logged out and gave the phone back.

The woman said, "We sell flip-flops and gum."

Her breath was toxic, and her feet were filthy. She went into the bathroom to clean herself up. Incredibly, Sophia didn't look traumatized, just hung over. No one would suspect she'd been drugged and possibly raped by a stranger. Her gaze settled on her eyes, usually her safe place. She peered into herself, and saw a shattered girl. Her stomach turned over again.

She washed her mouth out, and rinsed her feet. Then she went back into the store to ask the cashier, "What neighborhood is this?"

"Koreatown."

It wasn't too far from the studio in the Valley. The Uber car arrived and whisked her to the set. It was ten-thirty A.M. by then, and she was an hour and a half late. She ducked into her dressing room and showered. Her costume for the day was Valerie's work ensemble—jeans, boots, and a sleeveless blouse. Wardrobe always supplied underwear and bras that were custom made for the given outfit. Covering her parts with the thin scraps of fabric made her feel slightly less vulnerable. Slightly.

A PA knocked on her dressing room door, making Sophia jump. "Sophia? Are you in there?"

"I'm here," she said.

"We got a call from the Supperclub. You left your bag there last night. Do you want me to send someone to get it?"

"Yes, thanks." A small blessing: The bearded man didn't have her wallet and phone. She started crying with relief.

"You're wanted in makeup," said the PA.

She sniffed back the tears and had to psych herself up for a few minutes just to leave the sanctuary of her dressing room. But she did it. She took one step in front of the other, and moved all the way across the cavernous soundstage to the makeup area. She sat down in the chair, and Wanda, her regular, immediately got to work on her face.

"What's this?" she asked.

Sophia looked in the mirror where Wanda was pointing. Bruises circled both her upper arms.

Sophia swallowed hard, her salivary glands like a running faucet. "It's nothing. Can you just cover it?"

"Someone had a good time last night," said Wanda with a wink.

In a semitraumatized state, Sophia closed her eyes and let Wanda do her job uninterrupted. When it was done, Sophia examined her face. When she looked herself in her eyes, she could still see the hollowness. But when she examined her face as a whole, the foundation was a good disguise.

An intern arrived with her bag. Incredibly, nothing had been stolen. She started crying again. "Stop that!" said Wanda. "No crying until we wrap for the day. Then you can sob your heart out."

Sophia squirreled off to her dressing room, with her bag. She paced the small room, and tried to piece the night together, getting as far as the girl on the chair, singing, lipstick smeared. Then she hit a memory wall. She scrolled through her phone for photos, or to see if any names and numbers were added to her contacts. Nothing. A text from Demi came in. "Where were you last night?"

Sophia started to call, but hung up before it rang. She replied, "At the studio, can't talk. ☺"

Things were finally turning around for Demi. Sophia couldn't drag her down with this. Besides, if she breathed one word about it, especially to Demi, Sophia would completely lose it. She'd be hysterical; her makeup would be destroyed. Her composure, hanging on by a thread, would snap. That could *not* happen. It was the second day of shooting. She had to go out there and do her job. A personal unraveling was not blocked into the shoot schedule. She started panicking again, her insides writhing, terrified about breaking down with cameras and hundreds of eyes on her.

Scott would know what to do. He was an experienced actor, and might have advice. If she were sick, they'd give her the day off, right? She'd just say she was sick. She was, absolutely sickened by what she knew had happened, and more so by what she didn't know.

"Hey, Scott," she said into her phone.

"Sophia Marcus from Vancouver! How the hell are you?"

"Not so hot." Sophia quickly told him the whole story. "I'm supposed to do a scene comforting the victim of a sex crime today. I can't do it, Scott. I'll lose it. I'm going to tell Julie Chapman I'm not feeling well."

"You can't call in sick to stardom, Sophia. Two hundred people are counting on you to go out there and say your lines. If you beg off, they'll think you're a prima donna who can't handle a hangover. My advice to you, which you must take, is to say *nothing*. Don't rock the boat. Don't obsess about last night. You got some action, that's all. Pretend it never happened, and move on."

Another knock on the door. "Sophia? You're needed on set."

She said, "I've got to go."

An image flashed in her mind, the wheel of fortune turning and rolling right over her. *But I did my karmic duty*, she thought. It didn't protect her. She got crushed anyway. And now, she had to pretend that she was a functioning adult, a strong, beautiful woman who had her shit together.

You got this, she told herself, not believing it for a minute.

You never
know how
STRONG
you are
until being
STRONG
is the only
CHOICE
you have.

18

so many pints

Leandra and Harris's seven-hour drive from Scotland to London turned into a seven-day tour of the English countryside. Harris was a doer, not much of a talker. Thankfully, he didn't ask her too-personal questions, like, "Do you have any siblings?" That one always made Leandra's shields go up. Apparently, Harris didn't care about her family or background. He was living in the moment. Leandra was curious about his background, but she didn't push it, taking all conversational cues from him.

The first day, they walked along Hadrian's Wall which had been built thousands of years ago to protect the Roman imperialists from the Scottish barbarian hordes. For Leandra, it was a pleasant stroll along a pile of ancient bricks. But Harris went berserk, saying the ruins inspired the Wall in *Game of Thrones*. He described how it must have looked way back when, the orderly Roman army with gold helmets and red tunics on one side, and blue-faced *Braveheart* maniacs in skins and rags on the other. His excitement was infectious, and Leandra got into it.

For lunch, they ate meat pies and drank pints of ale. So many pints. In their room at the inn, Harris was too drunk to raise his standard, as it were. They slept nestled together, Harris as the big spoon, and woke up in each other's arms.

In the morning, as Leandra hastily applied her makeup in bed next to a sleeping Harris, she decided that not screwing on the first date was a refreshing change. It gave them both a chance to get to know each other before lust took the reins of the relationship. But one day was enough to hold off. *We'll do it tonight*, she thought.

They spent the next day shopping and having tea with scones and clotted cream in the medieval village of Hexham, and dined at another inn, with more pies and pints. The whole town reminded her of the movie *P.S. I Love You*. Her real life was a romcom. In bed, Harris held her until she fell asleep, but he didn't grab her boobs or ass, not once. In the morning, Leandra wondered if he was gay (unlikely). He might not be attracted to her (absurd). Or, she realized with surprise and delight, *He must be falling in love*.

Their days unspooled like a silken ribbon. They headed south, with several detours and stops in the Lake District. It was like driving through the fluttering heart and quivering loins of every romance novel ever written. The purple mountains, the blue lakes, and the electric green valleys took Leandra's breath away.

Harris said, "If you didn't fall in love with this part of the world, your soul is dead."

Leandra noted that he said, "fall in love *with* this part of the world," as opposed to "fall in love *while in* this part of the world." She agreed in both cases.

During their fourth night, they bedded down in the Beldsfield Hotel in Windermere. Leandra sat on his lap in front of their window, gazing dreamily at the deep blue of Windermere Lake. Harris kissed her for the first time. She was wearing khaki shorts and a

T-shirt bought at a tourist shop called Scrambles in Hexham. She was not at the height of fashion with minimal makeup and hair in a ratty pony, but Leandra had never felt more beautiful in the reflected glory of the lake, the heather on the hills.

"That was nice," she said, resting her head on his shoulder.

"Very," he said.

Leandra's mind quieted, and she felt all artifice fade. She wasn't Charlie's wife, or Oliver's spiritual advisor. She was just a girl in a half-poly T-shirt, kissing a boy in a half-poly T-shirt. This was as close to honest as Leandra had been with a guy, maybe ever, and she basked in it.

When Harris's legs fell asleep, they moved from the armchair in the window to the downy, inviting bed piled with chintz-covered pillows. Harris explored her mouth and touched her body, but he didn't try to remove her clothes. Leandra strained against his hands, willing him to go further. Although they were falling in love with each other, Leandra needed assurance in words or deeds that he found her sexy. His gazing moonily at her over hurricane lamplight and plates of bangers and mash in pubs wasn't enough. She needed heat. Her past relationships were forged in fire. A man's passion fueled her confidence. Harris denied her that power. He held off out of respect, probably. But it was starting to irritate her.

On their fifth night, they stayed in Liverpool, birthplace of the Beatles, Harris's favorite band. They went in and out of nostalgia shops and saw a concert of a pseudo–Fab Four performing the classic hits. Harris was in fan-boy heaven. That night, in the four-star Malmaison Hotel, Harris finally touched her naked skin. He bathed her in the claw-footed tub and shampooed her hair. He wrapped her up in a soft, thick bathrobe, carried her to bed. Slowly, he untied the cord of the robe. She lay back on the bed, open to him.

He drank her in with his eyes and then thrilled her with his mouth, making her come so hard and so loud, she rattled the crystal chandelier.

He kept his clothes on the entire time.

Leandra started to wonder if he even *had* a penis.

On day six, they drove to Stratford-upon-Avon, the birthplace of some minor, lesser-known poet and playwright. They took a tour of historic places around town ("Shakespeare Ate Here!" "Shakespeare Shopped Here!" "Shakespeare Shagged Here!"), which Harris loved. But Leandra was edgy, confused, and beside herself with impatience. She hovered on the brink of not-fucking madness. Kissing was bliss. Harris going down on her had been a religious experience, not just because she screamed, "Oh, god! Oh, god!" But, if he didn't slip it in *tonight*, she would lose her freakin' mind.

After an interminable Royal Shakespeare Theater performance of *A Midsummer Night's Dream* (Leandra liked the fairies and the magic, but the she-loves-him-he-loves-her relationship jumble was just nonsense), they went up to their suite at the twee Tudor-style Arden Hotel. As soon as the door closed behind them, Harris ripped the dress off her back, and threw her on the bed. He removed his own clothes piece by piece, the whole time staring at parts of her body. Finally breathtakingly nude, Harris crawled across the bed to her. If he gave a second's thought to her pleasure, she had no idea. He took his, and in his thrall, Leandra lost herself—and had the first multiple orgasm of her life.

She was so proud of herself!

When it was over, they lulled in the feathery softness of their King Henry bed. Harris fed her bites of chocolate and sips of champagne. "To think," he said, "we might have spent this week eating grass and sleeping on a cot."

Shocking herself, Leandra burst into tears. Did that mean their time together was over? When they arrived in London tomorrow, would they go their separate ways? He must have understood why she was suddenly so upset, but he didn't put her out of her misery with reassurance. Instead, he stroked her hair, soothing her insecurities by touch. Just like every night, they fell asleep in each other's arms.

The drive to London was rough. The Jaguar started acting funny. It might not make it to the drop-off location on the East End, and Harris was cursing and pissed off about it. Leandra sat in the passenger seat, quietly terrified of what would happen when they got through the traffic and drove into the city proper.

"Where do you want to go?" he asked.

"Kings Road," she said over the lump in her throat.

Leandra's stuff was still at Oliver's town house. Harris hadn't said a word about his plans and Leandra felt like she couldn't ask. Their original agreement was to drive south to London together. They'd done that. Leandra hated not knowing what would happen next. Like the *Midsummer* lovers in the play last night, Leandra agonized over the answers to unasked questions. She couldn't reveal her feelings to Harris—that she loved him and would like to be surgically attached to his side—for fear that he'd reject her and destroy her one chance at real happiness. Plus, she was flat broke and Oliver, if he had any pride, wouldn't take her back now.

The Jag sputtered to a stop outside of Oliver's town house. Leandra turns to Harris, tears in her eyes, ready to say farewell. He said, "How long do you need? If I come back in two hours, will you be ready to go?"

"I'll be ready in one," she said, and burst into tears *again*. Harris had to think she was a soggy female. "I'm usually an unfeeling shrew, I swear."

"You thought we were over?"

"I didn't know."

"I'm not letting you go," he said. "But I do need you to hurry. I have to get rid of this shit car and take care of some business. We're flying to Los Angeles tonight, so when you pack your stuff, make an overnight bag for the flight."

"Okay." She only cried harder now, snot indelicately dribbling out of her nose.

"Two hours."

She got out and watched him ride away. She waved idiotically on the street, and didn't care if Blinky and Spotty and Swanky happened to see her. Harris was her hero, her maestro, her lover, and her savior. Yes, he'd saved her from Holy Isle (there was an irony in there somehow). He had taken her to bliss, and tonight, he was taking her to Los Angeles, to his mansion in the San Fernando Valley. Maybe there was something to Sophia's crap about manifesting and vision boards. Leandra had acted like a Valley Girl for Oliver, and now she was going there.

She skipped up the steps of the town house, and rang the bell. Grimly the valet opened the door and said, "Grayson Manor."

"It's me," she said.

"Who is calling?"

"Leandra. From a week ago."

"Oh, yes," he said. "You're back. I hoped we'd seen the last of you."

Only in England was the help snottier than the people they served. "Just get out of the way," she said, pushing past him, and heading up to her room to start packing. "I need you to carry my suitcases downstairs."

Grimly said, "Dream on."

Packing took longer than expected. She'd acquired quite a lot of clothing and trinkets in Thailand and London—nine suitcase's worth. To think, she'd arrived in Phuket with one suitcase full of cheap dresses and ugly shoes. Now she had enough finery to fill Nordstrom. She couldn't resist trying on a few outfits as she packed, fantasizing about wearing them in LA, at movie premieres and dinners at Chassen's. Time flew playing dress up and, when the doorbell rang—it had to be Harris!—she wasn't finished. Leandra threw the remainder of her stuff into bags and cases, and then ran down the stairs to greet her American hero.

Grimly opened the door, but it wasn't Harris who walked through it. Oliver Bracknell strode into his home, and zeroed in on Leandra descending the staircase. The valet stood at his master's side.

Oliver said, "Thank you, Grimly. I misplaced my keys."

So Grimly had tipped Oliver off that Leandra was back. Slight adjustment to her plan. A note was no longer necessary. She'd just tell him what she would have written. "Oliver! I'm so glad you're here. I need help getting my suitcases downstairs."

The nineteenth Earl of Grayson stared at her, silently. He had a lot of practice on Holy Isle. Grimly said, "Will that be all, sir?"

"Yes, you may go."

Leandra wasn't going to get help with her bags until she made nice. So she walked down the stairs toward her ex-boyfriend. Or . . . was it possible Oliver didn't know she had dumped him? Escaping Holy Isle with another man should have been his first clue. She had sent him a text saying she was fine and he didn't need to worry about her. But could that be misconstrued? Brits seemed to fall in and out of love so quickly, he might not realize what was going on.

Leandra pecked him on the cheek. "You look well rested! Did you get what you were looking for on Holy Isle? I hope so. Um, yeah, I just wanted to say I appreciate everything you've done for me. I value our friendship. Thanks ever so much. If we don't meet again, just, you know, have a jolly ol' life."

"You're not really from Malibu," he said coldly. "I've been in touch with Charles Lemming in Bangkok. He told me you're really from Vancouver, Canada, and that you've never even been to California."

"Charlie doesn't know anything about me," she said, and realized how true that was. Neither did Oliver. Harris was getting to know her, but he'd only scratched the first layer of surface. The only people who *really* knew Leandra were her parents (who seemed kind of scared of her), and Sophia. Demi knew her, too, but didn't like her. So fuck her, basically.

Oliver seemed very pleased with himself for Sherlocking her other ex-boyfriend. "You're a fraud!" he announced, index finger raised to heaven. "You were faking all those ommms! I doubt you're spiritual at all."

"I am spiritual, just not about spirituality," she said.

"What the hell does that mean?"

It was a bit too late in their relationship to call her on her schemes. "Look, I wanted to tell you that Grimly was very rude to me. You should sack him."

"The ferryman told the Lama about you and the American, but

only after everyone at the retreat spent a full day searching the island for you. I was frantic with worry. I thought you drowned. Anyway, the truth came out. For the next five days, I meditated and chanted about forgiveness."

"That's nice," she said. "Look, my friend will be here very soon. So chop-chop with the servants. My bags? Upstairs?"

"During my meditation, I learned something important. You are a taker. And I am a giver. To forgive is to give. It's right there in the word. For-give. I am *for* giving. Do you understand? You are for *taking*. I am for *giving*."

Eating bark had softened his brain. "Okay," she said. "For-give away."

"That's what I'm doing," he said. "This is me, forgiving."

It looked like he was trying to hold back an elephant fart.

The bell rang again. "I'm just going to get that," she said, and skirted around Oliver to let Harris in. Fortunately, he came with a helper of his own, his limo driver. Leandra directed them to her room, and the three of them got all her luggage in the car in only a few trips.

Oliver continued to project forgiveness at her, which completely creeped Harris out. "You fucked that guy? Seriously?"

"If it weren't for him, we wouldn't have met," she said. "It's amazing how things happen, isn't it?"

"You're amazing," he said.

Once settled at the Virgin first-class lounge at Heathrow, Leandra FaceTimed Sophia, who answered on the first ring. "Hi!"

"Hey," said her best friend, who looked exhausted.

"Guess what? I'll be in LA tomorrow! I'm going to be staying in the Valley. How far is that from you?"

"With the earl?"

"Oh, no. That's over. He was just too snobby! I couldn't stand the phoniness and repression. The Brits keep all the feels locked up inside, stiff upper lip, keep calm, carry on. I'm just too self-aware and in touch with my feelings for London. I need a dose of North American realness."

"Great. Call me when you get here."

"Oh. Okay," said Leandra. "I thought you'd be more excited to see me."

"I am excited."

Leandra detected a great gulf separating them that had nothing to do with their being six thousand miles apart. "Are you mad at me?"

"No," said Sophia. "I'm just really tired. I've been dealing with a lot. We're shooting round the clock to have enough finished episodes for—"

"I can't wait to hear all about it." Leandra cut her off. "I've got to go. They're calling our flight."

"Our?"

"I'm with a new friend. Say 'hello,' Harris!" He leaned into the iPhone screen and waved at Sophia. "He's a movie director. I told him all about you, and he's dying to meet you. We'll be there in twelve hours. I'll text when we land."

"Yeah, okay," said Sophia, listless and dopey in the middle of the afternoon, her time. Was Sophia on drugs? She'd always been as pure as Canadian snow with that sort of thing. Leandra hung up, doubly assured that she was heading in the right direction.

"Is she okay?" asked Harris. "She seemed out of it."

"She misses me," said Leandra.

"You're a good friend."

"I just do what I can to help other people," she said. "I'm for giving. That's what it's all about. For instance, I'm all for giving you a blow job on the flight."

"Girl of my dreams," he said.

FORGIVE

anyway.

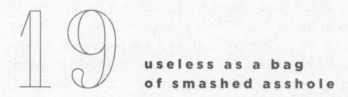

19

useless as a bag
of smashed asshole

Demi brushed her hair and tied it into a pony, her restaurant style. Dory was launching in a month, and she spent all day, every day there, building the website, planning a soft-opening party for Yelp superusers, running numbers for Internet advertising. Yesterday, she campaigned Aiden to invest in a permit to set up a picnic seating area. "Where?" he asked.

"Outback on a faux beach," she said.

"Enough with the outback jokes! But, yeah, I like it. That's my idea of California. A picnic on the beach."

It was hers, too. Every day during her lunch break, Demi walked along the boardwalk and on Venice Beach. It was a movie come to life, with girls in pink bikini tops and cut-off jeans on fixed-gear bikes, steroid junkie bodybuilders pumping iron, hippies selling friendship bracelets and hacky sacks, people of every color, class, and age, happily coexisting under the sky and on the sand. Smiles for miles. Even the bums were somewhat happy and healthy looking. It was paradise. To think that Demi had hesitated about moving out here. Catherine had gloated a bit when Demi thanked her profusely for kicking her out of the nest. Life *was* an adventure. You had to get out there and live it.

As Demi stroked on some light makeup, she gave herself a figurative pat on the back. She'd faced her fears, took a risk, and been rewarded. Working at Dory was her chance to prove herself. She was determined not to fuck it up.

Her very first task as an employee of Aiden Archer's had been to wait on line at the local chamber of commerce for an alcohol permit. The irony was not lost, and neither was the paperwork. She got the permits, double-checked the dates and location, dotted the i's and crossed the t's. When she brought it back for Aiden's approval, he said, "Good. Now create a mailing list." Grown-ups didn't need gold stars. Demi didn't need Aiden's praise to feel good about herself. Approval worth having had to come from within. Whether or not Aiden gushed about her creativity or efficiency didn't really matter, as long as she knew she'd done the job well. The mental shift might be small, but it felt seismic. Demi didn't need to please her boss, boyfriend, or father. She only needed to please herself, and her standards for what that meant were rapidly escalating.

Demi had lived and died for James's praise. It was what got her out of bed in the morning and into bed at night. She'd cooked for his approval, shopped for it, fucked for it. Demi didn't want to compare her relationship with James to hers with Aiden. But they were both older men who had authority over her. It was impossible not to. Demi and Aiden's dynamic was healthy, and mutually supportive. She knew she was building a friendship, as well as a business. It felt great to create.

Demi finished her makeup and chucked her used tissues at the bathroom trash can. She missed and picked them up off the floor. Low down, she noticed a white plastic bag of empty boxes shoved under the sink.

The bag was stuffed with boxes of over-the-counter STD tests, every type imaginable, and pregnancy tests, and some with spent swabs, pee sticks, and other panels, all of them negative.

Sophia had gone to a pharmacy, and cleaned out the home-test shelf. She must have spent hundreds of dollars. Demi wasn't even aware her friend was having sex with anyone.

There was David, but as far as Demi knew, they'd only made out that one night at Bar Marmont. Sophia had put him decidedly in the friend zone. The poor guy kept stopping by. "Just seeing what you're up to," he said when he wandered over nearly every night.

Sophia's usual blow off was "I'm going to bed."

David would sulk back downstairs like a kicked puppy. He was clearly heartbroken. Sophia really was exhausted. She would come home from shooting, eat whatever Demi made for dinner, and then crawl into her room. She seemed to sleep for ten hours a night, but it only made her more tired.

If Demi didn't know better, she'd say Sophia was depressed. But her friend had never been depressive growing up and she had no apparent reason to be upset. The show was hard work but she was doing well, living her dream. It was nearly impossible to be sad in this weather. Her mood was probably just a reaction to the pressure she was under. Demi was under pressure, too, and the demands of their jobs kept them from having time for a heart-to-heart. Demi mentally scheduled it for a month hence, as soon as *The Den* finished shooting its first five episodes, and the restaurant had its soft opening.

But then Demi found the box of home tests. The heart-to-heart just got moved up to ASAP.

Tracking back, Demi tried to figure out when Sophia might've hooked up with someone. She didn't come home after the First Night party. When Demi had asked her where she slept that night, Sophia said she'd crashed at Renee's. Renee was probably crawling with STDs, but Sophia wasn't into girls, no matter how drunk she got. Also, she wouldn't buy eight pregnancy tests if she slept with Renee.

Demi put the empty boxes back in the bag. Sophia was already on set, and wouldn't be available to talk until tonight. Taking a chance, Demi called her anyway.

"I'm in makeup," said Sophia. "I'm not supposed to move my mouth."

"Take me off speaker," said Demi.

"Okay," said Sophia. "Now my phone is caked with spray-on foundation."

"I had some time to kill this morning," said Demi. "So I thought, *What to do for fun? I know! I'll see what's under the bathroom sink.*"

"Knock yourself out."

"Is there something you want to tell me?"

"Mind your own business?"

"Something else?"

"No."

"Really?"

"I'm fine," said Sophia. "And I've got to go. We *won't* talk about this later." Then she hung up.

To the dead phone, Demi said, "We are *definitely* talking about this later." But for now, she had to get to Dory. Aiden was auditioning a new chef today, and she wanted to be there for the tasting. Demi struggled to let it go on the way to work. She had a tendency to ruminate. She was worried about her friend. Just like the bag of boxes and test strips, Sophia seemed to be trying to bury this. When Demi saw her later tonight, she'd try to pin her down about what was really going on.

"There she is!" boomed Aiden whenever Demi arrived at the restaurant. She smiled on cue despite herself. Aiden was a dancing bear of a man. Seeing him lifted her spirits, too.

"Good morning," she said, going into the kitchen to unload some groceries in the fridge. She'd gotten in the habit of shopping at Whole Foods on the way to the restaurant for ingredients to make dinner for them. They worked late so often, it only made sense to eat in. And he let her bring home the leftovers for Sophia.

"Demi, meet Chester Fangs—not his real name? Yes, it *is* your real name? Wow. Okay. Chester, meet Demi Michaels. She is my brilliant marketer, permit wrangler, and all-around, all-purpose right arm."

Chester Fangs nodded at her. He was skinny (always suspicious in a cook), tall, with a faux-hawk, a neck tattoo that was a crossbones of a knife and fork, and a "don't fuck with me" stare. Demi thought he looked familiar. "You were on *Top Chef*, right?" she asked.

"*Top Chef Baltimore*," he said. "I made it to the final four and then Colicchio booted me because he doesn't know what al dente means."

As Demi recalled, Chester threw a steaming bowl of tom yung goong soup at another cook during Restaurant Wars and was voted "the most hated cheftestant of all time" by fans.

Aiden asked, "What's *Top Chef*?"

"It's a cooking competition on TV," said Demi.

"It's rigged," said Chester. "Here's my résumé. You also asked me to make a sample menu." He handed a few neatly typed pages to Aiden, who sat down at the kitchen stool to read them. Demi scanned the pages over his shoulder. The résumé included big-name restaurants in LA and Chicago, and claims of tutelage under famous chefs. He'd won a few awards and had once cooked for the president, along with a team of other cooks from his then restaurant. The guy had chops, but did they want to rub shoulders with him every day? It was all coming back to her now, Demi remembered Chester making odious sexist remarks to the female chefs, how they should stick with noodle casserole and baby making, and leave cooking to the men, along those lines.

Aiden said, "Very impressive résumé. I love the TV stuff. We can get a lot of publicity out of this, right, Demi? Look here, Chester has two hundred thousand followers on Twitter!"

"Nice," she said. No doubt he was a talented chef and everyone knew those shows were edited to make people look bad. But he made a soft-spoken Japanese chef cry when she overcooked salmon on a team challenge. He called a chubby lesbian chef a "tranny who can't soufflé her way out of a paper bag." That was a quote, not a bad edit.

He'd once said, "Unless they're washing dishes, women in a kitchen are bad luck."

"Menu looks good," said Aiden. "High-end ingredients, complicated flavors. It's perfect for an upscale restaurant or a four-star hotel. But we're right on the beach. We want families to come in for a bite after swimming all day, *and* we want the foodies. Fine dining in a super casual environment. It's a delicate balance. Fish and chips should be on the menu, but they should be refined, light. Not the leaden greasy shite you get at fast-food places."

Demi added, "Ideally, Dory will get a reputation for having the best fish tacos on Venice Beach."

"I can do it," said Chester.

"Great! Let's see," said Aiden.

"I'll come back with a revised menu next week," said Chester.

Aiden said, "No." With his accent, *no* sounded like *nawr.* "Let's see what you can do on the fly."

"Like a *Top Chef* Quick Fire challenge!" said Demi. "Thirty minutes to make the best fish taco ever, starting now. It'll be fun."

Chester scowled at the idea. "That's not how I operate."

"You did it on the show," said Demi.

"That was for *money*, honey," he said. "I'm not going to cook on command because this girl thinks it'll be 'fun.'" Air quotes. The douche.

Demi couldn't resist trying to put this sexist prick in his place. "Let's make it interesting," she said. "We'll each make a taco. If Aiden likes yours better than mine, we'll hire you."

"We will?" asked Aiden.

Chester snorted. "Does she even know how to cook?"

"Take a chance, mate, and find out."

"Do you have ingredients here?"

As it just so happened, Demi had just put two mahimahi fillets in the fridge.

"I'll just step outside," said Aiden, standing up. "I'll be back in forty-five minutes."

When Aiden was gone, Chester said, "I'm not doing this."

"You refuse to share a kitchen with a *girl*? Only one of us is afraid of losing."

His face turned bright red, misogyny flared up. "You have no idea what you're doing, do you?" he asked.

Saying "Bring it" would have been superfluous. They both ran at the fridge and rummaged through the pantry. It wasn't fully stocked, but close enough. Demi's strategy was to make the kind of fish taco she always wanted but had never had before. Traditional taco with citrus, corn or salsa, turned the tortilla into a soggy mess that fell apart in her hand. Why couldn't a fish taco be eaten neatly, like a falafel? Inspired by that idea, she went about baking tortillas, mixing homemade cilantro cream, baking the mahimahi, and making her own recipe for a red cabbage coleslaw.

Over at his end of the kitchen, Chester grilled the fish, and diced perfect little pieces of mango and pineapple. By her estimation, diced fruit first appeared on a taco around the time fish grew legs and crawled out of the ocean a billion years ago. In other words, if Chester thought it was original, he didn't eat a lot of tacos.

They plated their dishes. Demi's taco wasn't nearly as pretty and refined at Chester's. Compared to his perfectly, artfully arranged construction, hers looked amateurish and thrown together. Demi started to doubt her rash suggestion that they do a Quick Fire. If she lost, she'd be stuck with this jerk.

Right on time, Aiden wandered back in from the beach with a beer in hand. "Can't have a taco without a beer," he said, sitting at the kitchen counter, looking at the two plates in front of him. "Looks good," he said.

He took bites of each taco. Demi was thrilled that hers didn't fall apart. She was even more excited that Aiden had to use a fork to eat Chester's.

"Well, they both have great flavor," he said, sounding eerily like *Top Chef* judge Curtis Stone. "The grilled mahimahi is fresh and light. But I'm going to give it to the baked fish with the cilantro sauce and cabbage slaw. I can picture every kid on the beach eating one of these, and Mom and Dad ordering it, too. It can use some re-finement, but the flavors hit every part of my tongue. Congrats . . . Demi?"

"This is horseshit," said Chester. "You knew it was her dish and picked it so you can fuck her. Screw you both. You can have each other and your amateur-hour baked shit tacos. I hope this place burns to the ground."

And then he made an inglorious exit, flinging his plate against the wall on his way out.

"Please pack your knives and go," said Demi at his back.

"Useless as a bag of smashed assholes!" said Aiden, making them crack up.

"Did you really like mine better?"

"I think we should open with it," he said. "It's fantastic!" He picked it up, and shoved the rest of it in his mouth.

"Don't choke!" she said. "We haven't put up the CPR posters yet."

He said, "It's easy. You just put your arms around the person's waist, like this"—he moved around to wrap Demi in his arms, and hold her back against his front—"and squeeze."

She spun around in his arms, threw hers around his neck, and kissed him. He accepted her kiss like her food, with gusto. "Thanks for liking my food," she said. Okay, she might've been flashing back to the rush she felt when James relished her cooking. Feeding people gave her a lot of satisfaction. But there were other kinds of satisfaction to be had, too.

Aiden said, "You kiss me if I like your food? What'll you do if I put you in charge of the menu? No, I mean it. You know what you're doing. You know what we're going for. We'll do it together."

"Okay," she said, registering the surge to her groin. "But I expect a raise. We'll talk terms after."

"After . . . we fuck each other's brains out?" he said, lifting her butt on the counter. "I've been hard since you said 'fish taco.'"

They went at it like starving people. Hungry mouths tasting each other, licking and savoring all the textures, the soft tongue, smooth teeth and swollen lips. Hungry hands skimming under clothes, grasping at skin and bones, like they were holding on for dear life.

Aiden unbuttoned her jeans and pulled them down over her butt. Then he stripped them off her legs. They fell onto the kitchen floor.

"Hey! Those are my favorite jeans!" Seven for all Mankind, and not cheap.

"They look great on you," he growled, "but even better off you." Aiden unzipped his own pants and grabbed her thighs, lifting them around his hips before he moved in, all of him, all the way in. Demi gasped, and clasped her ankles around his broad body, feeling a bit like she was being mauled by a bear, and absolutely loving it. At some point, he'd lifted Demi clear off the counter, like she was weightless, and lay her back down from the lengthwise end so her whole body could rest on it. He leaned over her, making the entire table shake, the wares stored underneath clanging away chaotically, like the rhythm of her heartbeat as her hunger for him grew, and grew, until the sweetness came.

A few minutes passed as they both recovered. Demi sat up, and looked around to find pots and pans all over the kitchen floor. Aiden was staring at her, grinning with wild eyes at her, nothing on his face but pure bliss.

"You're pretty," he said. "Did I ever tell you that?"

"And you're . . . lucky to have me," she said, beaming back at him, surprised by the uncomplicated joy she felt. Being with Aiden was easy, natural, just *fun*. Sophia would say sleeping with her boss was a recipe for disaster. But she didn't care. She deserved this.

"Damn right," he said, agreeing to her spoken and unspoken thoughts.

demi's fish tacos

SERVES 4

ingredients
red cabbage slaw (see below)
cilantro crema (see below)
4 fillets white fish
salt and pepper
cayenne pepper
1 avocado
12 small corn tortillas
sriracha hot sauce
feta or queso fresco

RED CABBAGE SLAW
1 head red cabbage
1 small bunch cilantro
⅓ cup lime juice
salt and pepper

CILANTRO CREMA
1 bunch cilantro
1 clove garlic
3 tbsps veganaise or low-fat mayo
¼ cups nonfat greek yogurt, plain
2 tbsps lime juice
½ tsp himalayn salt
½ tsp cayenne pepper

instructions
1. Start with the slaw. Thinly slice an entire red cabbage, chop a small bunch of cilantro, and put it all in a bowl with

lime juice and salt and pepper to taste. Toss the ingredients and set it to the side.

2. For the cilantro crema, add all of the ingredients into a blender or food processor and combine until there are just flecks of the cilantro and it is a nice light green color.

3. For the fish, salt, pepper, and cayenne to taste both sides to add some flavor and heat. Either grill or bake the fish for the proper cook time.

4. While the fish is cooking, slice the avocado into thin slices (a quarter per person, approximately 3 slices each).

5. Once the fish is done, warm the tortillas by wrapping them in tinfoil and either sticking them on the grill or in the oven for 5 to 10 minutes.

6. Toss the slaw a bit and make sure the cabbage is marinating in the acid of the lime juice; taste it to make sure it is seasoned correctly.

7. Put the cilantro crema in a basic dressing bottle that you can get almost anywhere (make sure it is squeezable). If you don't have one, put the crema into a little Ziploc bag, cut off the tip of one corner, and you have yourself a perfect piping bag.

8. Assembly time! Start with a warm tortilla, add ⅓ to ¼ of the fish fillet, top with some slaw and a piece of avocado. Then drizzle on the cilantro creme and sriracha (if you like things hot), and finish with just a little crumble of feta or queso fresco.

20 after the bomb

Sophia rode to work in her short-term-leased Ford Escape. She was superstitious about buying a car until she knew *The Den*'s fate. If she jumped the gun, and bought one now, surely the show would tank. The morning and evening rides gave her time to pull herself together before she had to act. At night, she acted to Demi like she was tired and stressed out, which was true. During the day, she acted for her costars, director, and the showrunner. No one would question that she was thrilled-beyond-thrilled to be part of the show, which she was, and the complete opposite of a diva/troublemaker/needy starlet. Her goal was to be easy and to give one hundred percent every day. She transmitted confidence. She was a positive force on set.

Inside her own head, it was like a bomb went off, and she was trying to piece herself back together.

The roofie maybe-rape was three weeks ago. Scott had told her to forget about it. But Sophia had been obsessed with remembering what happened. No matter how hard she tried, her mind turned to wool. She'd figured out who the actor at the bar was: Brody Reno, the star of a short-lived sitcom about an airplane pilot and his family called *What's Up?* Brody played the stud-muffin teenage son. Sophia only knew about the show because her brother watched it in high school to make fun of it. Reno's IMDB filmography began there and continued to limp along with bit parts on TV and in indie movies. She couldn't prove that Brody had drugged the shot he gave her, although it was likely. Whatever his role, he wasn't the guy she woke up with, but he was the only person who could shed light on her dark hours. She searched Brody's public pages for his friend's identity, but came up empty.

Not knowing tormented Sophia. If she'd gotten drunk and hooked up with a stranger, she'd regret it in the morning, but that would have been her choice, her mistake. What happened at the Supperclub had put her fate into someone else's hands without her knowledge or consent. She used to think being groped at CRUSH was dehumanizing. That was a cakewalk compared to this.

Every day for three weeks, she thought about calling Renee. She might have seen something. Sophia was pretty sure Renee and Brody made out that night. Maybe she could get in touch with him. Sophia held off on calling, though, waiting to see if she'd get over it and stop obsessing. Even in her current mental state, Sophia was still a cocky optimist.

But that Monday on the ride to work, she broke down and made the call.

Renee answered. "You're calling me," she said. "I'm so flattered."

Not a good start. "How's it going? What have you been up to?"

"Is it about a job?"

From the tone of her voice, Sophia got the idea that, unless it were about a job, Renee might hang up. So she lied. "I heard something. A movie. I'm giving the producer your name."

"That's awesome! Tell me about it. What's the title?"

"I can't say anything yet. I'll let you know when I have more info."

"Cool. Thanks! I have to say, I'm surprised. Last time I saw you, you were kind of a bitch to me."

Sophia's heart leapt to her throat. "About that night. I can't really remember what happened."

"You were *wasted*," said Renee. "Like, falling down drunk. Not a good look on you—on anyone, but especially you. You told those guys that I was the national spokesperson for 'old man erections.' It wasn't funny for the first ten times you said it, and really fucking annoying the next ten times."

"Sorry," said Sophia. "I wanted to ask you, did you talk to the guy with the beard? Brown hair, big teeth?"

"You mean the guy you were humping against the bar?"

Oh, god. "I think someone might've put a roofie in my drink. I drank the wine you gave me, and did a couple shots, and then everything went blank."

Renee paused. "Are you accusing me of drugging you?"

"No!" The thought had crossed Sophia's mind, as far-fetched as it might be.

"Jesus Christ. For the last time, Sophia, fuck you."

Renee hung up. Another dead end. It was possible she'd never know what happened to her that night. The private horror of wondering wasn't going away. Sophia lost it for a few minutes. (Thank god for LA traffic.) When she pulled into the studio, she had a tenuous grip on her emotions.

They were shooting episode 102 today. The premise: a female college professor is sexually assaulted by a male student, a football player. Valerie had an emotional scene to shoot, a flashback to when she was in college, and her boyfriend accused her of being a cheater.

So, yeah, Sophia had to deal with that today, a scene of begging someone to forgive her for making a bad mistake.

"Cut," said Henry Chapman, the episode director. "Sophia, more desperation. The love of your life is leaving you. Let's do it again. Action."

Sophia as Valerie was seated at the foot of her bed. Her "boy-friend" was standing with one hand on the doorknob. He said, "You did this. You ruined everything."

Her line: "I messed up. You have to give me another chance."

On the page, the line wasn't that exciting. But a great actor could turn it into a wrenching moment. Her character was full of regret and guilt, in abject terror of losing this man. Since regret, guilt, and fear had been dominating Sophia's thoughts, it wasn't difficult to bring those emotions into her eyes, her voice, and her body language.

Then she got off the bed, and rushed to him. "Please stay," she said, grabbing his wrist and pulling his hand away from the door-knob.

In her heart, she was begging for relief from very real pain. Her scene partner seemed taken aback by it, and spontaneously took Sophia's hands in his and said, "It's okay. It's okay. I'll stay."

She said, "Thank you."

"Cut!" yelled the director. "That was *incredible*, Sophia!" said Henry. The crew standing around the set applauded. "I really felt that. Great work. We need to do it again for a close-up, okay?"

She wiped her tears and nodded. "Yes. I'm good to go."

"Pick it up with 'Please stay.' Action."

Sophia channeled her emotions into the second take, and the third, and kept going until the scene was done. She played it cool all the way into her dressing room, running a gauntlet of applause and congratulations from the cast and crew along the way. As soon as she was alone, she crumbled.

When her tears subsided, she drew a few deep breaths, and put her legs up against the wall, an inversion pose from yoga that al-ways calmed her down.

"You got this," she said. It might take time to work through it. But, as the saying goes, *You're only given what you can handle*. She would handle this.

Part of her knew she shouldn't handle it alone. She had to tell someone. Another part superstitiously refused to open up. If Sophia kept the secret inside her, she'd be a better actor. Look at how Henry reacted to her scene. The crew applauded. She was proving herself to be worthy of the show. She'd turn acting into therapy, and therapy into art. Her scenes would be like a valve on a pressure cooker, letting off steam, releasing emotion, a bit at a time.

When Cassie and Paula asked her out for a drink that night, she thought, *If I were okay, I would go.* So she went. They suggested the Supperclub, and she thought, *If I had a great time there before, which I told them I did, I would love to go there.* So she agreed. A casual observer would have seen three women at the bar, having a blast, laughing. It was exhausting for Sophia to keep her smile painted on.

She was half asleep when she got home to Rosewood Mews. Pretending everything was fine was exhausting. If she could only remember the details, maybe she could one day forget them. She walked through the courtyard. The light was on in their apartment. Demi was home and awake. Sophia was in no mood to talk to her about her day, or listen to Demi's stories.

"Sophia, hold up," said David. He emerged from his apartment just as she walked by it. Had he been watching and waiting for her to get home?

There was no way she could deal with him now. "I've got a splitting headache. I'll talk to you tomorrow."

"One second."

"What?" she snapped.

"I just want to know what I did wrong."

"Nothing."

"Then why are you blowing me off?"

"I'm tired, David, okay? I'm working my ass off for twelve hours a day and when I finally get home, I just want to sleep. Why are you forcing me to tell you something's wrong with you? Look, just wait until the week's over. Don't take it personally. It's not you. But putting me on the spot doesn't make it easier."

He deflated before her eyes. "I was worried . . ."

"I'm fine. Really. I'm a big girl in big-girl pants."

Sophia ran up the stairs two at a time, and banged into her apartment to find Demi on the couch, a notebook on her lap and pen in her hands. "You're home," she said, stating the obvious, as she liked to do. It pissed her off, and gave her ammo. Usually, she'd come back at her, and they'd be bantering and laughing by now.

"I'm going to bed."

"I have news," she said. "Aiden is letting me develop the menu for Dory! It's like a dream I didn't know I had is coming true. I've always loved to cook, and I definitely have strong opinions about menus. But getting to conceptualize one from scratch, it's lighting up new parts of my brain."

"Is Aiden giving you more money for this?"

Demi looked down at her pad, away from Sophia's eyes. "We started to discuss it but we got sidetracked."

"Sidetracked, how?"

"You don't approve?"

"I'm sure Aiden is just awesome," said Sophia, finding any conversation excruciating after the day she'd had, but especially the subject of Demi's bad boyfriend choices. She could not be held responsible for whatever came out of her mouth. "He's an older man who holds all the power in the relationship. And you're falling right into line, turning him into some kind of hero savior who becomes the focus of your life. Sleeping with *your boss*, Demi? That's be a monumental mistake."

"Easy, tiger," said Demi, keeping it light. "He's not James, not even close."

"Well, if it all goes to shit, you can disappear into a bottle and wait for your friends and family to pull you back out."

Demi's face darkened. "Wow." It was all she could muster.

"Good night," said Sophia. She left the living room, and went directly into her room and locked the door.

Demi knocked on it, hard. "Open this door."

Sophia ignored her.

"We need to talk about all those tests in the trash and the way you've been acting. I know something happened. You have to talk to me. Open this fucking door."

The knocking and imploring continued for ten minutes, which felt like hours to Sophia. She just couldn't let Demi in. The door had to stay shut. If she opened up about her feelings and fears, it would be impossible to maintain any control of them. When Demi stopped knocking, the apartment became oppressively quiet. Sophia lay on her bed in savasana, palms up to receive gifts from the universe. She repeated her mantra, "You got this, you got this," until she stopped thinking at all.

STARS

can't shine

without

DARKNESS

21

a whipped cream emergency

It'd taken an hour in LA traffic to get from Harris's mansion in the Valley to Red O restaurant on Melrose Avenue. He sulked when she told him about her plans to have dinner with Sophia. He missed her terribly when they were apart, but for a couple of hours he'd just have to survive without her.

Red O turned out to be a Mexican restaurant where you felt like you're on vacation. A perfect place for cocktails with the girls. Inside, Leandra felt right at home. Everything, from the paint, seat covers, cushions, tablecloths, lighting, and fixtures, was gold. It was like walking into Fort Knox. The surfaces glittered. The light flattered her tanned skin, white-blond dye job, and rose gold jewelry. She caught her reflection in a gold-framed mirror and knew she had never looked sexier, as if her entire shopping and pampering life had been leading up to this moment.

Leandra followed the maître d', walking like she owned the place. Eyes followed her as she walked, as well they should. She kept her smile to herself, not sharing it with any of her admirers, just because.

She spotted Sophia in a cushioned booth table in front of a golden backlit bar with dozens of bottles of tequila. She could pick her out of any crowd, but her old friend jumped up and ran toward Leandra, wrapping her in a tight hug. "You made it!" Leandra melted into Sophia's arms. It'd been months since she'd had physical contact with a female and it felt great.

As exhilarating as it was to get a hug from Sophia, it was annoying to see Demi, also seated at their table. From the expression on Demi's face, she was just as surprised to see Leandra. Sophia had set them up, springing the reunion on them. Leandra put on her game face, which was as lacquered and placid as her basic bitch face. Demi, not nearly as skilled at hiding her emotions, looked like she could gnaw through her fork.

"You look amazing, Leandra," said Sophia. "Are those Louboutin boots?" Uh-huh and they retailed for $1,500, but price was of no concern for Harris.

"Hello, Demi," said Leandra, oozing charm and grace. "You look fab." She looked like a boy with her Fedora, T-shirt, and jeans. *If she was trying to make an antiglamour statement, it came through loud and queer,* thought Leandra.

Demi said, "You look great, like a real LA woman."

As usual with Demi, Leandra couldn't tell if she was being insulted. They air kissed politely. Sophia took a few pictures, capturing the all-too-awkward moment.

"My boyfriend got me this dress at the Gucci on Rodeo Drive. He's such a love." Leandra took her seat. "You'll never believe who did my hair. Ken Paves!"

"Who?" asked Demi.

"He cut Jessica Simpson's hair."

"Who?"

Leandra blinked. How could Demi not know . . . "You're fucking with me."

Demi smiled acidly. "Sorry. I can't help myself. It's like a mental disorder. I'm *compelled* to mock. Your hair looks good. Big and bouncy. You've got a lot more going on here than last time I saw you." Demi gestured to Leandra's exposed cleavage.

She was wearing rubber cutlets in her bra, just as a trial to see how she liked having bodacious hooters. Harris preferred a full rack, and even offered to pay for implants. "I thought they might like to get some air," she said, and arched her back.

Demi laughed. It seemed genuine. "It's nice to see them, and you."

"This is going well!" said Sophia. "I thought it'd be nice if we had a meal together. Okay? Weirdness over? Good. Now we can have some fun together, like old times."

Leandra smiled. Did Sophia really want to dig around in the past? What would be the point? They were adults with real lives, not kids in school with their petty grievances and jealousies. Leandra was too evolved and sophisticated to hold a grudge. She just didn't particularly like Demi. The feeling was mutual. But, if push came to shove, they'd stand up for each other. That was what old friends did.

"I can't believe I've been here for two weeks already and we haven't gotten together yet."

"I know. It's not like Toronto when we lived in each other's pockets."

"I've been so busy with Harris, going to dinners and parties. We had drinks last night with Jenna Jameson."

"The porn star?"

"She's very sweet in real life. Not a skank at all. She's thinking about doing a cameo in Harris's next movie."

"What's it about?"

"It's a love triangle. Passion, glamour, but deep emotion." That was the extent of what she knew of the project. Harris had been throwing tantrums about production costs and locations for weeks. Whenever he whined about his work, she tuned out. Truth be told, she was a tiny bit embarrassed by how upset he could get. His company made web originals, not *real* movies. How worked up could anyone get about some low-budget flick that went straight to pay-per-view? Leandra wasn't exactly sure how his indie movies could make as much money as they apparently did, judging by his house, cars, and credit card bills. Then again, Harris came from money, as he told her ten times a day.

Fresh out of names to drop, Leandra turned the conversation around to them. "How are you two doing as roomies?" she asked. In school, the three of them fantasized about getting their own house, with enough room for all of their boyfriends, even though only one of them, Sophia, was in love at the time. Now, only Sophia and Demi lived in an apartment somewhere, while Leandra lived with her love in a mansion. Life was so wonderfully unpredictable.

The two of them gazed down at their empty plates as if an appropriate and polite answer to her question could be found there. So being roomies wasn't a nonstop party? Something was definitely amiss. Leandra couldn't help relishing the tense moment.

Finally, Sophia said, "We're like family. We fight, and we make up."

Demi flagged down a waiter. "Can we order drinks, please?" she asked him. They each got a house margarita with Espolón Blanco tequila, and housemade limonade and scanned the menu. As usual, Leandra hunted for the most expensive item and ordered that. In this case, a ribeye steak with a lobster tail for $64. She got a few sides, too.

"Tell us about Harris! He sounds like a keeper," said Sophia.

Leandra described their trip through England, and his house in the Valley. "We have five bedrooms, a pool, a bowling alley, a tennis court. If you guys ever need to just get away from West Hollywood, come over anytime."

Demi was frowning, clearly holding back some obnoxious judgey comment.

"Something on your mind, Demi?" asked Leandra.

"Not a thing."

"I doubt that."

She paused, and then launched right in. "It's just that you told us where you and Harris went, what he buys you and how cool his house is. But you didn't say anything about *him*. His character."

His *character*? What did that even mean? "He's a very sweet, loving person, with deep respect for women."

"Good for him, and you."

"Are you guys seeing anyone?" asked Leandra.

Sophia interjected. "We're both focused on our careers right now."

O-kay. Sophia wanted to talk about her career, fine. "Tell me about your show!" said Leandra.

While she listened to Sophia describe *The Den*, Leandra made good eye contact. She nodded and laughed at the right moments. But she found it nearly impossible to concentrate on what Sophia was saying about the minutiae of her shooting schedule and the people she worked with. She was glad for her friend's success, but it made her uncomfortable by comparison. Sophia was a professional actor, and Leandra was . . . a professional girlfriend? A year ago, Sophia was struggling, and Leandra was the honors student. It was hard to keep her balance on the shifting platform of their friendship. Meanwhile, Demi quietly sipped her margarita and said nothing.

"It's overwhelming to keep all the balls in the air. I'm just trying to live in the moment," said Sophia. "Stay present."

"Me, too. My motto is Be Here Now," said Leandra, tuning back in, realizing she'd been here now for twenty minutes, and hadn't been in the moment for the entire time.

Demi laughed like she knew Leandra had pulled her motto out of her ass, and said, "My motto is 'Eat Here Now.'" Right on cue, the servers brought their food. Her steak looked and smelled scrumptious, but Leandra would limit herself to only several bites. She didn't want to get fat.

"Demi's opening a restaurant in Venice," said Sophia.

Then it was Demi's turn to blather about a job at some taco stand on a public beach, the kind of place Leandra wouldn't be caught dead in. Five minutes went by as she half listened to this drivel. Leandra tried several times to bring the conversation back to her glamorous life of travel, sex, romance, and adventure, but Demi intentionally blocked her, and dragged the discussion back to food and permits and loudmouthed Australians.

"I don't think the three of us have been in the same room since twelfth grade," said Sophia. "Remember the night we drove to English Bay Park and smoked a whole pack of cigarettes?"

"My lungs still ache," said Demi.

"We swore we'd follow our bliss, no matter what."

"I said I wanted a Wall Street or Capitol Hill husband," said Leandra. "I was so narrow-minded."

"Right. There're a whole wide world of douche bags out there," said Demi.

She didn't know the half of it. "I meant that I thought happiness would come from being taken care of. But I know now it's taking care of someone you love. If Harris lived in some apartment in West Hollywood, I'd still be with him."

"We live in an apartment in West Hollywood," said Demi, deadpan.

"I'm sure it's lovely," said Leandra.

Sophia said, "That night, I said I wanted to be an actor, and I'm doing it. The closer I get to bliss, though, the further away it seems. We've all been in constant motion since that night—different cities, apartments, jobs, relationships. It seems like we never stop moving, but where are we going? For what? Is there an endpoint, when you stop, look around, and say, 'Yup, this is bliss. Whew! Made it!'"

Leandra recited the line from a poster in her dorm at Holy Isle. "The search for bliss is inside ourselves."

"This enchilada is bringing me pretty close to bliss," said Demi.

"I'm serious, Demi," said Sophia.

"I think, that night, I said my bliss was finding a career I love doing, using my creativity and enjoying life," said Demi. "I took a long detour away from bliss in Vancouver, but I'm getting closer here, definitely, but I'm not sure bliss can ever be locked down. You might get there, and then wake up and realize bliss is somewhere else."

"I found my bliss in Harris," said Leandra. "He's adoring and smart, sexy, and deep! We're forever. It's permanent bliss with him."

Sophia said, "I can't wait to meet him."

Demi said, "He sounds like the total package."

Their praise felt genuine. Leandra basked in it. She'd earned it. After her wild journey across three continents, Leandra was reveling in the destination. She had no intention of leaving. "Just be patient, guys," she said. "One day I'm sure you'll be as happy as I am."

They polished off their plates—Leandra ate way more than she intended—and had another couple of margaritas each. By the end of the meal, they were laughing like the old friends they were, especially about the sagas of Charlie and Oliver (with minor edits to make Leandra look good). She held up her glass to make a toast. "To the girls we used to be, and the ballsy, sexy women we are now!"

They clinked and drank. Demi flashed a genuine smile at her, and Leandra remembered how tight they used to be. If it weren't for that one party, that one decision that Leandra had made for them, they'd probably still be BFFs.

Sophia's antennas were on high alert, sensing a thaw between Leandra and Demi. She smiled at them, back and forth, mentally willing them to kiss and make up. Was this what she hoped would happen tonight? Leandra was buzzed, and warmed by seeing old friends. So, sure, she'd bury the hatchet. Why not?

"We went our separate ways, but we wound up back together, here, living the dream. If James didn't cheat on you, Demi—not to bring up a touchy subject—you'd still be in Vancouver. And if Jesse and you stayed together, Sophia, you wouldn't have come to Toronto with me, or signed on with Agnes Chen, who heard about the audition for *The Den*. So it all worked out for the best. I'm *glad* we talked him into dumping you."

Sophia said, "You . . . *what?*"

"Shut up, Leandra," Demi warned. Man, she looked *pissed*.

At the time, they'd agreed to keep the secret, but it was the only thing they agreed on since that night. Demi was so drunk, she barely remembered what really happened; anyway, it was five years ago. The truth couldn't hurt Sophia now. She was way beyond that silly little high school fling. She might as well fill her in.

"You were having dinner with your parents or something, and didn't go to the big party at Maggie Rose's house," said Leandra. "Demi got wasted, almost passed out on the lawn, and I had to baby-sit her. Jesse was there, too. When you weren't around, Sophia, he wasn't very nice to us. He was kind of a prick, actually, like he was jealous of any time you spent with us. That boy was way too posses-sive. Anyway, he made some rude comment about Demi, like how could Sophia put up with her? That Demi would drag you down, would always be someone you had to carry through life. He was really letting it out, really gushing with hate, right, Demi? Oh, you don't even remember. Well, he was."

"What did you say to him?" asked Sophia, her voice flinty.

"I defended Demi, and our right to be in your life, and how creepy obsessed he was with you. I might've said a few other things."

"Like what?"

"That you felt suffocated by him and how you told us at the Bay that your bliss was to get as far away from him as possible. Demi slurred some other stuff, about how we made a pact to follow our bliss and help each other do the same, and that if there was only one thing Jesse could do, he should let you go to save his own dig-nity because he was just some pissant high school boyfriend, and you were going to be a star, and go out with rock gods and movie actors. And look at you now! You are becoming a star! Rock gods are next on the list."

"I'm sorry, Soph," Demi said, "I wanted to tell you, but . . ."

"I didn't. We discussed it, and eventually agreed that it was best if you didn't know what went down. If we told you we caused the breakup, you would have run back to him and dumped us. We made the decision that we were more important to you than he was. For your future. And this dinner tonight only confirms how right we were."

"You made the decision for me who was important in my life," said Sophia. She was smiling. Good! She understood.

Demi looked horrified at that smile. She said, "It just seemed cruel to tell you. You were crushed already. And if he'd leave you that easily he wasn't worthy. I might've rationalized from guilt. And I have felt terrible guilt for years about this."

Leandra remembered their heated arguments about the morality of manipulating other people's lives. Demi was then, probably still is, way too sensitive for her own good. She hadn't been toughened up by loss like Leandra. Easing Demi's guilt was just too onerous for Leandra to deal with. She refused to listen to it, which turned Demi's guilt into anger, and then antipathy. It was sealed when Leandra convinced Sophia to leave Vancouver behind after graduation, and start over again in Toronto with her.

Leandra's driver texted that he was outside the restaurant at their prearranged hour. "Oh, shit. Sorry to run, but my driver is illegally parked out front." She dropped $200 on the table and stood up. "You both look so upset! Don't be sad. We'll do this again very soon. It's so great to see you both. Kiss, kiss!"

She hugged them both and was a bit insulted Sophia didn't take more photos to document this wonderful clearing of the air between them. Leandra had finally gotten that pebble out of her shoe, metaphorically speaking, and could have skipped to the limo if it wouldn't make her look deranged. She sank into the leather seats and closed her eyes, a little drunk and warmed from the inside to have reconnected with old friends. Would they get together again, as promised? Who knows? They were childhood friends with little in common, moving at a rapid clip in different directions.

At least she knew that her love with Harris was real.

When Leandra got back to the mansion around ten P.M., it was overrun with girls. About half a dozen of them had been hanging out at the pool in thong bikinis all week. Harris was feeding them and letting them use the golf carts, the archery range, and the tanning beds. They swarmed the house, playing Grand Theft Auto VI in her living room at three in the morning, at full blast. But she put up with it.

They were actors. "If I don't keep them content and close," Harris explained, "they'd go suck balls for some other producer."

In Leandra's opinion, the girls lacked grace and intelligence. They weren't even that pretty. They did, however, have ridiculously perfect, smooth, and groomed bodies, like hairless Jessica Rabbits.

Cherri, a particularly vapid redhead, bounced over to Leandra in the kitchen, and asked in a baby voice, "Hi, Leah! Do you have whipped cream and chocolate sauce?"

"I don't eat sugar."

"Oh. I guess we'll have to order some."

They were addicted to calling Instacart to have random groceries like bananas and zucchini delivered at all hours. It cost a fortune! "Is it really a whipped cream emergency? It can't wait until morning?"

"We need it tonight!" she pouted.

Leandra ignored her, and went in search of Harris. She found him on the couch with Tammy, a short brunette with a tongue piercing. "Hey, babe," he said. "I was just telling Tammy about the time in high school me and my boy Cam cut school and destroyed my dad's Ferrari. Man, was he pissed!"

"That didn't happen to you, Harris," said Leandra. "It's the plot of *Ferris Bueller's Day Off.*"

"She's too smart for me," he said to Tammy. "But seriously, once, in high school, my parents went away for the weekend. I threw this huge party and the house got trashed!"

"I believe it," said Leandra. "It's also the plot of *Sixteen Candles,* but whatever." Sometimes Leandra wondered if every point of reference in Harris's childhood was a John Hughes movie. Did he really have a life, or spend his entire adolescence jerking off to the Molly Ringwald panties shot in *The Breakfast Club*? "Can we speak privately?" she asked.

Harris could tell Leandra meant business. So could the brunette, who jiggled out of the room. Leandra took her spot on the sofa. "I can't live like this. I had you to myself in England, and now we're surrounded by all these people." All these *girls.* "I want them gone." She wished Harris would act more like he had on their long drive—

romantic and worshipful. With her new perspective, his boyish-
ness had been evident on their travels. Pretending to do battle at
Hadrian's Wall. Insisting they wear Beatles wigs at the concert in
Liverpool and yelling, "Who goes there?" around every corner in
Stratford-upon-Avon.

He could still rattle her chandelier. But was that enough?

"The boys are on their way over with the equipment. I've had it
with Stirrup Studio. We're shooting the movie right here, at the house,
tonight. We're zoned for it. The whole county is zoned. I got the permit, so we're good to go," he said. "So after tonight, the girls are gone."

"I don't understand," she said. "How can you shoot a movie here?"

"We'll do it by the pool, in the cabanas, or right here, on this
couch." He got a text. "They're here. I'm going to help set up. Just chill
out for an hour. I'll text you when we're ready to roll."

This was absurd! Even a web original movie needed storyboards
and a scene schedule, right? Establishing shots? B-roll? What about
wardrobe and lighting? As far as she knew, they didn't have a final
script. She'd asked to read it, and Harris just laughed at her. An entire
story, with a beginning, middle, and end, all shot at the pool? At
night? It couldn't possibly work. But, then again, she wasn't an artist.
He'd made millions with this kind of impromptu problem solving.

She went upstairs to their bedroom, and took a quick shower.
Their king-size circular bed with the black satin sheets was neatly
made, thanks to the staff of maids who arrived every day at noon to
clean up after the "girls and boys," as Harris called his cast of female
and male actors. The "boys" were just as physically immaculate as
the "girls," with neatly hedged body hair and defined musculature.
All the actors were complete slobs. Empty bottles and ashtrays all
over the place, self-tanning spray smeared on the furniture.

One more night of this zoo, and then they'd be alone. The mov-
able feast would move on. Harris would turn off the Xbox, power
off the TV, shut down his computer, and stare at *her* for hours on
end. That was all she wanted, to be lavished with gifts, praise, and
sexual attention. She could wait a few more hours for that.

She put on the Versace outfit Harris had picked out for her, a black corset dress, with black patent leather super high heels, and went down to see movie magic in the making.

She exited the rear doors of the mansion to the pool. Sure enough, silver umbrellas and lights were set up around the chaise lounges where Leandra had sunbathed that very morning. She felt a rush of excitement. Her house was going to be in a movie! She couldn't see what was going on yet; the umbrellas blocked her view. She walked closer as quietly as she could.

Harris and a dozen other people were watching the scene, including a handful of the girls and boys, and some older men who were Harris's business partners. To be honest, when she thought of her future husband's partners, she envisioned Christian Greys, rainmakers in $10,000 suits. She didn't picture rotund middle-aged doofuses in Hawaiian shirts, sweatpants, and fat cigars.

"Action!" said Harris, just as she got close enough to see what was going on.

On one lounge, bikini'ed Cherri and Tammy rubbed coconut oil on each other's bodies.

Leandra's jaw hit the patio.

She watched in stunned silence as the emotionally deep love triangle plot unfolded. First, Cherri and Tammy did each other. Then Peter did Tammy. Then Peter did Cherri. Then the three did one another. Then Eric the Redwood entered the frame. He and Peter did Cherri while Tammy . . . Leandra wasn't sure what she was doing.

So it wasn't really a love triangle after all. It was a love erect-angle.

Of course, it was only too obvious in hindsight. Why did this always happen to her? Leandra willfully ignored the clues when they were splayed out in front of her, sort of like Cherri's body was right now on the chaise.

The love of her life was a pornographer.

The future father of her children made two-hankie spankies for fapsters.

This was a lot worse than being tucked away and forced to cook in Charlie's Bangkok house, or eating bark while counting backwards from one thousand on Holy Isle with Oliver.

She had to look away when Greta Gagglo joined in. Too many swinging body parts. The moaning intensified. Leandra worried the furniture might break.

Harris said, "On the face! On the face! Great, Eric. Nice, Greta. Okay, everyone. Cut."

The crew rushed in to give the actors water and towels. Harris's investment partners put their heads together to discuss the scene and blow smoke at each other. Harris came over to Leandra, and asked, "So? You like? I thought it was too much coconut oil, but our audience loves it when we edit in wet, slapping, sucking sounds."

She wanted to say, "You let those people sit on my couch," but instead, she said, "The lighting was good."

"You really like it?" he asked. His eyes sought her approval, like a child from his mommy.

"Very artistic," she said. "Taut dramatic tension."

"You know, babe, you're hotter than any of the girls."

Leandra kissed his cheek. "Thanks, hon."

She went back into the house, up to her room, and curled into a fetal ball on the bed (that had probably been used for a fivesome) to examine her feelings. The worst part was realizing that Harris thought she knew what he did all along, and that she approved. He hid nothing from her.

Earlier tonight, Sophia asked the question, for all their frantic movements, do they like what they were moving toward? Well, sometimes you moved frantically to get away from what you didn't like. Leandra was going to move out of this sleaze factory as soon as possible. She let loose one ragged sob, but that was all she could spare.

Think practically, she admonished herself. In order to get away from Harris and his coconut-oiled minions (meanwhile, why coconut?), she had to line up her next boyfriend. No blinders next time! She wouldn't idealize a scumbag! She was learning. This was good.

Or, as a gritty alternative, she could throw some clothes into a suitcase and go to Sophia and Demi's apartment. She could sleep on their couch, find herself a job, eat Demi's food, drink cheap wine, and date a man her own age who was also in the process of becoming. She could have the typical life of a normal twenty-one-year-old recent college graduate. How bad would it be to leave luxury and laziness behind and work toward making a positive contribution to society? The more she thought about it, the more she liked the idea. She'd wear jeans from Levi's and get her hair trimmed at Supercuts. There was a comfort to being a commoner. Look at Demi. She was chopping vegetables and cleaning fish for a living. It didn't get lower than that. Perhaps stepping down from the grandstand, figuratively, would be a relief. For a while now, Leandra had been thinking about her next adventure, the next man, where her next filet mignon was coming from. No wonder she couldn't live in the moment.

Leandra vowed to stay in the moment exclusively, starting . . . *now*.

She also made a mental note to have the maids scrub the pool chaises with bleach.

there is no

ELEVATOR

to success.

you have
to take the

STAIRS.

22 shining the knob

Demi and Sophia didn't speak for the entire ride back to their apartment. Sophia just kept that smile on, which Demi knew meant only one thing: She was furious. As well she should be! They'd caused the greatest love of her life to end, and then kept her in the dark about it for years. Demi couldn't count high enough the number of times Sophia had cried and asked, "Why did he do it?"

Well, now she knew.

They got to the apartment. Sophia charged into her room and slammed her door. Demi was prepared to slink off to her room, but Sophia came charging back out.

"How could you do that to me?"

288 SHAY MITCHELL & MICHAELA BLANEY

"I'm sorry! I was drunk and Leandra always seems so sure of herself."

"What? Are we talking about the same person? She doesn't have any idea who she is or what she's doing! Come on, Demi! You were her best friend for years."

Demi was confused. What now? Were they talking about how much she screwed up, or were they talking about Leandra? "About Jesse . . ."

"Fuck, Jesse! This isn't about him."

"What is it about?"

"It's about us. Me and you and Leandra. You lied to me, and you let her manipulate you. She screwed up with Jesse. Sounds like that situation got out of control. But she knew what she was doing with you."

"She bullied me into it."

"Bullshit! Leandra only messes with people who let her get away with it."

Demi shook her head. "And you let her get away with it! I know she's funny and she was there for you in Toronto. But she's a user. Those stories about the guys she dumped? That was brutal."

"You just don't get her at all."

"Then explain."

"Leandra is damaged. She's like half a person."

Demi sighed. "Stacy died eleven years ago."

"That doesn't matter. She is who she is because of it. Leandra operates on pure survival instinct, like an animal. If she feels threatened, she lashes out. If she feels unsure of herself, she adapts to fit in. You see her as phony and think her stories are self-serving. I hear them all as the desperate acts of a lonely woman."

Loneliness radiated from Sophia. Unlike Leandra, who didn't know how to connect, Sophia was deliberately disconnecting herself from the people who would make her feel less alone in the world. She'd been avoiding Demi for weeks, barely responding to texts. She flicked David out of her life like a fly on the butter.

"So you're not mad about Jesse," said Demi.

"Who gives a fuck about Jesse?" screamed Sophia.

"You are mad about Leandra?"

"I feel sorry for her."

Demi inhaled. That left only one person. "You are mad at me."

"Living together hasn't worked out the way I thought it would."

Oh, great. Now Demi was going to have to move? "Fuck you," she said. "I'm trying as hard as I can to reach you, but you won't talk. Fine! If you don't tell me what's going on, I'm leaving."

"Fine!"

Demi charged at the front door, opened it, ran through and slammed it. Realizing, at once, that she didn't have her purse, or shoes, or keys. She wouldn't get far. Tentatively, she knocked on the door. Sophia threw it open.

"What?"

"I forgot my shoes."

Then they started laughing, hysterically, landing on the couch in the living room. It was a huge relief, incredibly, the first belly laugh session they'd had in weeks. When Demi could catch her breath, she said, "We really need to talk."

Sophia nodded. "Okay."

"Is someone at the show harassing you?" Since the home test bonanza, Demi assumed there was a man in Sophia's life, but she had no idea who. "It's not David, is it?"

Sophia waved that way. "Not David. No one at work." She made eye contact with Demi, and said, "Six weeks ago, a guy at a bar drugged my drink and I woke up in some bed with no memory of what happened."

"After the First Night party," said Demi.

"I couldn't tell you. I couldn't tell anyone. I know I took my anger out on you, and I haven't been a good roommate or friend. I'm sorry."

"Jesus, you were dealing with this by yourself, all this time? No wonder you were depresso. Did you go to the police? We have to report this."

"No," she said. "I can't do that with the show about to premiere.

There's no way to prove anyone's guilt. I don't even know what happened. Maybe if I went to the police right after, but I didn't. I went to work."

"I'm so sorry that happened to you."

"Me, too."

"Do you know who he is?"

"I've tried to figure it out, but I can't."

Demi drew Sophia into a hug. She was shocked by the news, and even more shocked that Sophia tried to bury it. Leandra was proof of that. She tried to bury her feelings about her sister, and look what happened. There was no burying something like this. "I could have helped you," Demi said.

"How?"

"Just sitting here like this."

Sophia said, "You would have flown into a rage, and tried to find the guy and kill him. You would have made me take you to his house."

"So you know where he lives," said Demi. "What was that address?"

They laughed ruefully. Sophia said, "I just focused on work to get through the worst of it. The weight was heavy, but it didn't crush me."

"I could have taken some of it off you," said Demi.

"I get that now," said Sophia. "I feel lighter already. But you were doing well with the restaurant. I didn't want to put my problems on you. But, yeah, I see that it would have been better for both of us if I told you right away."

"I'm grateful to know the truth, whenever you're ready to share it," said Demi. "I'm guilty of trying to bury some secrets, too. I should have told you about Jesse the very next day, and about my DUI. But I needed to hide in a hole for a while and process it before I could stand to hear anything from anyone, even you. I already blamed myself, and felt horrible enough."

Sophia nodded. "I blamed myself about the roofie night. It was irrational, but that's how it was. That was another layer. I'd yelled at you about the drinking. I was doing shots that night. I felt like a hypocrite."

"Not the same."

"I know," said Sophia. "I wasn't thinking clearly for a while there. I needed to hide in a hole, too."

"In the future, let's honor each other's holes. Which sounds perverted, I know. We'll honor the holes, and pull each other out of them."

They sat on the couch like that for hours, Sophia telling Demi everything since the roofie night, the morning after, doing all those tests, the incredible relief to be clean, the challenge of filming scenes while so upset, how she poured her emotion into her performance. "It helped," she said. "This helps. I feel a lot better."

"Is there anything else you're not telling me?"

"That's it. What about you?" asked Sophia.

"I'm sleeping with my boss."

Sophia laughed. "I assumed."

"But it's only good. If anything gets weird, I'll tell you."

Demi and Aiden had fallen into a rhythm. When she got to work, they fooled around in the kitchen. When Carole, the newly hired chef, and her staff arrived, they chased each other around his office. When everyone else had gone for the night, they did it in the dining area.

"That's all you need to survive," he said. "Three hots a day."

Their fling *was* red hot and hilarious. She'd never laughed so much during sex before. Demi remembered that old adage from Woody Allen, that sex and comedy didn't mix. Wrong. With Aiden, it was another kind of release, from the core, a deep explosion of emotion that worked on Demi like good medicine.

During downtime, they'd disappear into his office and go, as the Aussie's put it, "up to the guts with nuts." They also cooked for each other, filling the restaurant with aromas and their mouths with flavor and textures. It was the most sensual relationship of her life. He engaged all of her senses—touch, hearing, smell, sight, taste—deliciously.

He seemed to like her a lot, too. A foodie with an oral fixation,

Aiden loved to kiss, deep soul passion that left Demi gasping. James, on the other hand, hardly ever kissed her mouth. He kissed other parts plenty, but she understood now that it'd been to make him feel like a master, not necessarily for Demi's sake.

Demi couldn't help comparing her ex with her boss. For the most part, she came up with dissimilarities. The only aspect of the two relationships to worry about: Demi's world revolved around Aiden. In the beginning, any new relationship swelled up and pushed everything else away. The phenomenon wasn't unique to Demi's, although it was her pattern to go to extremes.

She was ever hopeful that it was possible to fall for a man without losing herself. The trick, she decided, was to establish firm boundaries. She and Aiden didn't see each other outside the restaurant—by mutual consent. A couple of times, she asked him to come along on her daily lunchtime beach walk, but he chose to stay behind in his office to catch up on phone calls and emails.

Demi used her alone time to do the daily spot check on her life. She was going places, and not only on foot. After a long and annoying process of sitting through a class, and taking a written and a road test, Demi was the proud owner of a brand-new California driver's license. If she had a car, her life would be complete. Her salary was decent, but Ubering and the California lifestyle was expensive.

"I'm going for my walk," Demi said to Aiden. They'd just finished a meeting about the soft open with Carole. It was only a week away and the preparations were chugging along.

He said, "I'll be here."

Instead of going out the back to the beach, Demi snuck into Aiden's office and hid in the closet. Her plan was to jump out, naked, while he was on the phone, and surprise him. She quickly shed her shirt and shorts, bra and undies. Through a crack in the door, she watched him sit behind his desk and turn on his computer. Her perspective was of his back, the screen visible over his shoulder. He tapped away on the keys. The screen turned blue and she heard the sound of a dial tone and a phone ringing. He was Skyping? Okay, she couldn't burst out naked now. The person on the other end would see her.

"Hallo?" A woman's face appeared on the monitor, a pretty blonde around thirty.

"Morning, Sheila," he said.

"Can't talk long today," she said. "I'm running late. The transfer came through, so I paid off the contractor. But the washing machine delivery didn't happen. I spent all afternoon on the phone dealing with it . . ." She kept going, the details of life flowed uninterrupted. Aiden just sat and nodded.

A knock on the door. Carole poked her head in. "Boss? Can you come into the kitchen for a minute? I want you to taste the crab fritter."

"Two seconds." To Sheila onscreen, he said, "Got to go. Send the delivery guy's email address. I'll try you later, if I can. Otherwise, tomorrow. Love you." He made kissing noises. The woman kissed back. He ended the call, got out of his chair, and left the office.

Demi redressed quickly, crept out of the office, and onto the beach without anyone seeing her. Instead of doing her regular stroll, she doubled back to the boardwalk, and went into the nearest bar. She ordered a vodka on the rocks, and sucked it down in one gulp.

The last time she'd done the "Surprise! I'm naked!" ploy was when she found James with that Slavic bimbo. She had learned he was a cheater, and life as she knew it was over. This time, in a twist of fate, she discovered that *she* was a cheater. You could argue that she had no idea that Aiden was married or whatever he and Sheila were, and that he alone was the cheater. But not knowing didn't make it right. Ignorance wasn't absolution. Every lunch hour when she took her walk, he'd been Skyping with Sheila. Afternoon in Los Angeles was early morning tomorrow in Sydney. Aiden was an electronic presence at breakfast back home. If she weren't sleeping with him, she'd think that was sweet.

As close as they'd become, Demi didn't know much about Aiden. Her own fault. She didn't ask. She had the idea that he came as he was, without the encumberance of a past. He must have liked it, too, and didn't ask about hers either. Assumptions had been made on both their parts.

She ordered another drink. Sophia nailed it when she said, "If it doesn't work out with Aiden, you can crawl into a bottle." Sophia's remark was mean, and prescient. It was a reflex for Demi to reach for a drink to numb the pain. Aiden never got around to giving her a raise for developing the menu. In the end, Carole had changed most of it anyway. Had he flattered her and made her feel important just to get at her "joot"" (his word for it)?

She texted Sophia. "Can you talk?" No reply for ten minutes. She was on set. Since their confessional night, it was like the light behind Sophia's eyes when she looked at Demi was switched back on. That was a relief for them both. They couldn't change what happened to Sophia, but they could talk about it now, and had been every night for days. It seemed to help immeasurably.

Demi would have to tell her about Aiden's wife, girlfriend, whatever, and soon. But right now, she had to talk to someone else. She called Catherine. "I messed up," she said when her new old friend answered. They'd been checking in about once a week, so Catherine knew all about Aiden. Demi filled her in on the latest development.

"He's in love with someone else," she said. "So what?"

"That doesn't bother you?"

"Nope."

"I'm repeating patterns. From one cheater to the next," said Demi. "I thought things were changing for me, but they're exactly the same. I'm a fucking idiot."

"Where are you now? Are you drinking?"

"No."

"*That's* the dangerous pattern," said Catherine. "You're reacting the same way, the easy way. Did you think this through, really consider your options, or did you run right to a bar?"

"What's there to think through?"

Catherine said, "Do you like this man? Does he make you happy? Are you having fun at the restaurant? Can Aiden help you with your career, which, I can assure you, will last longer and be more important in the long run than any man? Aiden has been a huge positive in your life. You chose a winner this time, Demi. He's good for you. His being a cheater *protects* you. It's like protective covering for your heart."

Demi started to understand what Catherine meant. She'd been trying not to repeat the mistake of folding herself into Aiden's life, like she'd done with James. When she saw Sheila's face on the screen, a chemical chain reaction swept through her brain cells and reconfigured them. She'd initially felt betrayed and angry. But Demi had the ability, the hard-won self-awareness, not to fall back on easy emotions, but instead find inner strength. How can any situation work to my advantage? How to turn this negative into a positive?

"Do you get it?" asked Catherine.

"Aiden is safe," said Demi. "His being married or whatever makes him safe." There was no way she could fall in love with him now. And no chance of losing herself in an obsessive relationship. If she chose it, she could be free of fear, judgment, and ego. It was all gone. Demi could remove expectation from her reality. She'd just exist in the moment, enjoy it, or not, and float. No judgments, no pressure, no thoughts about a future together. Just fun, food, sex, and success. This could be the ideal situation for her.

"Are you too drunk to go back to work?"

"Maybe."

"Go anyway," said Catherine.

Demi left her third drink on the bar, and returned to Dory. She found Carole and Aiden in the kitchen, pulling apart the fritters and discussing ardently whether to put them on the menu or not.

"Taste this," he said, shoving the fried nugget at her.

Demi tried it, and loved it. "These hotcakes will sell like hotcakes."

"Are you sure?" he asked.

There wasn't a trace of mirth in his eyes now. No funny business about the business. He had a wife back in Sydney to support, so every decision about Dory was serious. If Aiden didn't value her opinion and her work, she wouldn't be here.

"I'm sure," she said. "But I worry about the oyster stew."

"Really?" asked Carole. "You never said anything before."

"I'm saying it now."

Aiden, Demi, and Carole spent the rest of the afternoon going over the menu item by item, tearing it apart. Maybe her two and a half cocktails freed her to speak her mind. Or maybe it was the revelation, thanks to her secret sage Catherine, that the only person Demi could cheat on was herself. The only way she'd do that was by discounting her worth. Alcohol was tied up in it, but Demi's most dangerous addiction was self-doubt. Her worst enemy was anxiety. She was going to take those traits off the menu.

If you want to make

your dreams come true,

you have to **WAKE UP**.

23

karma doesn't forget

The wrap party at the Abbey in West Hollywood might be a farewell party. The first five episodes were done. The first episode might not air for months. Despite the uncertainty, everyone was in a good mood, including Sophia. She knew how to dress this time, in a flirty cocktail dress from Alice + Olivia embellished with colored beads, and super-high Jimmy Choos she had gotten on sale.

Julie Chapman had to yell over the music, and her voice was getting hoarse. She thanked every member of *The Den*'s crew, from wardrobe to lighting, by name. Sophia hung back in the crowd with Demi (solo; Aiden was working straight until the opening), David, Leandra, and Harris (who was not at all what Sophia expected), and waited for Julie to single her out.

"And now, our incomparable cast! Paula Rosa, where are you? Get over here," said Julie. "Our grisly veteran." That made everyone laugh. Paula looked like she was eighteen. "Your leadership and creativity—"

"She's hot," said Harris. "Does she do any extracurricular work? I'm casting a big production right now called *Back Door Bitc*—"

"Not now, Harris!" said Leandra, too loud. "This is Sophia's night."

Gracious of Leandra to say. Only a minute ago, she'd asked Sophia, "What's the name of your show again?" Sophia just had to laugh at Leandra. No matter how selfish, she knew Leandra loved her and would fight for her. She already had, albeit in a misguided way.

Julie yelled, "Cassie Lambert, your turn!" Cassie looked like a goddess tonight in a white drapey dress. "Our local girl. Cassie's input, especially about the LA private school world, was invaluable—"

Demi whispered in Sophia's ear, "David told me he's shocked you invited him."

"I owe him an apology," she said. "Might as well do it here, in public, in front of everyone I know. Just to keep it intimate." Since Sophia pretty much accused him of semi-stalking, David backed off completely. When she did run into him, he waved, but kept his distance. In the last week or so, she wished he'd be less cautious, and talk to her again. If he did, she'd make sure to thank him for being a concerned friend, and to say she was sorry to cut him off at the knees.

Sophia glanced at David. He was drinking a beer from a bottle and talking to Harris. More like Harris was talking David's ear off about his screenplay idea, and David was patiently listening. Sophia liked how he hooked his thumb into the waist of his jeans. An inch of his tan, taut belly showed. Just then, David looked at her, and smiled. It gave her the melts. Sophia smiled back, and took a step toward him.

"Sophia Marcus!" called out Julie.

"You're on," said Demi. "Walk like a star."

Sophia cut through the crowd to join her boss and costars by the bar. It wasn't exactly like walking up the aisle at the Dorothy Chandler Pavilion to receive an Academy Award, but it was good practice.

It'd been eight weeks since the First Night party. Every home test that could be taken had come up negative, including the ones she had to mail in. She'd gotten her period twice, which, despite taking a dozen pregnancy tests, was a huge relief. By now, she'd gotten used to the idea that a complete stranger knew things about her she didn't. And, more important, would he, could he, reveal what he knew to others? She'd been out of it. He was a guy, therefore, he *must* have taken dozens of pictures of her doing just about anything. If the show was a hit, he could sell the images to the media. A night she didn't even remember could destroy her career before it even got off the ground.

"There she is," said Julie. She positioned Sophia between Paula and Cassie. "Our secret weapon. I'm going to let you all in on a little secret. We weren't sure about Sophia for *The Den*. Her audition and test were excellent. She's obviously gorgeous and talented. For the show's first iteration, she was a good fit. But when we shifted to a dramatic format, Henry and I had a few doubts. We didn't know if Sophia had the depth to handle the material. Well, from her first big scene, we knew she was something special. Sophia is the emotional anchor of the entire show. I'm just so proud of her."

Sophia was flattered, touched—and a bit horrified. They had doubts about her? Julie said, "her first big scene." Did she mean the "Please stay" scene? It had been a turning point for Sophia as an actor. She'd used her unspeakable experience to tap into the depth of emotion Julie was referring to. After that, Sophia knew how to turn it on whenever she had something powerful to express.

As her colleagues and friends applauded her, Sophia took a super low, jokey bow and flashed a big beautiful smile. No one had any idea what she was really thinking: The maybe-rape might have saved her career. It disgusted her that the worst experience of her life had a silver lining, even though she'd initially tried hard to find one. Sophia would untangle this emotional knot at some point, but not now. Tonight was a celebration. She'd spun misery into gold, by sheer force of will, completely on her own. *Yeah, I'm a badass*, she thought to herself.

Julie said, "Thank you, thank you, thank you, everyone! Henry and I are so excited about *The Den*. The network loves what they've seen. Hold on to your hats, people! We have an airdate! Episode 101 will have its world premiere at nine P.M. next Tuesday!" Gasps from the crowd. "The marketing blitz starts tonight!"

Paula and Cassie started jumping up and down. They squeezed her into a three-headed hug. Sophia wasn't quite sure why Tuesday at nine P.M. was such a cause for excitement, but she went with it.

After the crowd simmered down, Julie said, "Congratulations to everyone again. Enjoy the party! Enjoy your hiatus. It might be short."

"She said 'hiatus,'" said Cassie. "Hiatus implies temporary."

"What's she going to say? Enjoy unemployment?" replied Paula.

Sophia asked, "When will we know?"

"If the show gets decent numbers next Tuesday, we could be back at work on Wednesday," said Paula.

"I don't want this to end," said Sophia. It'd been kind of a blur, meeting everyone, shooting, the pressure of bringing it, struggling to hold it together. If/when the show started shooting again, she'd be more relaxed, more open to getting to know Cassie and Paula. Now that she thought about it, they'd all been holding back on a personal, protective level. The Hollywood way? Sophia was learning every day on this job. The only emotion she felt right now was gratitude. "Thanks, you guys," she said.

"For what?" asked Paula.

"I don't really know."

Cassie laughed. "I feel the same way! Thanks for whatever."

"We're only just getting started," said Paula. "More of everything good is to come!"

More of everything good. Sophia loved the sound of that. A moment later, Cassie's parents appeared, congratulating them all. Paula's boyfriend swept her up and carried her like Tarzan. Sophia wasn't alone for long. Demi and Leandra were suddenly there, hugging her, kissing her, making her feel loved. She hugged her old friends as tight as she could, letting happiness flow in.

Demi said, "You're strangling me."

"You're going to be a star," said Leandra.

"Knock wood," said Sophia. "Right now. Do it!"

Leandra rapped her head, and said, "Ouch. My ring!" Demi and Sophia snorted and laughed as Leandra untangled her absurdly large cocktail ring from her absurdly big hair. Even if the show tanked, she had this moment. This memory would be crystal clear, and locked for life.

David took his turn hugging Sophia. "Your showrunner just called you her secret weapon," he said. "If I were you, I'd ask for a raise."

"I'm glad you're here," she said. "I've been such a bitch to you."

"Enough of that," he said. "You don't have to apologize."

"I do," she said. "I'll explain it all one day. But for now, I'm sorry and I miss you." She leaned half an inch toward him, and he closed the distance in a heartbeat, kissing her decisively but not possessively, strong and gentle. She'd been afraid to kiss him or anyone; afraid she'd been turned off to sex entirely. But David felt familiar, safe and warm, like bread from the oven or her own bed. She sank into the kiss, putting her arms around him, and leaning into his lean body.

Harris said, "Wow! You guys are hot! I need video."

"Don't. You. *DARE*," said Leandra, spitting fire at him, reminding Sophia why it was great to have Leandra in her corner.

David said, "Much as I appreciate making up, I have to warn you. We're rivals now. *Sex & Murder: LA* airs on Tuesdays at nine."

No wonder everyone was freaking out. The network had a lot of confidence in *The Den* to put it up against the longest-running drama in TV history. It was the setup for a huge success or a dismal failure.

David must have been reading her mind. "TV is no place for weak tits. And I mean that in so many ways. I wish I didn't have to go, but I'm meeting some people in the Hills."

"Will you be home later tonight?"

"Definitely," he said.

"I'll see you then." Sophia kissed him good-bye, just a quickie, the promise of more of everything to come. He touched his lips, and left.

Harris said, "Sophia, I might have an opportunity for you during your hiatus. I run a website called TV T&A. Check it out, tvt&a.com. If you're into it, we can take some bikini shots, help get you advanced publicity for your show."

"He's joking!" said Leandra, fake laughing. "Harris, stop. Seriously. *STOP.*"

Demi was already typing tvt&a.com into her phone, and said, "Whoa! I'm not sure you want to T up your A for this one, Sophia." She showed her the screen with images of topless and bottomless actors.

Sophia zeroed in on one photo, of a bearded man in this birthday suit on a beach. "Harris, who is that guy?"

"That's Jared Greco. He was on a survivalist reality show called *Nude and Stupid* where they send you into the woods, bare-assed, with a lighter, a piece of string, and a bar of chocolate."

"Do you know him?" she asked.

"No, but he's right over there. I can go get him for you if you want to meet him."

Sophia looked where Harris was pointing. Right there, over at the bar in a group of model boys, stood Sophia's maybe rapist. Her blood turned to sludge. Brody Reno, the guy she suspected of drugging her, was also with him.

"You know him?" asked Demi.

"Oh, my god, isn't that the bartender chick from CRUSH in Toronto?" asked Leandra. "I remember her. She looks awful! This is what happens. Girls come to LA to get famous, and wind up aging ten years."

Renee was in Jared and Brody's crew. She'd lied to Sophia on the phone about not knowing them. Maybe Renee had drugged her drink, or helped the guy who did. Did she hate Sophia that much? Even if Renee had nothing to do with the roofie, she was still hanging with the guys who did. Sophia watched Renee throw back her head and laugh, then turn to look right at her. Renee smiled at Sophia, put her arm around Brody, and lifted her glass, an air toast. Or was she implying, *Want another drugged drink?*

"I'm going to be sick," Sophia whispered to Demi. "Get me out of here."

Demi didn't hesitate. "Bathroom break," she said loudly. "We'll be back in a few minutes." But she didn't take her into a crowded bathroom. Instead, Demi guided Sophia straight out of the bar's front doors to the street and then around the corner of the building.

Sophia tried to steady her breath. It hit her all over again. Just seeing them, Renee holding up the drink, it triggered the panic, if not any memories.

"Are you okay?" asked Demi.

"No," she admitted. "Panic attack."

Demi said, "Okay, let's do jumping jacks."

"*What?*"

"Seriously, I learned this on *Orange Is the New Black*. Let's go."

In the alley by the Dumpsters, the would-be TV star in her fancy sequined dress and six-inch heels, did jumping jacks. Two sets of ten. And it fucking worked! Her heart was beating, she was breathing hard. But it was due to the exercise, not the panic. Her whole body calmed down. She still had the shakes though. But was it from anger or fear?

"He's in there. *Nude and Stupid.*"

"So?" asked Demi. And then, her eyes narrowed and sharpened. "Is he the one? Holy shit, he's right in there. It's a gift from God. I can murder him now. I have been lifting vats of cooking oil for a month. I can so take that guy."

"No."

"I have to."

"Karma will get him," said Sophia. It was the only attitude to take. Inflicting violence on him didn't undo what happened to her. She had no evidence to accuse him with. All she could do was react to how she felt—freaked the fuck out—and decide what action to take.

"Beating on him would be faster." Thank god Demi wasn't drunk, or she'd be roaring back in there already.

Sophia shook her head. "That'll only call more attention to it.

Don't make me regret telling you." Demi froze. "I don't meant that. I'm so glad I told you, and I appreciate all the hours of talking about it since then. I needed that time with you to heal. I thought I was fine, but seeing him was like tearing out the stitches."

"What now? We just ignore him? Do you want to go home?"

"I don't know!" she cried. "I don't know what to do." That was it. The ultimate truth that she, and everyone, had to accept. There would always be more questions than answers, more problems than solutions. Maybe bliss was having lots of life experience, and getting comfortable about not having a fucking clue. If so, bliss was a million miles away. Sophia started crying, mainly from frustration. "I want to feel normal!"

"Okay," said Demi. "Under normal circumstances, we'd go back inside, have a good time with our friends, dance, drink, eat some food, and laugh our asses off. So I propose that we go do that. I will not leave your side."

"I'm not sure I can face him," said Sophia. "Them."

"I hate to say it, but I think you have to. Just once, to prove you can."

Sophia agreed. Hand in hand, they walked back toward the front door of the club. Right as they were heading in, Renee and her posse were coming out. Sophia and Demi stopped in their tracks on the sidewalk.

"I've got this," whispered Demi, squeezing her hand.

Renee saw Sophia, and didn't hesitate. She came right over and said, "Hey. How's it going? Congrats on your show. Good luck with that." The tone was snide.

Sophia tried to talk, but couldn't. Demi said, "I'm Sophia's friend from . . ."

"I know who you are. Demi. The fuckup."

Sophia said, "I never called you that."

Renee laughed. "Take it easy, Sophia. So sensitive. Anyway, it's dead in there. We're going to the Mondrian. Do you want to come?" Just then, the model boys followed Renee over to them. Sophia could feel their eyes on her, sizing her up, deciding if she were hot enough. Made her sick to her stomach.

Demi said, "We're going to stay."

Sophia lifted up her eyes. They zeroed in on the two men she believed were the architects of the worst night of her life. Brody, who drugged her without her knowledge. Jared, who took full advantage of that.

Jared said, "How's it going, Sophia?"

"Do I know you?" she asked, her heart thundering in her chest.

Demi said, "You're Jared from *Nude and Stupid*, right? I'm a big fan!" Then, to Sophia's astonishment, Demi went in for . . . a hug? She put her arms around him, but in the process, accidentally elbowed him in the face. He pushed her away to hold his nose, and Demi started rubbing his back, comforting him. What the fuck? A sneak attack? Sophia knew Demi might get physical. She couldn't help herself.

He stepped away from her. The whole crew took off, walking briskly away. Demi cracked up because they had to hold up their too baggy jeans. "Look at them go!" she said. "Fuckers."

Sophia asked, "What the hell was that? You just gave him a huge ego boost!"

Demi said, "I boosted something else, too." She held up a black iPhone. "I figured you might want this."

Oh, my god. His phone! With all his photos! "How'd you learn to do that?" Sophia asked, taking the device in grateful disbelief.

"Just a little something I picked up in jail," she said sarcastically.

"No screen lock," said Sophia, amazed. She could go right to his photo library and see it all, but she hesitated. "I've been obsessed about finding out what happened to me. But now that I have the answer in my hand, I'm not sure I want to know."

"Let's trash it."

"How?"

"First, I erase his photo library and his streaming photos on the cloud."

"How'd you learn how to do that?" asked Sophia again.

"Also something I picked up in jail," said Demi. "I just do. I've worked office jobs for the last four years, and learned how to do the basic stuff." She pushed buttons for a few minutes while Sophia's heart returned to normal. "Okay, it's done. All cleared out. Next, we shut it down, like so. We should destroy it, too. There are some high-powered blenders at Dory."

That sounded perfect. "Let's do that later tonight. I'm not ready to leave the party yet. We have to dance first."

Demi seemed surprised, but pleased. "Great!"

They went back into the club. Sophia felt shaken, but also stirred by her own strength. She'd faced them, and survived. She could survive anything with Demi at her side.

We've got each other.

Demi said, "Before we find them, what do you think of Harris?"

"Handsome," said Sophia. "But, am I crazy, or does he *reek* of coconut oil?"

Holding on
to anger is like
drinking poison and
expecting the other
person to die.

—Buddha

24

so go

Leandra had a bad night. The
Abbey with Sophia and Demi was fun. But when they arrived back
home, they found Tammy and Cherri on the couch, playing Halo,
with Instacart bags on the floor and a pint of ice cream oozing on the
table.

"Oh, I forgot to mention," said Harris. "We're shooting *Eiffel Tower
II* later this week, and the girls needed a place to stay."

"Absolutely not," said Leandra.

"It's just for a few days."

"Get rid of them," she said. "I mean it! It's a major turnoff to come
home to find crab-infested slags on the couch. If you expect me to
stay in this house, you're going to have to make some changes, Harris. No more bimbos. I want them gone, now. And no more porn.

You're out of business. I could have been married to a banker or an earl. You can't possibly expect me to settle for the lowest of the low, no matter how good you are in bed. Which reminds me. We are getting rid of that ugly, stupid round bed."

Leandra paused to draw breath. She noticed that Tammy and Cherri were staring at her now, the red-rimmed lips and fake-lashed eyes wide open. It was simply beneath her dignity to breathe the same air.

"If they're not out of here in five minutes," she said. "I'm leaving."

An hour later, Leandra and her fifteen suitcases were booked into the Days Inn on Sunset Boulevard. She'd never been dumped before, or sent packing, or given $100 and a kick in the ass on her way out.

Rejected by the scum of society. How could anyone recover from that? She'd just have to spin it, claim that she'd orchestrated the breakup, and that he'd just played his part in the script she'd written, which was more or less exactly what happened.

Leandra lay awake all night, thinking about what to do next. The obvious plan was to find another boyfriend. It was always easier to swing from one monkey bar to the next. She'd lost her grip this time, and would have to make a significant vertical leap to grab another rung. Where would she go to find a rich man? There was always Manhattan and Washington, D.C., but she didn't know anyone there.

She finally dozed off, and woke up to the sound of a vacuum and the knocking of the maid. It was one P.M., which meant she had missed checkout and would have to pay for the room for another night. The last time she woke up, dazed, in a cheap hotel room, she was in Phuket, alone, with nothing. Months later, Leandra was just as alone, but now she had fifteen suitcases full of stuff to lug around. Luggage, or baggage? Both? What difference did it make?

She could sell everything. The designer clothes and jewelry would net her enough to get a studio apartment, maybe in Sophia's complex. She could wait it out among friends until she found a new benefactor. Or she could always go home to Vancouver, live with her parents, write this off as a gap year, and apply for internships and entry-level jobs in Toronto in the spring like all her sorority sisters.

Leandra took out her phone to call Sophia, and saw that her friend had sent a text inviting her to Dory, Demi's restaurant, for its soft opening. At the dinner at Red O, Demi had described the owner as a big burly Australian who owned a bunch of places in Sydney. He sounded like a possibility.

She suited up for seduction in a skintight Hervé Léger bandage dress, stiletto sandals, and took a taxi to Venice.

Dory was on the beach side of the boardwalk. The building itself was a clapboard bungalow that reminded her of clam shacks in Maine. There was a line to get in, which confused her. She headed to the front of the line, catching a heel in the slats on the board-walk.

"Leandra!" said Demi. She was manning the door and handing out menus. "You made it."

"The place hasn't even opened yet," she said. "Who are all these people?"

"Between Aiden, Sophia, and I, we know a lot of people in town. We marketed to the right groups and partnered with a few brands for the launch," she said.

"How did you know how to do that?" Leandra wouldn't have known where to start, and she had a marketing degree.

"I worked my ass off! Sophia is out back. Come on, I'll show you."

Demi took her into the main dining area with modern yet simple picnic tables topped with a slab of raw wood and square iron rods crossing underneath to mount the tabletop, which elevated the rustic vibe. It was hard to get a good look at the furniture, though, because each bench was occupied, and the tables were laden with plates of yummy-looking food.

"We debated the bench seating. But hipsters think they're post-ironic and people love them. We're hoping to attract locals and . . ."

Leandra zoned out, her mind having to adjust to an elevated impression of Demi. Leandra had expected Demi to go down in flames, or wind up in prison, before her twenty-fifth birthday. Shouldn't she be passed out drunk somewhere, or in the kitchen washing dishes? It unsettled Leandra to bear witness to Demi's success, keenly so, given recent changes in her own life.

"Can I get you a drink? You look like you can use one," said Demi.

"A glass of rosé would be great, thanks. Just . . . where's Sophia?" Her voice cracked a bit.

"Right this way. You might have some trouble on the sand in those shoes."

Demi guided Leandra to the rear entrance of the building, to a fenced-in beachfront area with more tables, these weathered to silver. She spotted Sophia at a crowded table, sitting on the lap of that writer. What was his name? David? Sophia's costars were there, too, and some other people she recognized from the party last night. One of the girls was playing the ukulele. The barrel-chested older guy with the booming voice had an Austrialian accent. "Is that man the owner?" asked Leandra.

"Yup, stuffing his face when he should be helping me in the front of the house. Hey, Aiden!" Demi yelled. "A little help?"

The big man got up and walked toward them. He flung an arm over Demi's shoulder, and said, "Who's this?"

"A friend from home," said Demi. "Leandra, this is Aiden."

"What was Demi like at thirteen? Gawky? Braces?" he asked her. "Sophia won't tell me."

"Don't you dare say a word," warned Demi.

Leandra said, "She was cute. Sophia was exotic. And then, there was me. The sexy one." And she threw in a wink.

"Back off, Leandra," said Demi. "He's married."

Aiden froze for a second, his arm dropping off her shoulder like a dead weight. He turned to Demi and started to speak, but couldn't seem to. All he got out was "Ummmmm . . ."

"Yeah," said Demi. "It's like that."

Aiden said, "Can I see you inside for a few minutes? We have some important restaurant matters to discuss."

"Absolutely," said Demi, smiling at him. "Excuse us."

"You're excused." *What was that about?*

Leandra took one step toward Sophia, and sank into the sand. If she took off her Louboutins, she'd look even sillier. A waiter whipped by her with a huge tray of margaritas and tacos. He placed it on Sophia's table, and they all dove in. She'd have to sink low to get over there, in so many ways.

"Hey," said Leandra when she made it across the sand.

Sophia turned toward her with a mouthful of food. She held up a finger and finished chewing before she said, "So glad you made it! Did you bring Harris?"

"About that. We broke up, actually."

"I'm so sorry. What happened?" Sophia slid off of David's lap and stood up (on bare feet), to give Leandra a hug.

"It wasn't working," she said. Leandra almost made up a lie that painted him in the worst possible light, as was her way. "He pressured me to do anal," something like that. But what would be the point? "He wasn't who I thought he was," she said. "And I'm not who he thought I was." *I'm not who I think I am.* Was she one in a million, or just another girl who came to LA, hoping to find a man to take care of her for a while?

Leandra's wine arrived, and she drank half of it in a single swallow. Sophia said, "Have a seat."

The benches were low, and her dress was tight, she didn't think she could sit even if she wanted to. She also hated to eat and drink on the beach. Sand got in the food, and fleas and the taste of salt water on her tongue. Also, that redheaded girl kept plucking on the ukulele, which was beyond annoying.

"Ukulele and tacos on the beach?" asked Leandra. "I don't remember seeing this on your vision board."

"My vision board has beaches on it," said Sophia.

"But here? What about Bali? What about the villa in Tuscany?"

"I'll get there one day. But right now is pretty great, too," she said, sweeping her hand at the beach, the restaurant, the people at her table.

"But what about dreams? You said if we followed our bliss, doors would appear where there were only walls."

"This is the door," said Sophia. "Good food, good friends, music, a beautiful day."

"You can't be serious."

Sophia looked at her like she felt sorry for her. "Are you okay?"

"I'm *fantastic*," said Leandra, better than Sophia was, apparently, trading in her dreams for a skinny writer boy and a pitcher of margaritas. "I just wanted to say good-bye. I'm flying to Paris in a few days. I don't think we'll see each other again before I go."

"Paris?"

"I'm meeting my English friends at the Plaza Athénée. I'm sure the food won't be as good as this," she said, nodding at the tacos on the picnic table, "but we'll manage."

"I've never been."

"Me, either. But Cosimo and Jacques know the city inside and out. All I have to do is show up."

"I'm so jealous!" said Sophia, sounding like she meant it.

Telling a grand lie didn't give Leandra the rush it used to, though. "I'll miss you," said Leandra. "But we'll talk."

"Of course we will. You won't stay for one more drink?"

"I can't, really. Packing and shopping! Too much to do."

Over the next few days, Leandra researched Los Angeles's high-end consignment stores, and sold everything she owned, save a few of her favorite outfits and pieces of jewelry, one large suitcase worth. With $30,000 to her name, she booked a first-class Air France ticket from LAX to Charles de Gaulle. She couldn't help remembering how she felt all those months ago when she flew from Toronto to Phuket with one suitcase and $3,000. As cramped as it was in coach, she felt light and free, with her whole life ahead of her. Just like now.

Sophia called her earlier today, asking her to stay in town tonight. "My show is airing, and we're having a viewing party at the apartment. I'd really like you to come. You know you're welcome to stay over for as long as you want."

Leandra was tempted by Sophia's offer, but she had her plane ticket and was itching to fly. It wasn't in her nature to settle for uku-leles and bare feet like Sophia, or with a fat, married boss/boyfriend like Demi. Frankly, she expected more for her friends than they seemed to want for themselves. *What was wrong with them?*

"You've got your bliss," she told Sophia. "I'm searching for mine."

In the first-class lounge, Leandra ordered a dry martini. As she sipped her drink, she glanced up at the TV screen behind the bar—and saw Sophia's face on it! She looked gorgeous. The volume was down so she couldn't hear the dialogue, but Sophia sold it without words. "I miss you," she said to the TV screen, which might be the only way Leandra would see Sophia again.

No, they were old friends, and they would find a way to circle back to each other. Sophia and Demi would always be in her life. She was glad things were working out for them in LA. But she couldn't stay in one place or one relationship. Sophia and Demi were like sisters; they had each other. As close as she'd been with Demi and Sophia, she never felt as close to them as she had been with Stacy. She wished she could, but that kind of trust and love weren't available to her. After you'd been cut in half, you were never whole again. She could fool herself into believing a friend, or a man, or a place, could give her what she'd lost. But then she'd only feel more lonely and disappointed when she failed to find the unfindable. And yet, the powerful urge to search for it remained.

Leandra must have transmitted a beguiling *tristesse* because it caught the attention of the handsome man seated to her right.

"You look so sad," he said with a thick French accent. No wedding ring. Did they wear them in France? "Would you like to talk about it?"

She smiled with just her lips, a small sad smile, and arched her brows to accentuate the romantic misery in her face that he was attracted to, and said, "I'm sure you don't want to hear about my problems."

He said, "But I do!"

"Are you on the flight to Paris?"

"I am. Seat one-A."

"I'm one-B," she said. "I guess we have all night to talk about our problems."

"And perhaps solve some of them."

What was that? The sound of a door opening? Leandra turned away from the TV, and marched right through it.

"I'll drive," said Demi. Aiden
had given her a Fiat, and she was getting behind the wheel at every
opportunity, even to drive Sophia to a meeting for *The Den*.

"Do you know the streets yet?" asked Sophia.

"I like to get lost," said Demi, making them both think of that
night, almost five years ago, driving around Vancouver with Leandra. Seemed like a million years ago.

Sophia finished her makeup. "I'm nervous."

"Why? The show's a hit, after only two episodes! You're getting
amazing ratings. And now we can upgrade and get a real house. It's
all good!"

Sophia had learned to be cautiously optimistic about success, even while keeping a positive attitude. "You're right," she said, smiling. "Ready."

They headed east, toward the meeting in Hollywood. She'd been called to meet with the new publicity team. Now that the show was picked up and media calls were flooding in for the three stars of the show, the producers hired half a dozen publicists. Her image, her career, would be in their hands.

"Listen, Demi, what will happen if the show turns out to be huge, and I become really successful?"

"I don't understand the question."

"Meanwhile, the restaurant flops."

"Okay, I get it," said Demi. "You could ask the same thing in reverse. I'm a hit, and you're a flop. It doesn't matter which way it plays out. The issue is, what happens if we wind up moving in different directions?"

"Ideally, we'll both move up," said Sophia.

They stared at each other, imagining how big the friendship disparity would have to be to pull them apart. Ocean-size? Puddle-size?

"We won't let that happen," said Sophia. "Leandra was right about one thing."

"That Jenna Jameson isn't really a skank?"

"That whatever life throws at us, we'll catch it together."

Demi laughed. "Or get hit in the face with it!"

They drove along, and then Demi jammed on the brakes and pointed at a huge billboard over the highway. "Holy mother of fuck," she said. "Did you know about this?"

Sophia had not been told that her face and cleavage, along with those of Cassie and Paula, were going to be put on a billboard on Hollywood Boulevard to promote the show. She'd never seen her face with such objectivity. "I look good," she said.

Demi was flipping shit. "You look sensational!! Are you fucking kidding me? Look at you!"

A car horn blasted behind them, and they drove on. Demi went on about the billboard, and she dearly appreciated that, but it was such a strange feeling to see your image but not feel connected to it.

They pulled up at the studio in Hollywood, and Sophia got out. Demi would check in at the restaurant and pick her up later. A couple of girls on the street recognized Sophia, and took out their phones to snap a photo. Sophia felt a thrill, almost taking out her own phone to snap a photo of them taking her picture.

On that high, she sailed into the Silver Associates office and was immediately shown into a glass-paneled room to meet three elegantly dressed women and one nattily suited man. Sophia took a seat at the glass conference room table.

Introductions were made, but Sophia quickly realized she'd be talking to only one person, the man (which annoyed her; out of four people, why was the one man in charge?).

His name was Eric Silver, the firm's founder, and he reminded her so much of Ari Gold from *Entourage*, she wondered if he fashioned himself after the character. "We have been looking forward to meeting you, Sophia," he said. "We have huge plans for your career. It's our job to make you look good."

"Great," she said, not sure what else to say.

"Great," he repeated. "So. You really are gorgeous."

"Thank you."

He smiled. "We're going to make you famous. Not just here in America. You're going to be famous around the globe."

"Gulp," she said. They laughed. They were publicists, and would probably laugh at anything.

"So," said Eric. "Before we talk about what we have planned for you, we need to do some troubleshooting."

"Okay."

"Is there anything in your past, anything at all, that could become a problem for us down the road?"

Immediately, she thought about the photos that might have been on Jared's phone or, possibly, the cloud (whatever that was).

"What do you mean?"

"Any relationships that ended badly and could come to light? Any arrests, or questionable past careers? It wouldn't be so good for the show or the network if you were, just as a wild example, an escort or a porn star, in a previous life."

"No!" she said.

"Have you ever Snapchatted body parts to a boyfriend? I don't care if you have. Snapchat has its value. But we need to know now so we can head it off in the future."

Sophia just shook her head.

He said, "It's essential that you tell us everything, Sophia. We need to know about every skeleton in your closet. Every bad boyfriend who might want his fifteen minutes by making up a story about you. Every time you used your charms to get a job. Any friend you treated badly who might leak pictures and stories to Perez Hilton. So is there anything you need to tell us? Anything at all?"

"I understand," she said. "I can't think of anything."

"I'm going to ask you point-blank, Sophia. Are there nude photos of you floating around the Internet?"

"No," she said.

"You're sure."

"Yes."

"Then what are these?"

One of the women pushed a folder across the table toward Sophia. Her fingers trembling, she pulled it toward her. Terrified of what she'd find, she cringed when she opened it and found three prints, black and white.

"Oh, my god." She looked at the pictures, and then up at the four faces across the table from her. "I can explain," she said.

"Go right ahead," he said.

Sophia studied the photos again, and tried to calm her racing heart. How did they find them? "These were shots I did with a photographer in Canada when I was in high school," she said of the topless pics. Not completely topless. Her arms and hands covered most of the important bits. "They were for a local clothing store. After we did the bathing suits, he convinced me to do a few art shots. You can barely see anything."

Eric nodded. "But we were able to find them in one day, without looking too hard. So I'm going to ask you one more time. Is there anything in your past we need to know about?"

In her head, she weighed the pros and cons of telling them about Jared. She and Demi destroyed his phone. Jared didn't seem too tech savvy about storing any pictures he might've taken. It was just too awful to sit here and tell four strangers about that night. So she said, "Nothing at all."

"Okay, then," he said. "Let's talk about your upcoming cover shoot for *Elle* Canada."

"Really?" She used to read that mag in high school, and had put images from it on her vision board. And now she was going to be on the cover? Manifesting worked! All thoughts of Jared flew out of her head. Despite what Eric said, the past was the past. She only wanted to focus on the future, her bliss.

"*Elle* Canada, a Q and A in *Esquire*, a story in *Entertainment Weekly*— and so much more to come. This is just the beginning for you, Sophia."

Just the beginning. "I love the sound of that," she said.